WINNER TAKES ALL

"Julianna."

"Why . . . why do you call me that?" she asked, opening eyes that had darkened to a smoky gray. "My name is Penelope. Penelope Pickering."

Discarding her glove, he cupped her hand in the warm, intimate embrace of his own. "I prefer Julianna," he replied softly, looking down at her hand, which felt strangely naked and vulnerable beneath his gaze.

He turned her hand over and pressed his lips to her fingers. "We did not finish the game; I have not won. I know I have no right to claim my kiss, but . . ." He raised his head, his eyes black opaque pools. "I find I cannot help myself."

His movements were slow, deliberate, inevitable, as he drew her into his embrace, brushing her lips with the breath of a kiss.

"On the contrary, Lord Fairmont," Julianna whispered, raising her mouth once more to his. "I think the game is most certainly yours."

THE TIMELESS CHARM OF ZEBRA'S REGENCY ROMANCES

CHANGE OF HEART (3278, $3.95)
by Julie Caille

For six years, Diana Farington had buried herself in the country, far from the gossip surrounding her ill-fated marriage and her late husband's demise. When she reluctantly returns to London to oversee her sister's debut, she vows to hold her head high. The behavior of the dangerously handsome Lord Lucan, was too much to bear. Diana knew that she could only expect an improper proposal from the rake, and she was determined that *no* man, let alone Lord Lucan, would turn her head again.

The Earl of Lucan knew that second chances were rare, so when he saw the golden-haired Diana again after so many years, he swore he would win her heart this time around. She had lost her innocence over the years, but he swore he could make her trust — and love — again.

THE HEART'S INTRIGUE (3130, $2.95)
by Evelyn Bond

Lady Clarissa Tregallen preferred the solitude of Cornwall to the ballrooms and noisy routs of the London *ton,* but the future bride of the tediously respectable Duke of Mainwaring would soon be forced to enter Society. To this she was resigned — until her evening walk revealed a handsome, wounded stranger. Bryan Deverell was certainly a spy, but how could she turn over a wounded man to the local authorities?

Deverell planned to take advantage of the beauty's hospitality and be on his way once he recovered, yet he found himself reluctant to leave his charming hostess. He would prove to this very proper lady that she was also a very *passionate* one, and that a scoundrel such as he could win her heart.

SWEET PRETENDER (3248, $3.95)
by Violet Hamilton

As the belle of Philadelphia, spirited Sarah Ravensham had no fondness for the hateful British. But as a patriotic American, it was her duty to convey a certain document safely into the hands of Britain's prime minister — even if it meant spending weeks aboard ship in the company of the infuriating Britisher of them all, the handsome Col. Lucien Valentine.

Sarah was unduly alarmed when her cabin had been searched. But when she found herself in the embrace of the arrogant Colonel — and responding to his touch — she realized the full extent of the dangers she was facing. Not the least of which was the danger to her own impetuous heart . . .

Available wherever paperbacks are sold, or order direct from the Publisher. Send cover price plus 50¢ per copy for mailing and handling to Zebra Books, Dept. 3639, 475 Park Avenue South, New York, N.Y. 10016. Residents of New York and Tennessee must include sales tax. DO NOT SEND CASH. For a free Zebra/ Pinnacle catalog please write to the above address.

Queen of Hearts
Emily Maxwell

ZEBRA BOOKS
KENSINGTON PUBLISHING CORP.

To the memory of my mother and best friend,
Edna Caroline Schwab
Love and goodness live forever

ZEBRA BOOKS

are published by

Kensington Publishing Corp.
475 Park Avenue South
New York, NY 10016

First printing: January, 1992

Printed in the United States of America

Prologue

"Paste, my dear Julianna, paste!" Victor Marnay, Marquis of Ramsden, threw the emerald necklace on the dressing table and stared accusingly down at his stepdaughter.

Julianna Seaton paused, one hand still on the long auburn hair she had just finished braiding for the night. Her eyes gazed unseeingly at her reflection in the candlelit mirror before dropping to the necklace which glittered glassily up at her.

"I—I thought you had gone back to London," she stammered, one hand going to the neck of her faded cambric wrapper.

"And so I had, my dear." The marquis's thin mouth curved briefly into the travesty of a smile. "But when I arrived at Rundell and Bridges with the intention of selling this," he nudged the necklace with the tip of one manicured finger, "I was told that the necklace of my dear departed wife was worth no more than a few pounds. That the emeralds had, in fact, been replaced by paste copies some time ago. Now who do you suppose could have done such a thing?

"Surely not your much lamented mother," Lord Ramsden continued without waiting for Julianna's reply. "She was much too ill the last few years to do anything of the kind. And not Eleanor. My dear sister would have bungled things the way she always does. So that leaves only . . . you, Julianna."

"I have no idea what you mean," she said, rising slowly to her feet in a desperate show of bravado. "Perhaps the jewelers made a mistake."

"No, my dear stepdaughter, the mistake was yours."

Though they were much of a height, Julianna being tall for a woman, she felt dwarfed by the menace emanating from the marquis.

"I am badly dipped, Julianna. I have neither the time nor the patience to play these cat and mouse games with you. Besides, they bore me. If you were a woman of wit and charm, or even passable beauty, I might indulge you, but you are not. I want the jewels, Julianna. I want them now!" The words were whispered, a soft, ominous hiss in the quiet room.

Julianna rubbed her arms, feeling suddenly chilled though not with cold, fourteen years of living within the crumbling walls of Graxton Manor had inured her to that. "I do not have them," she said at last.

"Then you know where they are. Or if they have been sold, you know where the money is. As I recall, your mother received several fine sets of diamonds upon our wedding, and when her parents died, she inherited the emeralds as well as a sapphire necklace of particular beauty."

Julianna turned on him then, her carefully controlled facade crumbling with her anger. "You must know where the diamonds are," she said. "Did you not pry open my jewelry box and steal them, not six months past?"

"Steal?" Lord Ramsden raised finely plucked eyebrows in feigned surprise. "Surely you would not call it stealing to take what is rightfully mine."

"The jewels were left to me. You know that!"

"I know that you possess nothing but what I give you, stepdaughter. Nor did your mother. When Emily Seaton married me, her dowry, her very self, became mine to dispose of as I wished. Remember that, Julianna. The jewels are as much mine . . . as you are." The marquis smiled, enjoying her discomfiture.

"Did you not read the article in the *Morning Post* about the man who sold his wife at auction, my dear?" he asked, sitting down on the small stool by the dressing table. "No? Ah, I should have saved it for you. He was a butcher, I believe. His wife fetched a pound and sixpence." Lord Ramsden raised his quizzing glass and peered through it at Julianna, making her feel as if she were on the auction block herself. "But you need not worry. A woman of four and twenty with the figure of an adolescent boy would fetch so little, it would hardly be worth the trouble."

Julianna ran her tongue nervously over suddenly dry lips. "You are trying to frighten me," she accused, hoping that was indeed all he had in mind.

"Not frighten, Julianna. Warn. You have no money, nowhere to go. You are entirely dependent on me and should set yourself to please, yet do not. I wonder why?" he taunted.

Because I hate you as you very well know, Julianna answered silently. Because to please you in this case I would have to give up my every hope for the future. "I know nothing about the jewels," she said yet again.

"You are such a hopeless liar, Julianna. That is why you will never make a good card player. Despite your phenomenal memory and ability to calculate the odds, the hand you are playing is always revealed in your eyes for anyone to read. A pity, really. At one time I had such hopes for you."

"I remember," Julianna whispered, her eyes lifting to the dressing-table mirror where she saw not the woman

7

she had become, but a young ten-year-old girl innocently trying to please her new stepfather. "What you did was unforgivable."

Lord Ramsden laughed. "Not unforgivable, my dear. Amusing. A tableful of hardened gamesters playing cards with a fresh-faced schoolgirl who must sit on a book to reach the cards. Sir Montrose wouldn't believe you were my stepdaughter, you know. Kept saying you must be a dwarf. Quite the nine days' wonder you were."

"Like a two-headed pig?"

"Something like," the marquis agreed with a shrug. "But we stray from the point, and as I have said, I have not much time. The emeralds, Julianna. I must have them tonight. The moneylenders are after my blood."

"I have told you —"

"And I have told you! I am tired of these games. The emeralds, Julianna!"

"No." Julianna lifted the chin Lord Ramsden never tired of telling her was much too square for beauty and gave him back stare for stare. His threats were as empty as his pockets, she assured herself. And in any case she had not gone to the trouble of having the emeralds copied to meekly hand them over now. "No," she said again, all pretence of ignorance gone. "You must find some other means to pay your gambling debts."

"I think not, my dear. You see you are forgetting something, or should I say someone."

A sudden shock of fear jolted Julianna. "Paul," she whispered.

"Ah, how quick you are," Lord Ramsden said admiringly. "Yes, I refer to Paul, your little stepbrother. You see, if you do not give me the jewels, I shall be forced to rusticate at Graxton Manor. And naturally I should take more interest in my son. The son you have so enjoyed taking under your frustrated maternal wing. I believe the first thing I shall do is engage a new nurse for him from the village. Maggie, the barmaid at the Goose and Dragon would seem an excellent choice. With your shockingly bad memory for names, you probably do not remember Maggie, but I assure you she is well-known in the village for her many . . . talents, shall we say? It would be much more convenient for me to have her living at the Manor. And I am sure there are no end of things she could teach Paul."

"You would not—"

"And now Paul is . . . two? Yes, now he is two, it is really time I began to consider his education." The marquis took a quick turn about the room, his pale brow creased as if in deep thought. "The intricacies of hazard or faro may be too much for him at present, so I think I shall begin by instructing him in the gentlemanly art of playing at dice. It will relieve the boredom of country life for me, and I am sure Paul will enjoy it. In addition to Maggie's tuition, of course."

"You are totally despicable."

Lord Ramsden smiled. "I have never denied it, my dear. I am also at point non plus. If you wish to continue in your shabby little charade of domesticity here, you would be well advised to tell me where you have hidden the emeralds. I should find them eventually anyway, you know."

"You shall have them tomorrow," Julianna said in the choked voice of defeat. "It will take me some little time to retrieve them."

"I shall be leaving early," Lord Ramsden warned.

Julianna nodded and turned away, her hands clenching and unclenching in the folds of the faded cambric wrapper. Lord Ramsden was completely without conscience, without any shred of moral decency. She could not bear to look at him, could not bear to see the smirking look of triumph she knew she would see on his face. For if she did, she was afraid she would lose all control. And control, the ability to bury deep within her true feelings, was the ace Julianna meant to play in Lord Ramsden's game.

"And you will ensure that this time the emeralds are not paste copies?" the marquis prodded.

"Yes."

Lord Ramsden watched Julianna narrowly for a moment, then, apparently satisfied that he had won another battle with his recalcitrant stepdaughter, walked to the door. "A wise decision, my dear. The young vixen should never try to outsmart the old fox."

Julianna waited, back held ramrod straight, until she heard the door click shut behind her stepfather, then she collapsed on the small stool in front of the dressing table, shoulders slumped, as the tears she had been holding under tight control flowed freely down her pale cheeks. She had known the time would come when her stepfather would realize that in Paul he had the ultimate weapon.

When her mother had died of a fever shortly after Paul's birth, Julianna had assumed the care of her little half brother. Lord Ramsden might say it was a sign of frustrated spinsterhood, and perhaps it was. Julianna only knew that she loved Paul with a fierceness she would not have believed possible, and she would not allow her stepfather to ruin the little boy's life with his profligate ways.

For years, Julianna had dreamed of escaping from Graxton Manor. Marriage was out of the question. There was no money for a Season to introduce her to eligible men, and it was laughable to suggest to the marquis that he provide her with a dowry. He would simply say it was a waste of money.

"The girl will never take," he had said on many an occasion, not bothering to spare Julianna's feelings.

"She is too tall and too thin, and that red hair of hers is impossible. Not to mention those strange, colorless eyes which I can barely look at without shuddering. And while she may be able to conjugate Latin verbs and spout mathematical formulas as if they were poetry, she lacks every social grace. Her father saw to that." And then having reduced Julianna's mother, Emily, to tears, Lord Ramsden would bow politely and take his leave.

Julianna stared into the dressing-table mirror with those eyes so abhorred by her stepfather, eyes of a gray so light they seemed to change color with her thoughts, and allowed herself to remember for a moment her real father, Edward Seaton.

He had been a younger son of good family, a mathematician of some repute but little fortune when he had met Julianna's mother. Whether it was love at first sight, no one could say. What was certain was that within two weeks of their meeting, the young couple had eloped to Gretna Green. Emily's family never forgave her. Of the rich merchant class, they had long ago determined that their only child should marry into the aristocracy. That she should waste herself on a younger son was not to be thought of.

Still, the marriage endured for eleven years, and when Edward Seaton died, his wife was inconsolable. She made no demur when her family, taking her back into the fold once more, urged her to marry the Marquis of Ramsden. And much good the marriage did any of them, Julianna thought bitterly. Lord Ramsden shunned his wife's family and dissipated her inheritance. Aristocratic titles meant very little when the money that should have been spent on food and clothing was being wagered on which drop of rain would reach the bottom of the windowpane first.

If it had not been for her mother, Julianna would

11

have left Graxton Manor years ago. Not that she had anywhere to go, her grandparents being long dead, or any means of earning a living. And with the advent of Paul, the cards were stacked even more heavily against her, for who would hire a young woman with a lively two year old at her side? There was one thing she could do, however, and do very well, thanks to the combined efforts of her father and Lord Ramsden.

A small smile curved Julianna's lips. The Marquis of Ramsden was indeed an old fox, as he had said. But what he had forgotten were the desperate measures to which a young vixen could be driven in defense of her cub.

"You are wrong, my dear step-papa," Julianna whispered, her eyes darkening to slate. "I do not always reveal the hand I intend to play." For a moment more she remained seated on the small stool, then she rose briskly to her feet and wiped away the tears that still remained on her pale cheeks. There was no time for such costly emotions nor for any of the fears which had held her so long at Graxton Manor. There was too much to be done.

A soft knock at her bedroom door a few moments later caused Julianna to stiffen warily as she stood beside the opened doors of her armoire, pondering the meager wardrobe inside.

"It's only me." Lady Eleanor's head, topped by a frivolous and much mended lace nightcap, peered around the door. "I can tell by your frozen look that you were afraid it was my brother."

Julianna let go of the breath she had been holding and nodded, turning as casually as possible from the armoire. As much as she liked Lady Eleanor, Julianna did not want the marquis's sister to get wind of her plans.

"He's in the library, drinking the last of Father's

brandy, and looking very pleased with himself. Did you give him money? He was looking the veriest thundercloud when he arrived, you know. So it must be money. Is he all to pieces again? Faro was never his game; I keep telling him that. Not that he listens to me. Thinks I'm hen-witted."

"Not just you," Julianna assured her. "He thinks most women have more hair than wit."

Lady Eleanor nodded, her blue eyes, so unlike those of her brother, crinkling suddenly at the corners. "I don't deny I'm a bit of a fribble," she admitted. "But there's a great deal more than curl wrappers beneath this cap." She nodded briskly again and walked over to the fireplace, shivering slightly and drawing her pink silk wrapper more closely about her stout little body. "Well?" she asked, turning and parading in front of Julianna again. "What do you think? I made it out of the bed curtain in the Queen's room." Lady Eleanor indicated the pink wrapper. "You've got to admit it looks better on me than on the bed. And it's not likely that we'll be entertaining any queens in the near future."

"It looks delightful, Lady Eleanor. You certainly have very clever fingers."

Lady Eleanor smiled, her cheeks flushing to match her wrapper. "I could make something for you too, Julianna. There's a lovely bit of blue curtain in the second withdrawing room that's just going to waste."

"Thank you, Lady Eleanor, but I don't think—"

"You'll need something a bit more fashionable in London."

Julianna sat down with a thump on the end of the fourposter. She could not have been more surprised if one of the dragons in the threadbare Oriental rug at her feet had risen up and bitten her.

"Told you I wasn't a flea-wit." Lady Eleanor pursed

her lips complacently, enjoying Julianna's look of non-plussed amazement.

Recovering herself after a moment, Julianna schooled her features to their usual blandness. "I really don't know what you're talking about, Lady Eleanor. I have no intention of going to London."

"Pish-tish. I always know when there's something afoot. And if it's not London, it's somewhere else then. I don't mind where we go, so long as it's some place with a bit of life. What about Bath then? Not as fashionable as it was, but I daresay we could contrive to enjoy ourselves."

"Lady Eleanor, I—"

"I know," that lady interrupted ruthlessly. "You had no intention of taking me along nor, I imagine, of letting on that you were even thinking of leaving. Fact is, you have no choice. Oh, I don't intend blackmail, Julianna." Lady Eleanor held up one small hand larded with goose grease and encased in a cotton glove. "But you must cut your cloth to suit your gown, you know, and you'll need me. As much as you love Paul, you've never had the tending of him day in and day out. He's more of a handful than you imagine, my love. And don't bother denying the fact that you intend to take him with you. It's plain as the nose on your face that you wouldn't go anywhere without him."

"Definitely not flea-witted," Julianna said.

"Then it's settled." Lady Eleanor gave a nod of satisfaction. "When do we leave?"

Chapter One

Taking Paul's hand, Julianna looked quickly down the street and around the small enclosed square that faced the house they had taken for the Season. Though it had been more than a month since their arrival in Bath, Julianna still sometimes expected to see Lord Ramsden bearing down on them, demanding the return of both the jewels and his son, and could not forbear glancing nervously about whenever she ventured out with Paul.

Though she had styled herself a widow with a young son when first arriving in Bath and had carefully meted out her story to various gossips during early visits to the Pump Room, Julianna was quite aware that her resemblance to Paul was slight. At first, she had expected someone to remark on this, to ask if the little boy with golden curls and bright blue eyes was indeed her son. But as the days passed and no one did, Julianna began to relax, beginning to feel more and more at ease in her new role. Still, Lord Ramsden was an experienced gamester, and as Julianna knew all too well, the game was never won until the last card had been played.

Now, reassured by the relative absence of foot traffic outside the small house, Julianna stepped lightly over the threshold and, with her little stepbrother skipping happily along at her side, headed in the direction of the Spring Gardens. It was a lovely day, and Julianna enjoyed being outside. The buildings, made of stone quarried nearby, gleamed whitely in the early morning sunshine. It looked as if the frequent spring rains had ceased for awhile, and Julianna felt quite content with her lot.

As they entered the Gardens and began to stroll down one of the many paths, Julianna gazed happily about at the newly green grass still sparkling with dew, and the flowers bursting into many-colored blossoms. It was still quite early, and there were no public breakfasts that morning, so few people were about. Julianna began to softly hum one of the melodies she had heard at a concert the night before. Though she could barely carry a tune herself, Julianna enjoyed music and enthusiastically attended the subscription concerts that were part of Bath's social life. Paul giggled, and Julianna stopped humming to smile down at him.

"I know I am not musical," she acknowledged, "but it is not nice of you to point it out to me."

Paul giggled again, his blue eyes slanting endearingly upwards at the corners, and skipped over to one of the many benches dotting the park. Sitting down next to him, Julianna adjusted the folds of her blue cambric walking dress which Lady Eleanor had fashioned from a pair of hangings in the south bedroom of their rented house.

"For they are wasted there," Lady Eleanor had said, unpicking a seam. "The material is quite good, and we are not even using the south bedroom because of the smoking chimney. And as soon as we come about, we will replace the hangings with new, so what is the harm?"

What harm indeed? Julianna thought, smoothing the fabric with one hand. Though if things did not soon improve, they might find themselves without the wherewithal to put food upon the table, much less replace the bedroom hangings. For all Lord Ramsden's talk of fortunes made and lost over the gaming tables, there was precious little changing hands in Bath, which was no longer the fashionable watering place it had been in the previous century. Now the residents were mainly retired military officers, much too cautious to gamble for large stakes. Still, London was the first place Lord Ramsden would search for them, so it had been quite out of the question that they should stay there.

Paul wriggled off the bench, much too active to sit still for long, and began to explore under Julianna's watchful eye. She was doing all this for him, really. All the subterfuge, creeping away in the middle of the night, the stage first to London and then the circuitous route to Bath, all had been done for Paul or Pog as they called him.

Julianna smiled as Paul bent down to carefully examine a daisy he had found in the grass. He had begun calling himself Pog as soon as he could talk. Pog was close enough to Paul in his mind and easier to say. Julianna had immediately begun to make up stories about Pog, the Pollywog, much to Paul's delight. Almost every day last spring, Julianna had taken him down to the little pond in back of Graxton Manor. Being part of the entail, it was the only land Lord Ramsden had not sold or heavily mortgaged, and Julianna had taken pleasure in showing Paul what real pollywogs looked like.

Sudden sobs interrupted her bittersweet memories, and Julianna looked up to see that Paul's pursuit of a yellow butterfly had resulted in a fall. Though the only apparent damage was a small scratch on the palm of one hand, Paul cried piteously and demanded her at-

17

tention.

"Pog hurt," he sobbed. "Pog broke self."

Crouching beside her small stepbrother with little regard for her dignity or dress, Julianna took a lacy handkerchief from her reticule and did her best to staunch the little boy's tears. Sensing sympathy and perhaps a way to wrangle an extra Bath bun for tea, Paul's sobs increased in intensity. Julianna straightened, knowing that Paul was already dangerously close to being intolerably spoiled, and hardened herself against the sight of those big blue eyes swimming with tears.

"Pollywogs never cry," she said firmly. "Especially ones named Pog."

"N-never?" Paul sniffed and rubbed at his nose with his hand.

"Never," Julianna repeated, wiping his nose with her handkerchief and thinking that no one looked less like a pollywog than Paul. He was almost completely his mother's son with a daintiness of feature and a cherub smile that were already proving dangerous to feminine hearts. "Do you remember the time Pog was attacked by a big fish and almost lost his tail?" she asked.

Paul shook his head. "Fish big like this?" he asked, holding out his arms as he peered up at Julianna.

"Even bigger," Julianna confirmed. "Quite enormous, in fact. I will tell you about it as we walk back." She took Paul's hand and turned, only to find her way blocked by an elegant gentleman who suddenly appeared in their path.

"Excuse me," she said, grasping Paul's hand so tightly he began to protest. The man stared down at her, his dark eyes so opaque and cold they made Julianna shiver as if a cloud had suddenly passed over the sun. For a long moment the man stood unmoving, his eyes studying Julianna with what was surely more than

18

the casual curiosity of a stranger . . . then he silently stepped to one side allowing them to pass. It was all Julianna could do not to run back to Taylor Street. She was almost certain the man turned to watch their departure. Who had he been? Someone who just happened to be passing and had stopped when he heard Paul's sobs? Or someone sent by Lord Ramsden?

When she sat at a gaming table Julianna's demeanor was always cool, and despite Lord Ramsden's sneering words to the contrary, she knew her expression rarely gave away the hand she had been dealt. It was only where those she loved were concerned that Julianna ever lost control. And she had come very close to losing that control in the park.

Her heart still beating unsteadily, Julianna somehow managed to regale Paul with the story of the pollywog on the walk home, though she did it absently, her mind unable to shake free of the panic that had gripped her during that strange encounter in Spring Gardens. If the man had not been sent by Lord Ramsden, if, indeed, he were merely a passing stranger, why had he stared at her so?

"Because you look uncommonly fetching in the blue cambric I so cunningly fashioned for you," Lady Eleanor said later as they sat in the small parlor sipping tea and eating cakes. "This morning, I think I almost convinced Mrs. Norbert to have her drawing room refurbished. I certainly hope so, for she has satin moiree curtains at the window that would look most fetching on me."

"Have you heard a word I said, Lady Eleanor?" Julianna put down her teacup in exasperation. At times the woman seemed as fluff-brained as the meringue on her favorite dessert.

Lady Eleanor gave Julianna an affronted look. "Of course, I have. It is merely that I do not believe in

19

meeting troubles halfway. Do the chickens come out to greet the fox? There is no way my brother could have traced us to Bath."

Julianna was not convinced. Paul had been more difficult than they had anticipated on the trip to Bath. She was sure they would be remembered by the other coach passengers. Why, after two days of enduring his whining cries and demands, even Lady Eleanor had been moved to say that she quite understood why some people sold their children or allowed them to be stolen by gypsies.

"And in any case Ramsden would never associate what we were with what we are." Lady Eleanor patted a crimped curl complacently. She had spent hours in her room with a bowl of sugar water and a curling iron, and her mirror had convinced her she looked nothing at all like the dowdy, middle-aged woman who had fled Graxton Manor. "I am sure no one will ever connect Julianna Seaton and Lady Eleanor Marnay with Mrs. Penelope Pickering and Miss Prudence Partridge. We have covered our trail more than adequately."

"That may be, Lady Eleanor, but you were not in the Gardens this morning. You did not see the man. He had the most piercing brown eyes, dark as . . . dark as the very devil's." Julianna gave a little shudder. She was not given to dramatics, but there had been something about the stranger on the path that morning she could not easily dismiss.

"Did you get his name?"

"I beg your pardon?"

"The man's name, Julianna. We might invite him to tea if you had gotten his name. He sounds most interesting."

"Lady Eleanor, this is not a romance from the circulating library!"

Lady Eleanor bit into a teacake with pink icing.

"Whatever else you may say about the cook, and last night's joint was so overdone it might have served as a barrow wheel, her pastries are really quite good." Lady Eleanor licked a bit of icing from one finger. "Remarkably good, in fact. And . . ." she held up her hand to silence Julianna who seemed about to speak, "of course it is a romance. Midnight escapes, wicked stepfathers, mysterious strangers . . . what more could one ask, Julianna? If you are not interested in the gentleman, then you might think of me."

"We do not know that he *was* a gentleman. And I certainly hope I know better than to speak to a strange man in the park. Besides, we stray from the point."

"I thought meeting a marriageable gentleman was the point." Lady Eleanor reached for a piece of gingerbread. "I know I should not, but there, lean and mean go together, and some men like ladies with a bit to them, you know."

Julianna sighed. When Lady Eleanor was in one of her woolly-headed moods there was no talking to her. Still, Julianna found herself persisting. "You may have come to Bath with thoughts of romance and marriageable gentlemen in mind, but I did not. We live a lie, Lady Eleanor. We could never tell a gentleman the truth for fear of betrayal. Would you have love without honesty?"

"Honesty often precludes love, my dear. Of a certainty, it is injurious to romance."

"I do not believe in romance," Julianna answered with some asperity. "Nor marriage . . ."

"There will be many a man to agree with you there, Julianna."

". . . for myself," Julianna finished with a frown. "I saw what marriage did to poor Mama, and I would not put myself under any man's thrall. For only see how they abuse their power. First Mama married Papa . . ."

21

"I thought they were quite happy."

". . . and though they were quite happy, just see what happened when he had the misfortune to die."

Lady Eleanor frowned. "It was most inconsiderate of your father, I have always thought."

"Indeed," Julianna agreed. "For Mama was never herself again. She no longer smiled or laughed, and I daresay would have forgotten to eat had not I or one of the servants reminded her. And then to marry Lord Ramsden, who cared only for her money. No, I do not believe in marriage and shall be quite content can I but provide for Paul. I leave romance to you, Lady Eleanor. You think only of the happiness it might bring, I think only of the sadness I saw in poor Mama's eyes."

"Marriage is a lottery." Lady Eleanor nodded. "But even so, some must win."

Julianna smiled. "Ah, but you know I do not believe in playing games of chance, only games of skill," she said, putting down her teacup to take up one of the invitations that had arrived that morning.

Julianna and Lady Eleanor had been careful to call upon the Master of Ceremonies as soon as they arrived in Bath and had entered their names in the subscription books for the balls, public teas, and concerts held in the Upper Rooms. These, along with daily visits to the Pump Room, walks on the Parade Grounds, and frequent forays to the circulating library for the latest novel, had assured them entry into Bath society, though their fear of meeting an acquaintance of Lord Ramsden kept them from entering as wholeheartedly into the social whirl as Lady Eleanor would have liked. Still, they could now claim a large, though superficial, acquaintance with many of the residents and visitors, a necessity were Julianna to be invited to the social gatherings where gambling took place.

"Lord Fairmont," Lady Eleanor said now, frowning down at a calling card with corner bent to indicate it had been delivered in person. "Do we know a Lord Fairmont, Julianna?"

Busily sorting through the invitations, Julianna shook her head. "I don't believe so, unless . . . I think I may have met a Lady Fairmont at one of the card parties I attended last week. A rather large lady with orange hair, if I remember correctly."

"Would there be any reason for her husband to call?" Lady Eleanor asked, one eyebrow raised questioningly. "Especially as you seem little acquainted with the lady?"

Julianna shrugged, placing an invitation on her pile of possibles before replying. "I can think of no reason, though I should like to further my acquaintance with his wife. If I am not mistaken, she lost an enormous sum quite cheerfully at Lady Palventon's soiree. I suppose we should attend this breakfast that Mrs. Remange is giving, though it is unlikely there will be cards."

"No, but it will be an opportunity to broaden our acquaintance, and I have heard tell of her excellent pastry cook."

Julianna glanced at her step-aunt's plump figure and smiled, for there was no denying Lady Eleanor had a well-developed sweet tooth. At Graxton Manor the food had been healthy but plain, there being little money to spare for the sweetmeats and cakes upon which Lady Eleanor thrived.

"Then we shall definitely accept," Julianna said, adding the invitation to the little pile on the small rosewood table at her side.

"Of course, we shall need new morning gowns." Lady Eleanor's small face lit up, her blond ringlets fairly quivering at the thought. "I saw some material on one of those vendors carts only this morning that would make up beautifully.

Julianna sighed, her usually erect shoulders sagging slightly as she shook her head. "I am afraid new gowns are out of the question, Lady Eleanor. Our pockets are quite to let, and if we do not come about soon, I shall have to sell Mother's garnet set, which I hate to do since they will not fetch near their worth in Bath."

Lady Eleanor nodded. "It was a good thing you sold the emeralds and those other pieces in London," she agreed. "But don't despair. You will have another big win soon, I am sure. You have been biding your time, after all. It would bring too much notice were you to win a sum equal to that you had off Lady Davina Greyling last week."

"It would frighten away the pigeons as my dear steppapa would say." Julianna made a small moue of disgust. "Sometimes I feel I am quite as bad as he."

"Nonsense, you are much the better player," Lady Eleanor said complacently.

Julianna laughed and picked up the pile of invitations again. "Let us hope so. That last win went entirely to pay the rent and the servants' wages. Mrs. Perkins hinted there were to be cards after her dinner party tonight, however. I think she wants to try her luck against me. I shall win a small amount and look around for bigger birds to pluck."

"Another Lady Davina perhaps?"

"Yes, but . . . you know, Lady Eleanor, as much as we need the money, I still feel vaguely guilty about that. It was quite a large amount."

"Even a small dog may be rich in fleas, Julianna. Do you have any reason to think she could not afford it?"

Julianna frowned and shook her head. "No. Lady Davina was dressed in quite the height of fashion and seemed more amused by her loss than anything else. It is just that she plays so badly it is almost as if she wishes to lose. It seems too easy."

"I am afraid you are not a true gamester at heart, Julianna, for all you are so skilled. It is the plumpest pigeon that the gamekeeper chooses, you know. And a good thing, for a scrawny one is good only for flavoring soup and that, not well. If it were not you, it would be someone else winning the lady's money, and we have real need of it . . . especially if I am to purchase that lovely lilac silk the vendor promised to save for me," Lady Eleanor added with a mischievous grin.

"What a complete hand you are, Lady Eleanor," Julianna replied with a chuckle. "Let us hope that there will be many a plump pigeon in our future."

"Indeed," Lady Eleanor agreed as she popped the last teacake into her mouth.

Who would have believed the timid Lady Eleanor Marnay would turn out to be such a minx, Julianna reflected later as she dressed for Mrs. Perkins's dinner party. Not that what Lady Eleanor had said wasn't quite true. They were certainly in need of the money, and Lady Davina had seemed more than willing to part with it. Julianna pulled her hair up into a high knot on her head, securing it with pins, and viewed her reflection in the dressing table mirror with something akin to resignation.

"If only my hair were not quite so red nor quite so bone straight," she addressed the face in the mirror. Large, light gray eyes looked back at her and blinked at such foolishness. One was what one was, and it was best to accept it and be done with it. But there were times when Julianna could not help but wish for the glossy blond curls of a Lady Davina.

"Perhaps if we could afford a lady's maid as Lady

Eleanor has been hinting, it might be possible to have my hair dressed more fashionably," Julianna told herself as she went to stand in front of the cheval glass. "Still, at least my dress is unexceptional."

Julianna turned this way and that as she admired the elegant lines of the evening gown Lady Eleanor had finished sewing only the day before. It was a dark gray silk overlaid with lace cut to minimize the faults of a too-thin, too-tall figure. And where Lady Eleanor had happened upon the material Julianna did not wish to know, for she quite expected someone to recognize their old bed hangings in her gown some evening.

"You look stunning." Lady Eleanor swooped into the room to admire her handiwork. "Just as I knew you would. Of course, you have one of those figures that can wear anything." Lady Eleanor glanced ruefully at her own plump reflection in the glass.

Julianna shook her head slightly in denial, quite aware that she was much too thin and tall for beauty, but grateful nevertheless for her stepaunt's attempt to bolster her ego. Not that Julianna set much store by her own appearance in any case. The important thing was her skill at the card table, and in this Julianna was supremely self-confident.

It was all due to her father, of course. Julianna pulled on her evening gloves, remembering the way he had sat at his desk, brow furrowed, hair awry, eyes alight with excitement as he taught her mathematical theory with the turn of a card or the toss of the dice.

"What is the probability of the die turning up seven, three times in a row?" he would question her. "The chances of your drawing an ace to beat my queen?"

Her father had been a born teacher as well as a brilliant mathematician, and Julianna had enjoyed the challenge. She could do complex sums in her head before she could read and was an expert at whist and piquet before she was eight.

And always in the background there had been her mother, lovely, petite, blond Emily Seaton, smiling and shaking her head over her husband's intensity with things she could never hope to comprehend. Her parents were opposites in so many ways, Julianna thought, and yet complete in each other . . . until Papa died.

"Julianna, are you quite all right?" Lady Eleanor asked, brow furrowed with concern. "You look so sad, my dear. Is anything wrong?"

Julianna blinked and reached for her reticule. Such a love as her parents had had was not given to many. "I am fine, Lady Eleanor, just a fit of melancholia, is all. Shall we look in on Paul and the new nursemaid before we leave? He will ask us to bring him a pony again, of course. But perhaps I shall win a fortune tonight, and he may have one after all."

Chapter Two

It was but a short walk to the house where the dinner party was to take place. Lady Eleanor spent the interval trying to cheer Julianna by repeating the gossip she had heard that morning in the Pump Room.

"Can you imagine? They almost called off the wedding. Mr. Keller said he would not wed with anyone who kept savage beasts as house pets, and Miss Armstrong vowed she would not give up her beloved Poopsie no matter what the consequences. I believe her parents settled the argument by sending Poopsie to the country on a repairing lease."

"Having met Mr. Keller, I can only say that I think I would prefer Poopsie," Julianna replied as they entered Mrs. Perkins's elegant townhouse and stood in line to greet their hostess.

Fortunately, Mrs. Perkins made no pretense that her dinner party was anything more than an excuse to indulge in a game of cards. As soon as dinner was over and the gentlemen had rejoined the ladies, the tables were moved from the sides of the room, and the playing commenced.

At first Julianna played hesitantly, as if not sure of the rules of the game, and lost a small sum to the other players. It was a calculated effort on her part, since it would not do to become known as a card sharp. Soon, however, Julianna was gathering in her winnings, a deprecating smile upon her face as she mentally did sums in her head calculating the probable cost of the lilac silk, their ever-present bills, and how much must be put aside for Pog's future.

"I compliment you on your card play, Mrs. Pickering." Mr. Wilmot, a huge bear of a man with side whiskers, joined Julianna as the game ended, and she took a brief turn about the drawing room. "Though I must say I still do not see how you could have known about my king."

Julianna looked up sharply. Knowing which cards Mr. Wilmot held had been a simple matter of deduction and logic based on the cards which had already been played. Surely he was not accusing her of cheating? But no, he was smiling. The remark had been no more than a casual one. "Ah, but you are such a kingly man, Mr. Wilmot," she answered lightly, returning his smile.

"The type of man a woman of queenly bearing might admire?" he asked.

Why, I do believe he is flirting with me, Julianna thought in some surprise. It was a new, but not unwelcome thought, that someone might find her pleasing to the eye. Having no idea what to reply, however, she simply continued to smile.

"Will you be attending the dress ball, Mrs. Pickering?"

"I do not usually attend," Julianna said. It was quite true. After a token appearance when they had first arrived in Bath, Julianna had felt free to spend Assembly nights at home since there was no opportunity for card play. It was a welcome respite to someone unaccustomed to the social whirl and time to spend with Paul. Still, would it be so wrong to attend? Lady Eleanor would welcome the idea. And while love and marriage had no part in Julianna's plans, she found she rather enjoyed Mr. Wilmot's attention. Surely a mild flirtation could do no harm?

"Perhaps, in this case, however, I shall make an exception."

Mr. Wilmot smiled, obviously flattered. He had been a widower for four years now, and he was beginning to think it was time he found someone to take care of him again. Mrs. Penelope Pickering might do quite well. Of course, he had heard there was a child, a young boy, and he was not overly fond of children. Mr. Wilmot resolved to call upon her and inspect the child. If the boy proved to be quiet and well-behaved, perhaps something could be arranged.

"Ah, Mrs. Pickering, I was hoping I might find you here."

Julianna turned at the touch of a gloved hand on her arm and looked down into the sparkling blue eyes of Lady Davina Greyling.

"I have just been made to endure the most insufferable dinner party given by a friend of my brother's. Fairmont insisted that I go. It is really too bad of him. But then I should be used to it. Fairmont never thinks of anyone but himself."

"Fairmont? Is . . . could Lord Fairmont be your brother, then?" Julianna questioned with a puzzled frown.

"Yes, more's the pity. Ah, Mr. Wilmot, I neglect you." Lady Davina held out her hand, causing that gentleman to blush a most unbecoming shade of pink as he bent over it.

"And the lady with . . . that is, Lady Fairmont is your . . . ?"

"My mother, the dowager," Lady Davina supplied. "She pleaded a headache and was allowed to stay home, though I very much doubt that is where she remained." Lady Davina looked about the room as if expecting to see her mother suddenly appear from behind one of the damask chairs. The tea being brought in at that moment, Lady Davina sighed and turned a woeful countenance once again in Julianna's direction.

"I had hoped to arrive in time for cards," she said. "But I might have known Fairmont would see to it that I was too late. Ah, well, we shall have a nice coze instead, shall we, Mrs. Pickering?"

Julianna, still puzzling over why Lady Davina's brother should have called upon them earlier, nodded absently and followed the diminutive figure to a settee placed in a corner of the drawing room. Mr. Wilmot was sent to fetch tea and cakes, and then summarily dismissed. "For one can hardly talk freely when he is about," Lady Davina said. "Wilmot has a terrible reputation as a gabblemonger and would like nothing better than to run to Fairmont with some juicy tidbit he has heard."

"Mr. Wilmot is a friend of your brother's, then?"

"Would like to be is more the case," Lady Davina answered, sipping her tea. "But come, let us talk of more interesting things. Not that much of interest occurs in Bath, of course."

"Oh?" Julianna's eyes crinkled slightly at the corners as she hid a smile. Clearly Lady Davina found any subject other than herself a source of ennui. "Bath is not to your liking then?"

"It is the height of the Season," Lady Davina replied between set teeth. "London is the only place to be."

"But then why . . ."

Lady Davina snapped at the bait. "My brother, of course. He absolutely delights in tormenting me. I was forced to marry Greyling, you know. He is Fairmont's closest friend. I think Grey was in need of money, so

31

my brother made sure he would have full use of my dowry. I was only seventeen at the time, and Fairmont refused to let me have a Season. What else could I do? He would have kept me locked up in that dreadful house in the country forever had I refused."

"Locked up?" Julianna asked.

"A virtual prisoner." Lady Davina nodded. "You cannot imagine the conditions. What can I say? My brother dislikes women, holds them in contempt, in fact. You see, he was engaged once, and the woman cried off. Well, who could blame her? And it is not as if Fairmont were in love with Clothinda. I doubt he is capable of the emotion. But ever since he has had this near hatred of our sex. Still, I am his sister, and there is no reason for him to treat me so. At any rate, Fairmont broke my spirit at last, and I agreed to marry Edgar Greyling. If I had not, well, there is such a thing as marriage by proxy, you know."

Julianna nodded and sipped her tea. It had grown quite cold, so enraptured had she become in Lady Davina's story, which was as good as any novel from the circulating library. Was it true, she wondered, or merely the result of a young girl's overwrought imagination?

"And I had thought that once Grey and I were wed, I would enjoy the freedom of a married woman, so I was not as reluctant as I might have been. But instead I find myself more under Fairmont's thumb than ever." Lady Davina made a small moue of disgust, thrusting out her lower lip so that Julianna was forcibly reminded of Paul when he was denied a treat.

"It is most unfair, do you not think so, Mrs. Pickering?"

"Well, I must say I do not understand why Lord Fairmont continues to have such influence over you. Surely that is now your husband's prerogative."

"Oh, I knew you would understand, Mrs. Pickering."
Lady Davina leaned forward and touched Julianna's
gloved hand impulsively. "And so I have told my
brother, but my husband is a military officer, you
know, and while he is away, Fairmont says I am still his
responsibility. It is all most discouraging."

Julianna set her cup of cold tea carefully to one side
and wondered what to say. She could certainly sympa-
thize with Lady Davina, having been so recently under
the thrall of Lord Ramsden.

"There is nothing to do in Bath," Lady Davina continued in a choked voice. "Fairmont will not even allow
me to ride. It is all most unfair. I am only nineteen,
after all. Everyone else in Bath seems to be in their dot-
age." She lifted tear-drenched eyes to Julianna. "Except
you, of course. I had hoped we might be friends,
though I am afraid my brother may forbid it. He dislikes my gambling, you see. Says I have neither skill
nor wits enough."

Julianna smiled uneasily, feeling in total agreement
with Lord Fairmont on this point. Still, it was certainly
to Julianna's advantage that Lady Davina continue to
grace the card tables with her presence.

"And it is not as if Grey cannot afford to pay my
gambling losses."

Julianna frowned. "But I thought you said he was in
need of money."

"That was before he married me. My dowry was
vast. It is almost as if I gamble with my own money,
don't you think?"

"Yes, I suppose."

"Oh, do say you understand and will be my friend,
Mrs. Pickering. It would mean so much to me." Lady
Davina's brow was creased with concern, her pixie little
face anxious as she leaned toward Julianna.

"Of course I shall stand your friend," Julianna promised, though with some misgiving. She had no desire to become involved in a family brangle, her whole objective being to live a quiet and unobtrusive life in Bath. What if this Lord Fairmont should prove to be an acquaintance of Lord Ramsden? What if he knew about Paul's disappearance, had, in fact, been asked to be on the lookout for a little boy of his description?

"Why the frown?" Lady Eleanor asked, joining the two of them on the settee. "Did someone tell you I lost to Mrs. Leacock, then?"

Julianna shook her head. "It would not matter if they had. I doubt you could have lost a great deal in any case." She looked hopefully at Lady Eleanor. It was a sad truth that Lady Eleanor was much like Lady Davina, lacking both the skill and wits for cards. The only difference was that Lady Eleanor always felt terribly guilty about her losses.

"Whist at a penny a point. A paltry sum." Mrs. Leacock sat down in a brocade chair near the settee. "I shall give it to the Society for Superseding Climbing Boys of which, as I have mentioned to Miss Partridge, I am a charter member."

"I was telling Mrs. Leacock of our problems with the chimney in the south bedroom," Lady Eleanor explained.

"Indeed?" Julianna asked, noting that Lady Davina was beginning to look bored now that she was no longer the topic of conversation.

"I highly recommend the services of Mr. Wibberting," Mrs. Leacock said. "He uses a new sweeping machine invented by a Mr. Smart in London. I could not condone any other method."

"And Mrs. Leacock says Mr. Wibberting is most careful to spread a cloth in front of the chimney to contain the soot," Lady Eleanor added.

"He keeps himself quite presentable, too," Mrs.

Leacock said. "No tracking dirt in or getting ashes all over the furniture. I shall give you his location, and you may have him call."

Julianna said she would be most agreeable to having Mr. Wibberting inspect the chimneys. "It is a nuisance not being able to use the south bedroom, but I have not liked the thought of some poor child, scarcely older than my Paul, being forced to climb through the chimneys. The climbing boys always look so thin and ill cared for, poor things."

"But of course they are thin. A plump child would not be able to get through the chimney," Lady Davina said matter-of-factly, and stifled a yawn.

Mrs. Leacock frowned. Julianna was quite sure that if Lady Davina were not a member of the quality, she would be subject to a strong lecture from the charter member of the Society for Superseding Climbing Boys. Instead, Mrs. Leacock contented herself with a disapproving look.

"I am sure you will be quite satisfied with Mr. Wibberting's work," she said stiffly. "Though even he may not be able to eliminate the smoke in that house. Always assuming it is smoke, of course."

"But what else could it be?" Julianna asked.

"What else indeed?" Lady Eleanor echoed Julianna's question. "It emanates from the chimney, it is dark gray in color, and only in evidence when we attempt to light a fire."

Mrs. Leacock's eyes looked at each face in turn, clearly relishing the suspense she had created. "Has it never occurred to you that it might be . . . the marquis?"

"What? Here?" Lady Eleanor shrieked, jumping to her feet and looking wildly about for Lord Ramsden.

"No, no." Mrs. Leacock chuckled heartily at the brouhaha she had caused. "I did not say it *was* the

Marquis of Carlborne, only that it might be. For there are those who believe in such things, you know, though I am not so gullible."

"Never say you have taken Lord Carlborne's house for the Season?" Lady Davina asked, ennui forgotten.

Julianna sat rigidly erect, one hand clasped to her breast where her heart still lurched madly about. "Who is Lord Carlborne?"

"Why . . . but surely you know?" Mrs. Leacock's eyes widened at this unexpected opportunity to dispense such a choice bit of gossip. "He is the owner of your house. Was, I should say, for he died quite tragically at the age of six and twenty."

"But I don't understand." Lady Eleanor had subsided onto the settee once more, though the feathers in her headdress still quivered slightly. "At least, I am sure it is too bad and all, but what has this marquis to do with our chimney?"

"Some say he still haunts the house where he met his untimely end," Lady Davina whispered with ghoulish glee.

Mrs. Leacock frowned at this usurpation of her story but refrained from comment, waiting instead for the inevitable question.

Julianna was the first to take the lure. "How did he die? That is, I surmise he died in the south bedroom, but may I presume he did not expire in bed?"

"Indeed not." Mrs. Leacock leapt in before Lady Davina could open her mouth. "You see the night of the tragedy, Lord Carlborne had been gambling heavily. He lost everything. Everything. Feeling that all was utterly hopeless, he went back to his house, the very house in which you now reside. He climbed the stairs to the south bedroom . . . and hanged himself with his own cravat!"

"But whose cravat should he have used?" Lady

Eleanor wanted to know. "I mean, if I were going to hang myself, which I have no intention of doing, but if I *were* going to, I should certainly use my own sash rather than borrow one from someone else. For after it had been used for such purpose, no one would want it again, and then a perfectly good dress would be ruined. It would be very difficult to find another sash that matched, you know."

Mrs. Leacock looked a bit taken aback at this pronouncement. "Well," she said at last. "Well, I suppose . . . I mean, I have never really given it much thought . . ."

"That's the problem these days," Lady Eleanor continued. "No one considers the practical side of things, and the ragman grows rich as a result. Not that I am complaining," she added as an afterthought.

Julianna smoothed the gray silk of her gown nervously, wondering if the material had come from just such a source, and willing Lady Eleanor to silence before she revealed her rather extensive acquaintance with those who earned their livelihood selling used clothing.

She need not have worried, for Lady Davina was fairly bursting to take over the conversation once again. "What Mrs. Leacock has not revealed is the identity of the man who won the fortune from poor Lord Carlborne," she said, a gleam of knowing mischief in her eye. "But she need not have been so circumspect; it is, after all, common knowledge, and I would certainly not defend his character. The man who was so callous as to ignore the pleadings of poor Carlborne was my brother, Lord Fairmont.

"Those who were there that night say the devil stood by his favorite's shoulder, for Fairmont could not lose. And when Lord Carlborne begged more time to pay his debts, for he had a young sister and aged mother who would suffer most cruelly, Fairmont laughed and said the wolf and lamb would never lie down together without the one devouring the other."

"I believe that to be quite true." Lady Eleanor nodded sagely.

"Of course it is true," Lady Davina said crossly. "Do you question my word?"

"Indeed not," Lady Eleanor said. "It is just that I doubt your experience has been pastoral. Nor has mine, for that matter. But I remember reading somewhere that shepherds arm themselves with rocks and such to keep wolves away, so I am sure it is quite true that they rarely lie down together without the most dire consequences."

It was Lady Davina's turn to look nonplussed, but she quickly recovered. "At any rate, my odious brother used to be called "The Devil," you know. The Devil Fairmont. And a fitting sobriquet it was."

The man sounded exactly like Lord Ramsden, Julianna found herself thinking as a shiver coursed down her spine. What a horrible coincidence should they prove to be acquainted.

Lady Eleanor's thoughts were following the same course. "Why, what an odd coincidence," she said.

"I beg your pardon, Miss Partridge?"

"That we should both have devilish brothers." Lady Eleanor nodded thoughtfully. "It is amazing how many things we have in common, is it not?"

"Indeed?" Lady Davina looked from Lady Eleanor's frizzled curls, plump figure, and furrowed brow which had obviously seen more than forty summers, and raised arched eyebrows. She had been looking for sympathy, not comparison. "I fail to see a resemblance. And, in any case, Fairmont is no longer called The Devil. He has become as strait-laced as any prosing vicar."

"Lord Fairmont is much respected in Bath," Mrs. Leacock concurred.

"I believe some now call my brother "The Angel," though not to his face, of course. And since his first name is Gabriel, I suppose it is fitting. I preferred him before he got so high in the instep, however. Now, he seems to find fault with everything, especially if I find it amusing." She frowned and peered over Julianna's shoulder. "But you shall have a chance to decide for yourself, for here is my brother come to fetch me home."

Julianna turned. The same cold, dark eyes she had encountered in the park that morning looked down at her, seeming to pierce to her very soul.

Chapter Three

The smell of beeswax and lemon scented the air as Julianna vigorously applied cloth and Lady Eleanor's homemade paste to the Hepplewhite table in the parlor. Lady Eleanor had left early that morning to purchase the coveted lilac silk, and Julianna had decided it would be a good time to set to work. Since the house had been vacant for the past two Seasons, there was a great deal to be done. Much more than could be accomplished by the few servants they had been able to hire.

Julianna had been working on the badly neglected furniture for the better part of two hours, but thought the results well worth her efforts. She paused for a moment to look down at her reflection which shone from the now gleaming surface of the table. Her arms ached, the towel she had wrapped around her hair to protect it from the dust was coming undone, and she had a discernible smudge on her nose, but for the first time in more years than she cared to count, Julianna felt truly happy. She undid the top two buttons of her dress — it was a warm day and polishing furniture hot work — and gave her wooden image a quick smile before proceeding to a small glass cabinet of cherry wood in one corner.

Humming out of tune as usual, Julianna applied a goodly dab of Lady Eleanor's paste to the wood strips that crisscrossed the clouded glass of the cabinet. The glass was in need of a good cleaning as well, though it was a task Julianna had decided to postpone. The cherry-wood cabinet contained, among other things, a large stuffed owl with a predatory gleam in its eyes. It reminded her rather forcibly of Lord Fairmont. Though his eyes were brown rather than yellow, they were just as piercing, and made one just as uncomfortable.

Julianna gave a little shiver, remembering the way Lord Fairmont had looked at her last night. He had said nothing about having seen her in Spring Gardens with Paul that morning, but she had been quite sure that he recognized her and remembered the incident. Lady Davina had been forced to make introductions, though they were so cursory as to be just short of rudeness, and then had almost leapt to her feet, ending any opportunity for further conversation. Which was just as well, in Julianna's opinion. She was not sure what Lord Fairmont's game was, but that it was a dangerous one, she was certain.

With a final rub of her cloth, Julianna stepped back and surveyed the cabinet and then the room. It was certainly looking much better than it had a month ago when they had moved in. Then, she had wondered at the neglect; now, she had reason to understand. Julianna sat down in a giltwood armchair, one hand absently polishing the fluted support, as she thought over what she had learned last night. She could well believe that Lord Fairmont would show little mercy to anyone who thwarted him, but still, to refuse so small a thing as Lord Carlborne's request for more time to pay his debt seemed callous in the extreme. And how dreadful to have a man's death on one's conscience.

Julianna shook her head and carefully folded her polishing cloth into a neat square. Gambling was a means to an end for her. She rarely got so caught up in a game that she forgot all else as she had seen so frequently happen to Lord Ramsden. Oh, every now and then, when she was pitted against a truly skillful player, Julianna enjoyed the mental challenge, but she did not think she would ever lose control to the extent of gambling away a fortune. Especially when others depended on that fortune as well. Julianna frowned down at the folded cloth in her lap. She supposed Lord Carlborne was at least partially to blame. And at six and twenty he had been no callow youth but a man who should have known better than to risk his future and that of his family on the turn of a card.

Do you then defend Lord Fairmont's actions? she asked herself. No. Julianna shook her head, causing the towel wrapped around her hair to slide even farther askew. She could not defend the man's actions. Not that Lord Fairmont would consider his actions in any need of defense. He seemed a man supremely self-confident, a man who made decisions and then forgot them, whatever the consequences to someone else.

How wounding it must have been then when his betrothed, Lady Belinda or Clodhillda or whatever her name was, had cried off from their engagement. Julianna smiled just a bit gleefully at this thought, remembering with some chagrin the dismissing way Lord Fairmont's eyes had passed over her last night. Though truly, Julianna would as soon Lord Fairmont did not dwell overly much on her or Paul. And she should be used to men's indifference. Other than Mr. Wilmot, none had ever shown an interest.

Mr. Wilmot. Julianna got to her feet, smoothing the towel she had tied around her waist to protect the skirts of her faded blue muslin. She was still of two minds about attending the Assembly. Did she really wish to encourage Mr. Wilmot? When she was younger she had thought of marriage as a means of escape from Graxton Manor. But as the years passed, and the only men she met were those invited to the Manor to gamble with Lord Ramsden, Julianna realized that the life of a spinster was much to be preferred over marriage to one of the so-called gentlemen her stepfather entertained.

No. Julianna decided firmly. No. Marriage was not for such as her. Better to make one's own decisions, one's own way in life, than to be dependent on a man. Especially now, when any serious attachment could place them all at risk. Julianna unfolded her polishing cloth and began to attack the curved back of a nearby armchair. The front door knocker, suddenly echoing down the short hallway at the bottom of the stairs, caused her to frown and put down the jar of Lady Eleanor's paste.

Whoever could be calling at this hour? she wondered, glancing at the small brass clock on the mantel. It was much too early for a social call or for Lady Eleanor to be returning from her shopping expedition. Then Julianna remembered Mr. Wibberting, the master sweep Mrs. Leacock had promised to send round. It was odd that he was not using the servants' entrance, but then, Mrs. Leacock had said the man was unusual.

Julianna wiped her hands on the towel wrapped around her waist and walked onto the small landing at the head of the stairs, waiting for one of the servants to answer the door. Besides Kitty, the young girl hired as nursemaid to Paul, there were only two other servants: Hawkins, employed as butler, footman, and general factotum, and Edna Gardning, hired as housekeeper-cum-cook. Lady Eleanor had insisted on being the one to hire them, and neither had references.

"But those can be forged, you know, so I discount them," Lady Eleanor had said. "The most important thing is that they were willing to work for the wages you said we could afford. I am sure they will suit us very well."

After two weeks of finding the two servants seldom about when needed, Julianna was not so sanguine. With a sigh, she hurried down the stairs. If Mr. Wibberting was as eccentric as Mrs. Leacock hinted, he very well might leave if she did not answer his imperious knock at once, and then they would never clear the smoke, or Lord Carlborne, from the south bedroom.

The front of the small rented house looked out on a square of greenery surrounded by a low iron fence and shared equally by the inhabitants of the neighboring homes. Julianna could see none of this when she opened the door, however, for the man standing there was so tall and broad shouldered he completely blocked the view. Added to this was the fact that the light was behind him, so Julianna could make out little of his shadowed countenance. Little except the dark brown eyes which had so unnerved her last evening and the hair above his shadowed face which caught the sunlight and glowed a deep guinea gold, forming an aureole about his head.

"If you have looked your fill," Lord Fairmont said, brushing past Julianna and depositing his high-crowned beaver on the hall table she had finished polishing only yesterday, "you might inform your mistress, Mrs. Pickering, that I have called. I imagine she is expecting me."

"Mrs . . . ? Oh. Oh, yes." Julianna took the card Lord Fairmont was holding out, wondering why he thought she would be expecting him. He had turned slightly so that the light from the doorway now fell full upon his face. It was the same well-chiseled, haughty countenance of the night before with high cheekbones, thin aristocratic nose, and cold, cold brown eyes. Lady Davina was right, Julianna thought as she shut the door. Despite the golden halo of hair, it was Lucifer, the fallen angel who came to mind.

"Come, girl." Lord Fairmont snapped his fingers. "Tell your mistress I am here. I haven't all day to waste on this business."

Julianna looked up; her large, light gray eyes darkened and narrowed. He thought she was a servant, the downstairs maid perhaps, whose job it was to answer the door in the butler's absence. Did he not recognize her then? No, Julianna realized, it was simply that he had not looked at her. Lord Fairmont was apparently one of those men who considered servants no more than chattel to do their bidding. Lord Ramsden had been another such, treating them as bits of furniture to be ignored, creatures without intellect or feeling.

A quiet rage began to build within Julianna's bosom against all such men who thought the distance between servant and master a vast chasm that could not be bridged and who judged only by outward appearance. Had I been dressed as I was last night, he would have recognized me at once, she thought. But now, the high-and-mighty Lord Fairmont does not even deign to look at me. Her lips tightened for a moment and then relaxed, her light gray eyes opening wide once again as if a mask of innocence had suddenly dropped in place.

"If you will come this way, milord," Julianna said, turning and leading the way up the stairs. Lord Fairmont followed, expecting, Julianna knew, to be taken to the parlor to await Mrs. Pickering. Julianna smiled slightly to herself. You are in for a bit of a surprise, Lord Fairmont, she thought. And no more than you deserve. For Julianna was beginning to believe that Lady Davina had not exaggerated last night, and all that had been said to her brother's disservice was true.

Julianna continued up another flight of stairs and threw open the door to the south bedroom. "I was expecting Mr. Wibberting," she said, her voice and demeanor one of total innocence. "Not that I object to using your services, Lord Fairmont, but I notice you are not equipped. I had hoped you would be able to begin immediately."

A slight smile appeared on Lord Fairmont's face. "I assure you that I am quite well-equipped and have yet to hear a woman complain about using my services."

"Good. I am sure you will do." Julianna nodded and preceded him into the bedroom. "And I assure you, I am sympathetic to the fact that times and the perversity of fortune have forced you into trade."

"I beg your pardon?"

"I hope you are not afraid of ghosts, however." Julianna ignored Lord Fairmont's raised eyebrows. "The house was closed up for two years before I leased it. Apparently no one wanted to take it because it is rumored to be haunted. I believe the last owner hanged himself in this room after having lost his fortune at hazard. Still, I doubt it is his ghost that causes the chimney to smoke." She nodded toward the empty grate, causing the towel wrapped about her head to slide precariously to one side. With an impatient hand, Julianna pushed it back in place.

Lord Fairmont frowned. "I see you know the story or at least the more scandalous parts of it. I am surprised to find such stale gossip still being repeated, however."

"The best of cakes is still worth eating," Julianna quoted Lady Eleanor. "Though not as tasty as when first baked."

"No doubt." Lord Fairmont looked at her for a moment, his eyes narrowing slightly. Then his frown turned to a smile as without warning he reached out and swept the towel from Julianna's hair.

"What do you think you are doing!" Julianna stepped back, one hand going to her tousled hair. "Have you gone quite mad?"

He continued to smile at her, casually twisting the towel in his hands into the shape of a garrote. "Not I," he said softly.

Julianna swallowed nervously, one hand going to her throat. Had she thought to teach this man a lesson? He was quite right. She was the one lacking in wits, not he.

"So, it is the red-haired Mrs. Pickering again." Lord Fairmont said. "I should have known." He threw the towel onto a chair and reached for her. Julianna bit back a scream.

"It was about to fall out."

"What?" Julianna looked at the comb he was holding out to her.

"It was about to fall out of your hair," Lord Fairmont explained, looking mildly amused. "You must be a devotee of Mrs. Radcliffe. You looked as if you thought I was about to strangle you." He strolled farther into the bedroom and looked around before turning to Julianna once again. "I am sorry I did not recognize you at once, Mrs. Pickering, though, in any case, I should think you would be flattered."

"Flattered?"

Lord Fairmont nodded. "And may I say that I too am sympathetic to the fact that times and the perversity of fortune have forced you into this particular trade."

Julianna, whose heartbeat had just begun to slow to normal, frowned in puzzlement.

"However, I am afraid the servant-girl guise has never particularly appealed to me. Though I imagine," his eyes roved slowly over her, "that beneath the faded gown you might not be without merit."

Julianna's carefully controlled facade slipped completely as she comprehended his meaning. "Are you suggesting—Do you mean— How dare you!" she sputtered.

Lord Fairmont shrugged. "What else was I to think? You answer the door in dishabille, you escort me to your bedroom, you begin a lewd conversation regarding my equipment . . ."

"I never! I—I—" Julianna's face flamed as she looked down at herself, realized the top buttons of her dress were still undone and quickly redid them, before haphazardly stabbing the comb she still held back into her hair.

"Not quite up to last night," Lord Fairmont said, looking at her in a considering way, "but an improvement."

"Thank you." Julianna's tone was icy.

"You are most welcome. But perhaps we might discuss this in less hazardous surroundings."

"Hazardous?" Julianna frowned at him. "There is nothing . . . oh, I see, you refer to the specter of Lord Carlborne. I did not think you the sort of man to be affrighted by such things." Julianna took a deep breath, trying to regain her scattered wits. "I assure you the marquis has not appeared to any of us, and as far as I am aware, presents no danger."

"No," Lord Fairmont agreed. "I believe Carlborne presented a danger only to himself. But I refer to more material hazards. I have not gained the age of six and thirty without realizing that being entertained in a lady's bedroom is one of them. Surely you are aware that with my reputation it will take more than a smoking chimney to catch me in a parson's snare?"

Such conceit! "I know nothing of your reputation," she said untruthfully as she marched stiffly from the room. "Nor do I care to."

"You surprise me," Lord Fairmont said softly behind her. "Most women find such things quite fascinating. Or should I say, challenging?"

The parlor, with its scent of lemon and beeswax, was reached in stony silence. Julianna walked to the gilt armchair and sat down, her mask once more in place.

"You wished to speak to me, Lord Fairmont?" Julianna asked, her words precise chips of polite ice.

Not a whit put off by this, Lord Fairmont strode over to the table on which Julianna had so recently been expending her efforts and after a moment of apparently perusing his image in its polished surface, turned to face her. All trace of amusement was gone, though his chiseled mouth was curved in a slight smile. "As we have already dispensed with the social niceties, let us get down to business, shall we?"

"Business?" Julianna returned his smile with a cold one of her own. "What possible business could you have with me, Lord Fairmont?"

"It is quite simple, Mrs. Pickering, and since I do not believe in roundaboutation in such matters, I shall tell you in straightforward fashion. Stay away from my sister."

"I beg your pardon?" Julianna could not believe she had heard correctly. The man spoke as if she were some unsavory suitor for his sister's hand rather than a chance and slight acquaintance of the lady. "I barely know Lady Davina," she said, thinking perhaps he had made some mistake.

"You know her well enough to have won several hundred pounds from her last week," he corrected. "You will not do so again."

"It is almost impossible not to win money from your sister, so poor a player as she is," Julianna protested. "And she did not seem distressed by her loss, far from

49

it."

"Of course she was not distressed," Lord Fairmont snapped impatiently. "She only does it to irritate me."

"Then your quarrel is with Lady Davina. You can hardly warn away half the population of Bath, and I doubt I am the only player to have gained by your sister's ineptitude."

"The others need no warning." His voice and eyes were steel, though the slight smile remained. "You have been made aware that I have something of a reputation, Mrs. Pickering. Do not attempt to cross me, or you will learn how it was earned."

Insufferable man! Lady Davina had not exaggerated in the least. Julianna could well believe he would imprison his innocent sister to gain his own nefarious ends. He was as bad as Lord Ramsden. Worse. But unlike poor Lady Davina, Lord Fairmont had no power over her. Julianna rose to her feet. Despite the towel still wrapped about her waist and the smudge of dust on her nose, Julianna's innate dignity and courage were evident in her proud carriage and the direct look she leveled at Lord Fairmont from those great gray eyes. "I must ask you to leave, Lord Fairmont. I will not be threatened in my own home."

"No?" Lord Fairmont's eyes narrowed. "I think you are forgetting something, Mrs. Pickering."

Julianna raised her eyebrows in disbelief. "I think not. Now if you will kindly take your departure, it will save me calling the butler to—"

"Jules, Jules." They both turned as the little boy came hurtling through the open doorway of the parlor. "Look, I—" Catching sight of the stranger, Paul stopped, eyeing Lord Fairmont with curiosity but none of the bashfulness one might expect from so young a child.

"This is Lord Fairmont, Paul." Julianna performed

50

the introduction stiffly. For all her bravery, she was still wary of Lord Fairmont and knew he would quickly realize her vulnerability where Paul was concerned.

Lord Fairmont bowed. "The young man I saw in the Gardens."

Paul did a credible imitation of Lord Fairmont's bow, and the two took stock of each other for a few minutes while Julianna's heart did a rapid flip-flop of fear. Lord Fairmont did remember their meeting then.

"I'm that sorry, mum." Kitty, the new nursemaid, bustled into the room full of apologies. "Just a minute I turned me head, and when I looked again off he'd gone. He's that fast there's no keepin' track of him."

"Yes, Kitty, I am quite aware of the fact," Julianna said, knowing full well that Paul's angelic appearance belied his behavior. "I am sure it is not your fault."

"I'll just take him back to the nursery, mum." Kitty reached for Paul's hand, but he danced quickly out of reach.

"Show, Jules," he said, his blue eyes growing stormy. "Show, Jules, first."

"What is it you wish to show me, Paul?" Julianna asked, bending to his level and forgetting both Lord Fairmont and her outrage at the man's insufferable behavior.

Paul held up one chubby fist. "For Humbert," he said, opening his hand to reveal a small ball of yellow cheese. Humbert was a brown field mouse which resided beneath the cellar steps. Paul had adopted it despite the cook's threat to quit if "that vermin gets into my kitchen."

"Some cheese for Humbert? How thoughtful of you, Paul," Julianna said.

Paul nodded, quite pleased with himself. "Come see?" he asked, tugging at Julianna's hand.

"In a minute, Paul. As soon as I have finished talk-

51

ing to Lord Fairmont."

"Him come too?"

Julianna straightened and glanced at Lord Fairmont. "Humbert is a field mouse," she explained defensively. "A poor pet for a boy, I know, but at the moment the pony he covets is quite out of the question."

Lord Fairmont frowned. "Women never understand what is truly important," he said cryptically.

"Come see?" Paul demanded again.

"I'm afraid not," Lord Fairmont replied, looking almost as if he were actually considering the matter. "I have an appointment in a few minutes. Perhaps I can meet Humbert another time."

"Bring buns," Paul said. "Humbert likes them."

Lord Fairmont's frown gave way to a smile. "Next time," he promised, and stood watching, lips slightly pursed as Julianna tenderly smoothed back one of Paul's wayward curls before the nursemaid led him away. After a moment, Lord Fairmont turned back to Julianna, one eyebrow raised in silent inquiry.

"My son," Julianna supplied quickly.

"Little resemblance."

Julianna nodded. "He takes after his father, Mr. Pickering," Julianna said, the lie, frequently rehearsed, coming easily to her tongue.

"And Mr. Pickering is . . . ?"

"Dead." Julianna let the word lay leadenly between them for a moment. "He died in a carriage accident two years ago. Paul barely remembers him." She knew her face showed a very real distress, for whenever she told the story, Julianna thought of her own father's death in that awful carriage accident when she was nine. After almost fifteen years, she could barely conjure up her father's face, but the remembered grief and confused sense of loss she had felt as a child were still quite clear.

"I'm sorry." The conventional words were uttered automatically, almost as if Lord Fairmont knew her grief was no more real than the late Mr. Pickering.

"Yes." Julianna nodded, head bent. "Thank you."

"None of this touching family situation alters my reason for calling on you today, however," Lord Fairmont continued in a voice once more edged with steel. "My sister is, I am afraid, a compulsive gambler. Her husband, Edgar Greyling, is a captain in the Light Dragoons, and while he is away on the Continent, I act as Davina's guardian. If you sit down to cards with her again, you may find that her promissory notes are worth no more than the paper on which they are written."

Julianna looked at him in amazement. "You would not redeem them?"

He shook his head. "I have warned Davina, and now I warn you. There is to be no more gambling."

"You may so advise your sister, and she may heed you if she wishes," Julianna began, feeling the heat rise in her face, "but I am a different matter."

"A different matter, indeed," Lord Fairmont agreed. "But you would still do well to consider my warning carefully. An addiction to gambling is not to be taken lightly."

A fact Julianna knew only too well. Hadn't Lord Ramsden gambled away her mother's inheritance as well as Julianna's own? Was it not just such an addiction that had caused her to flee with Paul and Lady Eleanor from Graxton Manor? Julianna was well aware of the evils of gambling, yet what other recourse had she? It was either gamble or starve. Either gamble or allow Paul's innocence to be consumed by his father's profligacy. Who was this high-and-mighty Lord Fairmont, who had doubtless never known what it was to do without, who was he to tell her to stop what had become her livelihood?

Her gray eyes darkened to slate as she raised them to his. "I thank you for the warning," she said, "and bid you good day."

Lord Fairmont bowed slightly and allowed himself to be ushered into the hall where he picked up the high-crowned beaver he had left there earlier. "Before I go, there is one question I would like to ask, Mrs. Pickering."

Julianna looked up at him warily. A hint of danger seemed to lurk in the opaque depths of the brown eyes looking down at her. "W-what is it?" she asked, hating the slight quaver in her voice but quite unable to control it.

"If your name is Penelope Pickering as you have given out, why does your son call you Jules?" A slight smile and he was gone, not deigning to wait for an answer.

Chapter Four

Lady Eleanor returned from her shopping expedition triumphantly laden with packages and tales of successful haggling.

"You will not believe what I paid for this green shot silk," she exclaimed, sweeping Julianna before her into the parlor. "Such a bargain and the perfect color for you. I have already decided on the design. Mrs. Grumbel was good enough to let me look through several of her fashion books when last I visited. I think a slightly dropped waist with a bit of that white piping I got for next to nothing, because as I said to the shopkeeper: the end is soiled and no one will pay full price for such. Though it only needed a bit of sponging as he should have known."

Lady Eleanor began ripping the paper from the packages, still talking excitedly. "And the lilac silk is as lovely as I remembered." She held up a bolt of cloth. "Do you not think so, Julianna? I am so glad that Mr. Wilmot was such a poor player. Though it is too bad Lady Davina arrived so late or I might have been able to buy that silver gauze as well."

"It is lovely and suits you very well," Julianna agreed, holding up her hand to stem the flow of Lady Eleanor's words. "But—"

"And I am sure I will be able to finish something in time for next week's dress ball. We shall attend, shall we not?"

Julianna nodded and allowed Lady Eleanor to continue in full spate, deeming it all but impossible to halt the words cascading forth. And though Julianna could feel her mind begin to flounder in the depths, she truly did not wish to dam the flow of Lady Eleanor's happiness.

When everything had been unwrapped and duly exclaimed over, Lady Eleanor bustled over to the bellpull and declared that they must now have a cup of tea and a cozy gossip. "For I want to hear all that Lord Fairmont had to say."

"Lord Fairmont?" Julianna straightened from her lounging position on the settee. "What do you know of Lord Fairmont?"

"It was he that was leaving as I arrived, was it not? So laden with packages was I that I had to hire a hackney. And he was so kind as to pay the driver when I discovered I had insufficient funds left over. It was the paste shoe buckles I think, though such a bargain could hardly be overlooked."

Julianna frowned. "You allowed Lord Fairmont to pay for your hackney?" She hated the thought of being in any way beholden to that insufferable man.

"Yes. He is so much more flush in the pocket, it seemed the sensible thing. He was most kind, said he remembered me from last night. It is Miss Polly Partridge, is it not? he said. I was most flattered that he remembered me, though . . . did we not decide that my name was to be Prudence, Julianna?"

"You know I can never keep our names straight," Julianna said, a small, anxious shaft of fear stabbing at her and causing her to frown. "I think having them all begin with P makes it more difficult, not easier as you suggested."

Lady Eleanor settled herself comfortably in the gilt armchair. "I daresay," she replied agreeably. "But since no one else can remember them either, it will not seem amiss that we forget them as well."

"People rarely forget their own names," Julianna pointed out.

"Well, practice makes perfect," Lady Eleanor said. "And I doubt not that we shall soon remember our names as well as anyone." She got up and went to the bellpull again. "I swear I am quite parched for a cup of tea and feeling in great need of some of Mrs. Gardning's delicious biscuits. Shopping is so tiresome."

Julianna's anxious frown was replaced by a smile. "If you are going to put it about that you dislike the task, you had best droop more, Lady Eleanor. You look entirely too vigorous to be taken seriously otherwise."

"Ah, well. I cannot wait to begin working on the lilac silk, I must confess. I may borrow Kitty again, may I not? She sews a very fine seam."

"Of course. You must just tell me when, and I will take Paul in charge. But, Lady Eleanor, what else did Lord Fairmont say to you?" Julianna could not quite quell her suspicions that Lord Fairmont had not paid off the hackney out of kindness, but for some reason of his own.

"Why, nothing much. The merest commonplaces, actually. He asked if I were not Miss Polly Partridge, and when I agreed that I was, he asked if I were a relation of yours."

"And you said . . . ?"

"Well, I was about to say that I was your stepaunt, when Lord Fairmont suggested that we must be sisters."

"Sisters?"

Lady Eleanor nodded, her face wreathed in smiles. "And then he mentioned the resemblance between me and Paul. He said it was quite striking and that Paul was a beautiful child." Lady Eleanor patted a crimped curl complacently. "A most charming man, Lord Fairmont. And so handsome. If only I were ten years younger."

"Since we are sisters, there is no reason you can't be," Julianna rejoined, feeling unaccountably irritated.

"Why, Julianna, it is not at all like you to be so dog in the mangerish," Lady Eleanor said. "It is hardly my fault that Lord Fairmont finds me attractive."

Julianna smoothed her skirt, realized she was still wearing the towel wrapped around her waist, and quickly removed it. "I simply do not trust the man," she said, staring down at the crumpled towel in her hand. "I think he does nothing without purpose."

Lady Eleanor raised her eyebrows. "I found him quite charming."

"He turns the charm on and off like a spigot," Julianna protested.

"That may be," Lady Eleanor surprised Julianna by agreeing. "But when the spout is turned in your direction, it is most gratifying. Now, wherever can Hawkins have gotten to?" She rose and gave the bell-pull an impatient jerk.

Julianna frowned, though not over concern for Hawkins and the whereabouts of the tea tray. She was thinking instead of Lady Eleanor's remarks and wondering to what purpose Lord Fairmont had engaged her step aunt in conversation. That the man was a practiced rogue and used flattery to put a woman off her guard was without question. But why had Lord Fairmont decided to employ his arts on Lady Eleanor?

For the rest of the day Julianna worried the matter like a cat with a ball of yarn but could come to no conclusion. When it was time to dress for the party they were to attend that evening, Julianna was tired and disinclined to go, a nagging headache tensing her brows into a half frown. Still, their hostess had promised cards, and Lady Eleanor was looking forward to the evening, having refurbished one of her old gowns with new ribbon and some artificial flowers.

"Of course, if you do not feel well, we shall not go," Lady Eleanor said, looking so woebegone that Julianna had to smile. "But I thought, perhaps, if you took one of my powders you might feel more the thing."

"I am sure I shall be fine, Lady Eleanor, and of course we shall attend. I must win enough to cover the purchase of that silver gauze, must I not?"

Since it was not an Assembly night, the party was well-attended. Flexing her fingers unobtrusively in their white kid gloves, Julianna looked around the room assessing the possible gambling prowess of the guests. To her surprise and delight, she quickly spotted Lady Davina Greyling standing to one side of the drawing-room windows.

Lady Davina was dressed in the first stare of elegance, her petite, though somewhat plump, figure encased in a gown of deep blue silk trimmed with gold lace and with a rather daring décolletage. Though not beautiful, Lady Davina had an air of breathless anticipation about her that lent a deal of countenance to her small, heart-shaped face. She turned to speak to the gentleman at her side, and the candlelight from the wall sconces glinted on the golden hair so like her brother's. Julianna frowned and found her earlier headache returning. Should she risk Lord Fairmont's wrath by gambling with Lady Davina?

I would be sure of winning a goodly amount, Julianna thought, for Lady Davina is not only a terrible player but reckless as well. Compulsive, Lord Fairmont had said, which gave Julianna momentary pause. She had no wish to encourage anyone to gamble, but if she did not have another large win soon, she must bid her mother's garnets adieu.

The decision was soon taken out of Julianna's hands, for no sooner did Lady Davina glance in her direction, then she was strolling to Julianna's side.

"I hope you will give me a chance to redeem myself, Mrs. Pickering," she said to Julianna with a careless smile. "I know my skill at cards is as yet no match for yours, but how improve if I do not practice?"

She speaks as if she were taking lessons on the pianoforte, Julianna thought, agreeing quickly to a game of piquet. Well, I am afraid they shall prove to be very expensive lessons, but if I do not win the lady's money someone else will. And I am most in need of it.

It was almost impossible to lose. Julianna did her best to allow Lady Davina a point or two, but it was not easy. The other woman seemed determined to part with her money as quickly as possible. The game was hardly a challenge to Julianna's skills, and she soon grew bored. The other guests wandered idly about the room, watching some of the card play or sitting down to new games of their own. Few stopped at the small table in the corner where Julianna and Lady Davina played, though Lady Eleanor came by once to whisper in Julianna's ear that she had actually won two pounds from old General Benefort.

"He is even a worse player than I," she confessed. "Which is a good thing, since I lost five pounds to Mrs. Grumbel." Lady Eleanor looked anxious about adding to their already precarious financial situation, and Julianna reassured her with a smile, noting Lady Davina's discard as she did so.

"I shall not buy that silver gauze, of course," Lady Eleanor continued, as if this would somehow make up for her loss. "It is not at all necessary."

Julianna said nothing, not wishing to argue the matter in public, but she would see to it that Lady Eleanor bought the silver gauze and whatever else she needed. For while it was quite true that Lady Eleanor was a bit of a dither brain, it was also true that she was invariably good-natured and seldom bitter about the deprivations she had had to endure due to Lord Ramsden's profligacy.

Lord Fairmont need not speak to me about the evils of gambling, Julianna thought. I know them only too well. Only this time, they shall work to my favor, and Lady Eleanor shall buy whatever fripperies she wants. Julianna concentrated on the game, mentally reviewing the cards that had been played and the ones Lady Davina probably still held.

"No wonder you lose so easily."

Startled, Julianna looked up, her eyes locking with the dark brown ones of Lord Fairmont.

"And has my dear brother arrived to save me from

the clutches of penury?" Lady Davina asked, turning to greet Lord Fairmont.

"I sometimes think I should let you go to debtor's prison were it not for Grey's sake."

Lady Davina's smile was icy. "That comes as no surprise. You have always placed greater value on Grey's friendship than on your family."

"If that were so, I wonder why I allowed him to marry you?"

Julianna flushed. She hated being a second party to this public washing of dirty linen. Neither of the combatants seemed to have noticed her discomfiture, however. Lady Davina appeared poised to throw her cards in Lord Fairmont's face, while he stared down at her, the worst insult of all, that of boredom, writ plainly for anyone to see."

"Damn you, Fairmont," Lady Davina said at last. "Your habits may have changed, but your tongue is as devilish as ever."

"Thank you, my dear." Lord Fairmont gave a slight bow. "Now if you will finish losing to Mrs. Pickering, I shall escort you home. I promised Grey you would take care of your health."

"And if I do not choose to go?"

Lord Fairmont smiled. "That would not be wise, Davina, as you have cause to know. Do not forget, I hold the purse strings while Grey is away."

Lady Davina's blue eyes narrowed in fury, but she turned to her cards, selected the one that would give Julianna the game, and threw it on the table. "I have lost nearly a hundred pounds," she said, smiling up at her brother sweetly. "Since you hold the purse strings, you will have to pay, will you not?"

Julianna was quite prepared for Lord Fairmont to refuse as he had threatened to do earlier, but he merely glanced at his sister's vowels before counting out the money on the table. "Since I do not see our esteemed mother present, may I assume you came alone, or did one of your many cicisbeos accompany you?"

"Monty," Lady Davina supplied. "He is somewhere about, I suppose."

"At least you know enough to pick the least dangerous ones." Lord Fairmont nodded. "I shall have one of the footmen fetch your wrap."

Lady Davina glared at her brother's broad shoulders as he walked away. "The devil!" she hissed. "Now you see what he is like, Mrs. Pickering. Do you blame me for hating him?"

"At least Lord Fairmont paid your gambling debt," Julianna answered in an attempt to mollify her.

Lady Davina shrugged. "He will get it back from Grey, and even if he does not, it is no more than Fairmont deserves."

Julianna did not reply since Lord Fairmont returned at that moment to claim his sister. Lady Davina's face was set in a sulky pout and Julianna could not but feel a momentary flash of sympathy for the man. Lord Fairmont turned to take his leave, and for an instant their eyes met and held before Julianna quickly looked away. Coward, she chided herself. Though it was not Lord Fairmont's anger she feared but the curious sense of kinship which had seemed to flow between them with an unmistakable and not unwelcome warmth.

Ridiculous, she told herself. You are being as fanciful as Paul when he imagines monsters beneath his bed. Only Lord Fairmont had not seemed at all monstrous. Quite the opposite in fact. Julianna drew the strings of her reticule firmly together and went in search of Lady Eleanor. It would not do to dwell on such matters. It would not do at all.

Lady Eleanor seemed to have acquired a beau in the course of the evening, for a Colonel Cramden, late of His Majesty's army, was busily chatting to her. Julianna paused, not sure if she should intrude when Lady Eleanor was so clearly enjoying herself. Frizzled curls dancing about her head, Lady Eleanor nodded vigorously in agreement with something the colonel was saying. Flushed cheeks and sparkling blue eyes made her seem much younger than her years. Perhaps we might be sisters after all, Julianna thought with a sad, reflective smile, feeling suddenly very old, and as if she had much more than four and twenty years on her shelf. Was it her responsibility for Paul, for all of them, that made her feel so? Or was it seeing the becoming flush on Lady Eleanor's cheeks which made Julianna feel as if she should set a cap upon her head and play chaperon.

"Ah, it is Mrs. Pickering, is it not?" the colonel asked, looking up and spying Julianna hovering a few feet away. He rose gallantly to his feet and reached for a cane, whereby Julianna could see he had a slight limp. "I have just been enjoying a tête-à-tête with your dear aunt. A most charming woman."

"Yes, indeed," Julianna agreed, looking down at Lady Eleanor who was blushing with pleasure.

"I hope you will allow me the pleasure of escorting you home. Miss Partridge has been telling me it is but a short walk, and if you will put up with my slowness, I should be glad of it."

"How kind." Julianna smiled, liking the colonel at once.

"I have been telling Colonel Cramden about Paul,"

Lady Eleanor said, beaming up at this gentleman as he helped her to her feet. "He has a grandson about the same age."

"Oh?" Julianna could not stop the feeling of edginess which crept over her at the mention of Paul's name. She knew she was being overprotective, but she still felt it best to keep Paul in the background as much as possible. It was not unusual for children to be raised almost entirely by nursemaids, and it would not seem odd for visitors to seldom see the boy. The fewer people who met Paul, the less likely it was that reports of him would find their way back to Lord Ramsden. And Julianna was already uneasy about Paul's meeting with Lord Fairmont.

"I thought the child might enjoy a carriage ride in the country sometime," the colonel said. "Most children enjoy that sort of thing."

Julianna forced herself to relax. What harm could there be, after all? "I am sure Paul would enjoy that. He misses the country, I think."

"Ah, yes? What part of the country do you and Miss Partridge call home then?"

Lady Eleanor looked anxiously at Julianna who silently cursed her own too-fluid tongue. "At the moment, home is in Bath," Julianna supplied after a momentary hesitation.

Thankfully, Colonel Cramden seemed to find nothing amiss with this answer and after taking leave of their hostess, the small party descended the stairs to the vestibule where a footman waited with their wraps.

A dark figure stood leaning against the passage wall as they entered, candlelight glinting upon fair hair and deep, shadowed eyes.

Julianna's smile wavered, the lighthearted comment

65

she had been about to make fading upon her lips. "Lord Fairmont?" Julianna breathed the question. "I thought you and Lady Davina had left some time ago."

Lord Fairmont straightened from his lounging position and stepped forward. "I sent Davina home in a sedan chair," he said. "I thought you and Miss Partridge might be glad of an escort considering the weight of your reticule."

Julianna's apprehension quickened into anger. "Colonel Cramden has already offered to escort us," she said coldly. "There was no need for you to wait."

"Apparently not," he agreed with a careless shrug. "How are you, Colonel?"

"Quite good, quite good, my boy. I find the baths quite beneficial, though I can't say much for drinkin' the stuff." The colonel smiled, his bristling, gray moustache curling up at the corners.

Lord Fairmont took Julianna's pelisse from the footman and held it for her. "If I am not to have the pleasure of escorting you home, perhaps I may call upon you later in the week?" he asked.

Certain that he wanted to further upbraid her for gambling with his sister, Julianna leapt to the defensive. "I assure you, Lord Fairmont, that it was your sister who approached me. Lady Davina suggested the play and the stakes, not I."

"You had but to agree?" he asked, his voice a deep, threatening purr behind her.

"Why not?" Julianna asked, swinging around to face him. "If not with me, Lady Davina would have gambled with someone else."

"I thought I had made my wishes on the matter quite clear."

"And so you did," Julianna agreed. "I simply saw

no reason to follow them."

"Then allow me to suggest a reason." Dark eyes regarded her narrowly. "You have already heard the gossip concerning my somewhat reprehensible past, a past which includes many things of which I am not particularly proud. One of these concerns Lord Carlborne."

"The man who hanged himself in the south bedroom." Julianna nodded warily.

"Do you know why he hanged himself, Mrs. Pickering?"

Julianna frowned. "He lost everything to you in a card game."

"Precisely. He lost *everything* to me." Lord Fairmont waited silently while Julianna mulled over the implications of this statement.

"But my dealings have been with Mr. Basset."

"My agent."

"Then you own the house in Taylor Street?"

Lord Fairmont applauded lightly, his eyes mocking her. "How quick-witted, Mrs. Pickering. And have you also deduced that if you wish to remain in that house, you had best do as I say? In other words," his voice hardened perceptibly, "you will not gamble with Davina again. Is that clear, Mrs. Pickering?"

What a thoroughly detestable man, Julianna thought. He reminded her forcibly of Lord Ramsden, which was about the worst she could say of a person.

"Do you understand, Mrs. Pickering?" he asked again.

"Yes." Julianna's lips curled around the word. "I understand quite well, Lord Fairmont. My education in men of your sort has not been lacking." She drew the pelisse about her and began to edge past, as if the very thought of touching him filled her with repugnance.

Almost casually Lord Fairmont stepped into her path. Removing her hand from the pelisse, he brought it to his mouth, brushing her gloved fingers lightly with his lips. "Until we meet again, Mrs. Pickering," he said, his eyes once more mocking her.

Julianna snatched her hand away and with lips pressed tightly together, marched past him. The nerve of the man! She all but shook with the indignity of it. It was fortunate that her experiences at Graxton Manor had taught her to conceal her emotions, or she swore she would have wiped that mocking look from his face with the back of her hand. Julianna smiled, imagining the surprised expression on Lord Fairmont's face had she dared to do so. His actions had probably never brought such retaliation in all his privileged life, she thought. He looks to have been a spoiled child from birth. Well, Julianna had not escaped from her stepfather's control only to be treated thus by another man. She had bested Lord Ramsden, had she not? Lord Fairmont would find her a formidable opponent as well.

Chapter Five

In vain did Julianna await Lord Fairmont's promised call. Not that she was anxious to see him again, not that the memory of warm lips searing through the glove upon her hand had anything to do with it. It was simply that now she knew he was the owner of the house, she was anxious to discuss the state of the chimney in the south bedroom, that was all. And Lord Fairmont had said he would bring Bath buns for Paul. Julianna hated to see Paul disappointed.

"He probably thinks a promise made to a child is easily broken," Julianna said, glaring at her mirrored image as she dressed for the Assembly some three nights later.

"Who?" Lady Eleanor asked, looking up from her attempt at arranging Julianna's poker-straight hair into some semblance of the current style.

"Oh, be done with it, do," Julianna said. "I hate to be fussed over, and there is no way you can turn me into a raging beauty, so you might as well give over."

Lady Eleanor sighed. "If only you would allow me to use some sugar water and curl papers, or perhaps the curling iron . . ."

"It is much simpler to pull it back into its usual style," Julianna replied, putting up her hands to do so.

Lady Eleanor rapped her smartly with a fan snatched from the dressing table. "You will not undo what has taken me an hour to achieve. If you will but refrain from taking part in the country dances tonight, there is no reason why the pins should not hold."

Julianna eyed the loose upswept curls dubiously. True, it was more flattering than her usual style, but still . . . "It will be in my eyes before the evening is out," she declared. "And there are so many pins stuck in my head, it is quite impossibly heavy. I shall act top-lofty the whole evening and alienate all our friends.

"There is no gainsaying the fact that what we need is a lady's maid," Lady Eleanor said with a smile.

Julianna swung around on the low stool to face her. "We cannot spare the expense."

"It would be an investment." Lady Eleanor moved to the fourposter with its curved pilasters, badly in need of dusting, and sat down. The front bedroom was so small the hem of her lilac sarcenet brushed against the yellow silk of Julianna's gown. "We cannot go about looking like dowds."

"Do we?" Julianna asked, an anxious frown drawing her brows together as she turned to face the mirror once again.

Lady Eleanor rose quickly to her feet. "We look as fine as fivepence," she said firmly. "It is just that a real lady's maid could make us look as fine as . . . as a guinea."

The melancholy that seemed to threaten Julianna was swept aside as she rose to give Lady Eleanor a swift hug. "I think you already shine like one," she said. "Is it that Colonel Cramden you met the other night?"

"Now, Julianna . . ."

"I could tell he was quite smitten."

Lady Eleanor blushed, raising shiny blue eyes to Julianna. "I am sure he is nothing of the sort, but I must admit I found him vastly attractive."

Remembering the erect figure of the colonel, despite the war injury that caused him to use a cane, the warm brown eyes, and the pleasant smile beneath the enormous moustache, Julianna had to agree. "There is something quite pleasing about him," she affirmed. "And if you were not my most beloved stepaunt, I should quite try to steal a march on you."

"Nonsense," Lady Eleanor protested with the suspicion of a giggle. "It is Lord Fairmont who attracts you, and not to be wondered at."

"You are quite wrong." Julianna pulled on her gloves and buttoned them firmly. "I am interested in Lord Fairmont only because it is he who owns this house. I should like to speak to him about having the chimneys cleaned and about the fact that he has not kept his promise to pay a visit to Pog. That is my only interest in the man."

Lady Eleanor picked up her reticule from the bed. "Even were I still in leading strings, I would not believe that faradiddle. There is not a woman alive who would not be interested in a man such as Lord Fairmont."

"What about the woman who was engaged to him and then threw him over for another?" Julianna asked, her voice casually indifferent.

"I can think of no explanation save that the woman suffered from a brainstorm or some malady as affects our poor, mad king. What other reason could there be?"

Julianna picked up her own reticule and proceeded

71

to the stairs. "I am sure I do not care," she said with a shrug. "Come, we had best leave; it does not do to be late."

As Julianna had told Mr. Wilmot, they did not attend the dress balls on a regular basis, but tonight each had their particular reason for wishing to be present. Lady Eleanor had certain knowledge that Colonel Cramden planned to attend, and Julianna secretly hoped Lord Fairmont might also be there so she might discuss the merits of various chimney sweeps with him.

Entering the Upper Rooms through the octagon-shaped anteroom, Lady Eleanor and Julianna turned to the left where the dancing was held. Each searched for the face they were seeking among those assembled, no easy task despite the magnificent chandeliers hanging high above which reflected the jewels and satins of the dancers.

After a moment, Julianna spotted Lady Davina standing to one side flirting outrageously with a young man, but there was no sign of Lord Fairmont.

"Ah, there he is."

"Where?" Julianna asked, her eyes avidly seeking the tall figure amidst the crush.

"Along the west wall," Lady Eleanor replied. "Come, let us walk in the opposite direction so that we might happen upon him by chance."

Julianna, recognizing the snow-white hair and military bearing of Colonel Cramden, swallowed her disappointment and agreed. They nodded to acquaintances, paused to exchange a word or two, and slowly circled the large oblong of the ballroom.

"Miss Partridge." Colonel Cramden rose stiffly to his feet with the aid of his ebony cane. "What a pleasure to see you again."

"Why it is . . . Colonel Cramden, is it not?" Lady Eleanor asked. "I did not realize you meant to attend."

Colonel Cramden flushed and looked down at the cane on which he leaned. "Despite the fact that I can no longer participate, I enjoy watching the dancing."

"Oh, but I did not mean . . . that is, I am sure it makes no difference." Lady Eleanor struggled with her embarrassment.

"It is just that we so seldom attend ourselves," Julianna said, coming to the rescue. "Miss Partridge was surprised at our good fortune in meeting you."

"Ah, Mrs. Pickering." The colonel limped forward to bow over Julianna's hand. "But you are wrong, you know. I am the fortunate one. May I persuade you two young ladies to join me in the tearoom for refreshments?"

Lady Eleanor and Julianna accepted with alacrity, though Julianna intended to excuse herself as soon as politeness would allow. There was no reason for her to play gooseberry in so public a place. Upon entering the tearoom, however, the small party encountered Mr. Wilmot.

"Ah, well met, well met." Mr. Wilmot stood and gestured them to a place at his table. "I have been wondering if you would attend, Mrs. Pickering," he said coyly, "for you mentioned that you are an infrequent visitor."

"We only attend when we have particular reason," Lady Eleanor replied, her eyes on Colonel Cramden so that she missed the blush that quickly stained Julianna's cheeks.

Mr. Wilmot smiled and puffed out his chest, looking a bit like a pouter pigeon with side whiskers. "I have been meaning to call upon you, Mrs. Pickering.

I thought you might enjoy reading a book of poetry entitled, *Rhymes Of Rustication or Odes Upon the Theme of Rustic Beauty Composed While Immured in Rural Appleton*. I found it quite charming, and one poem, especially, comes to mind since it concerns the poet's encounter with a lovely woman named Beatrice at an Assembly. It is by a Lord Fitzhugh."

"It is most kind of you to think of me."

"Yes," Mr. Wilmot agreed. "I shall write down the title so you may request it the next time you go to the circulating library. I found it most refreshing to read the work of a real poet after that scandalous drivel by Lord Byron. I am sure you will find there is no comparison."

Julianna, who secretly admired Lord Byron's poetry despite his reputation, nodded and said she would do her best to obtain a copy of Lord Fitzhugh's work.

"Excellent." Mr. Wilmot's side whiskers bristled in approval. "I have been privileged to attend one or two of the author's readings in London, you know. A most superior gentleman. I have even written to Lord Fitzhugh in the hopes that I might persuade him to give a reading in Bath. It would be a wonderful opportunity to hear a poet of the first rank."

"Indeed." Julianna smiled tightly and took herself to task for allowing a man's taste in literature to color her opinion of him. So Mr. Wilmot did not care for Lord Byron's poetry? There were no doubt many people who felt the same. Mr. Wilmot was still kind and worthy. Yes, and attractive too, if one liked side whiskers.

The fact was, however, that Julianna preferred the clean-shaven aspect of such a man as . . . as Lord Fairmont, albeit the odds of one so endowed with good looks and good fortune throwing his handkerchief after her were ones no gambler would accept. Not that I wish for his interest, of course, she told herself firmly. Certainly not. Considering their present circumstances it would, in fact, be her duty to discourage such a thing. For however attractive Lord Fairmont might be, he was not a man to be trusted. Not with his reputation.

Still, knowing that the probability of Lord Fairmont's singling her out was . . . Julianna glanced about the room and did a quick calculation in her head . . . was a good twenty to one was so lowering a thought that her head began to ache. She blamed it on the hairpins digging into her scalp and, when Mr. Wilmot later asked her to dance, quite crossly refused.

"I am sure it is to your credit that you continue to honor your husband's memory," Mr. Wilmot replied. "I believe someone said that he died on the high seas?"

The high seas? But surely they had decided on a carriage accident, had they not? Was it possible Lady Eleanor had changed stories midstream thinking the high seas a more romantic demise?

"Still, it has been well over two years since his death, I understand, and a year of mourning is considered sufficient by even the highest sticklers. Excess in all things is to be avoided."

"A worthy sentiment to be sure," said Lord Fairmont, having sprung, as far as Julianna could tell, from the side walls. "And since I am sure you do not wish to insult Mr. Wilmot's sensibilities, Mrs. Pickering, you must stand up with me for the next dance."

It was one thing to calculate the odds of engaging Lord Fairmont in dalliance, quite another to confront him in the flesh. "I am afraid I do not dance," Julianna said, repeating her earlier refusal to Mr. Wilmot.

"Nonsense." Lord Fairmont would not be so easily dismissed. "I am sure you dance quite well. A set is just forming; shall we join them?"

Not for the world would Julianna admit to Lord Fairmont that her dancing skills were of the most rudimentary. Had it ever been suggested to Lord Ramsden that a dancing master be hired for his step-daughter, he would have laughed and said it would be a waste of blunt, for who would wish to stand up with Julianna? She might have joined one of the dancing classes after her arrival in Bath, of course, but to be surrounded by young misses barely out of the schoolroom could only lead to further embarrassment and comment.

No, to Julianna's mind it was much better to sit quietly on the side watching, than be judged an ape-leader. "I would truly prefer not to dance, Lord Fairmont," she said. "Though there is something of a particular nature which I must needs discuss with you."

Lord Fairmont's eyebrows rose. "You intrigue me, Mrs. Pickering," he said, taking one of the chairs by her side. "What is of such import that you must forego the pleasure of dancing to speak of it?"

Mr. Wilmot, seated on Julianna's other side, leaned forward attentively.

Julianna flushed and found herself quite unable to speak of smoking chimneys. "I . . . it is not that . . . I do not dance because I have . . . have . . ."

"Ah, I understand," Mr. Wilmot broke in sympathetically. "You have injured yourself in some way?"

"Yes." Julianna nodded and turned gratefully to

Mr. Wilmot. It was almost the truth, for the shoes she wore, considered a wonderful bargain when purchased, were beginning to pinch quite abominably.

"Cold compresses," Mr. Wilmot advised. "And rest, of course. I have found that even the most severe injury to the . . . ah . . . limbs, can be treated quite successfully in this manner."

"If the injury is slight, however," Lord Fairmont broke in, "gentle exercise may serve to prevent stiffness. Shall we walk together for awhile, Mrs. Pickering?" He stood and offered his arm in such a way that Julianna felt she could not refuse.

Nor, despite the discomfort of her new shoes, did Julianna want to refuse. It was a wonderful thing to walk beside a man so tall and broad shouldered that he made her feel quite small and feminine. Julianna was sure no more than one man in forty-nine point eight could make her feel so. Only as they entered the ballroom and began to slowly circle the dance floor did Julianna begin to feel uncomfortable. Was it her imagination that all eyes turned to them, that there was a sudden cessation of talk as they approached, a buzz of lowered voices as they passed?

Julianna was suddenly quite sure that someone had recognized her gown as their former bedcurtains and that the pins had begun to fall from her hair and would soon rain down upon the dance floor in a virtual torrent. If only there were a trapdoor such as she had read about in the London theater, so she might be swallowed up and escape the wall of eyes that seemed to surround her.

The ground beneath her feet remained solid, however, and Julianna soon found herself tilting her chin and forcing a mask of composure over her features. It was her gambling trick and the way she had always dealt with her stepfather or with anything that had threatened to overwhelm her. Emotion was weakness. Julianna had learned that lesson well. She turned her head, her lips forming a smile.

"If we sit here, it will afford everyone the chance to stare at us quite openly without craning their necks," Lord Fairmont said, stopping beside a pair of chairs in the center of the room. "And the music and general noise will keep us from being overheard."

The smile froze upon Julianna's mouth, her gray eyes opened wide. So Lord Fairmont was also aware that they were providing the evening's gossip.

"I am quite used to it by now," he said, as if she had spoken her thoughts aloud. "One can hardly reach the age of six and thirty and be a member of such a family as mine without realizing that one is easy fodder for the gossip mill. I am sorry if it makes you uncomfortable, however."

Once again the man surprised her. She would have thought him above noticing such things, or caring, for that matter. Be careful, Julianna, she warned herself. It is one thing to find such a man attractive. But if you begin to like him as well, you will be lost indeed. He thinks you a widow with a young son. He does not, cannot, know your true identity. Romance is not for such as you. In any case, however much Lord Fairmont might seem to single you out for attention now, you must remember the laws of probability and not be taken in by his charm.

"You are wearing your hair differently, are you not?" Lord Fairmont asked. "It is most becoming."

"Thank you." Julianna's voice was tight, and she did not look up at him. She knew his dark brown eyes as well as his lips would be smiling at her, blinding her to whatever his reason in searching her out might be. And, as Julianna knew only too well, men seldom did anything that did not suit their own purpose. The fact that she did not yet know what lay behind Lord Fairmont's charming behavior, did not alter the fact. Julianna's eyes swept the room, encountering those of Lady Davina, who raised a questioning eyebrow before turning back to her companion.

"I see you have allowed Lady Davina to attend."

"Yes. As long as Davina does not participate in the more boisterous country dances or flirt too outrageously, I see no harm in her attending.

"How generous of you." Though Julianna did her best to keep her voice flat and unemotional, she was conscious of the sarcasm that underlay her words.

As, apparently, was Lord Fairmont. "I am not quite the wicked ogre my sister has painted, you know."

"Of course not."

"And I, at least, believe in withholding judgment until I know the facts."

Julianna did look at him then. He was no longer bantering with her, trying to charm with honeyed words. His voice was harsh, his demeanor serious, almost formidable, as he looked down with eyes as cold and unsmiling as the lips pressed into a thin line.

"I . . . do not think I understand," she said. It was true that she had judged Lord Fairmont and found him wanting, judged him solely on the words of a woman with her own hen to pluck, a woman who would shred his character to someone little more than a stranger. Yet Lord Fairmont had never denied Lady Davina's accusations, had by his behavior, in fact, given evidence to the truth of her words. Did he not even now admit to denying his sister the basic pleasures of a young woman: the enjoyment of a country dance and a harmless flirtation?

"Did you not say there was something of a particular nature you wished to discuss with me?" Lord Fairmont asked, apparently deciding to abandon the discussion in favor of a more innocuous one.

"Yes. But first I must say that if I judge without knowing the facts, it is only because they are not given me."

"Or you do not wish to see them," he countered.

"Really, Lord Fairmont. You seem intent on insulting me this evening for faults which I do not claim as mine. Was this your sole purpose in asking me to walk with you?"

Lord Fairmont put a restraining hand upon Julianna's arm as she made to rise. "You will remain seated, and you will smile," he instructed.

Julianna did as she was bid, realizing the wisdom of his words. She had allowed emotion to rule her, and the results had almost been disastrous. It would not do for her to become a source of gossip. Her livelihood depended on her being invited into the homes of those rich enough to gamble recklessly. To create a scene in so public a place as the Upper Rooms would not raise her social standing, quite the contrary. What was there about Lord Fairmont that caused her to so forget herself?

"I wished to discuss the state of the chimneys," she said, shaking off his hand under the pretense of rearranging the folds of her gown. "They are deplorable."

"Are we discussing particular chimneys or those of the nation as a whole?"

"We are discussing—" Julianna took a deep breath. Was the man deliberately trying to rile her, even after his warning? "We are discussing the chimneys at Taylor Street. As you have informed me that you are the owner, the chimneys are your responsibility."

"And the inhabitants?"

Julianna turned to glare at him, her outrage met by amused insouciance. "You need not concern yourself with the inhabitants."

"Then perhaps I might call tomorrow and you can give me a tour of the chimneys so that I might see the problem for myself."

"It is the chimney in the south bedroom that smokes, and that you have already seen." Julianna refused to acknowledge the flush she could feel warming her cheeks as she mentioned their earlier meeting. "I shall hire a Mr. Wibberting to clean it, as recommended by Mrs. Leacock, and have him send the bill to your direction."

"Ah, Ju . . . Penelope, there you are." Lady Eleanor, her hand upon Colonel Cramden's arm, greeted them. She seated herself with a sigh, rearranging the skirt of her lilac sarcenet to keep it from wrinkling, and then leaned forward conspiratorially. "We meant to follow you from the tearoom at once, but Mr. Wilmot would ply me with questions and then Mrs. Leacock appeared. We have been virtual prisoners of her tongue for the last twenty minutes, have we not, Colonel?" Lady Eleanor turned to her companion.

Colonel Cramden nodded, his moustache curling in amusement. "I have learned more than I ever cared to know about cesspools and such," he said, addressing Lord Fairmont. "Mrs. Leacock holds strong opinions it seems."

"Indeed she does," Lady Eleanor agreed. "There was something about the hinged valves of a Mr. Bramah that she found particularly exemplary, though I could not tell you what it was."

"I was much more interested in the rumor Mrs. Leacock mentioned concerning a benefit performance by Mrs. Siddons at the Royal Theatre," Colonel Cramden said. "Know anything about it, Fairmont? Must confess I wouldn't mind getting a ticket if they were to be had."

"Actually the rumor should be fact by tomorrow. I believe Mrs. Siddons is to perform as Lady Macbeth, which should gladden the heart of any true lover of the theater. I look forward to seeing her in the role again and comparing it to her earlier performances."

Julianna's eyes immediately narrowed and took on the distant look that meant she was busy doing mental sums. Theater tickets could hardly be called necessities, especially when one could barely afford the rent and servant's wages. Still, Julianna had always dreamed of seeing Mrs. Siddons perform.

"Penelope, Lord Fairmont is addressing you."

Recalled both to her surroundings and her new name by a discreet nudge from Lady Eleanor, Julianna blushed and apologized for her rudeness.

"I merely inquired whether you enjoyed the theater, Mrs. Pickering."

"Yes, oh, yes," Julianna affirmed with a vigorous nod that endangered her new hairstyle. "That is, I have never attended, but I have always wanted to do so. And to think of seeing Mrs. Siddons as Lady Macbeth, one of her most celebrated roles."

"Justifiably so," Lord Fairmont said. "Though Mrs. Siddons is no longer at the height of her powers, I think no one can surpass her."

"Remember seeing her once in *Isabella*," Colonel Cramden reminisced. "When she spoke those words near the end before she kills herself, that part about sleeping so soon, she had near everyone in the audience weeping."

"Ah, yes." In a soft voice, Lord Fairmont began quoting,

Asleep so soon! O happy! happy thou!
Who thus can'st sleep: I never shall sleep more.
If then to sleep be to be happy, he
Who sleeps the longest, is the happiest;
Death is the longest Sleep. O! have a Care,
Mischief will thrive apace. Never wake more;
If thou didst ever love thy Isabella,
Tomorrow must be Dooms-day to thy Peace.

Colonel Cramden sniffed and blinked rapidly for a moment. "One of the most moving things you ever want to see," he said in a voice suspiciously hoarse. "To see Mrs. Siddons perform is a privilege I shall not soon forget."

She would forego that new gown Lady Eleanor was insisting upon, Julianna decided, and simply refurbish one of her old ones. This might very well be the last chance they would ever have to see the great actress perform.

"It is surprising that you have never seen a theatrical performance, Mrs. Pickering," Lord Fairmont said. "Even in the provinces there are many fine companies. Did your husband then, disapprove?"

"No, my father," Julianna said, still caught up in the magic of his recitation. "Father was a scientist, a mathematician who had little time or appreciation for that sort of thing. I believe he took my mother once, but I was too young to attend."

"And your father's name was . . . ?"

"Edward Seaton," Julianna supplied before she quite realized what she had done.

Lord Fairmont smiled. "Edward Seaton? Ah, yes. He lectured once while I was up at Oxford, I remember. A brilliant mathematician."

Julianna nodded, suddenly aware of the precipice that yawned before her. If she were not careful, she would find herself handing Lord Fairmont her true identity on a silver salver. Fortunately a vigorous boulanger commenced at that moment, the noise making speech all but impossible, and afterwards Mr. Wilmot came to claim her attention.

Lord Fairmont rose to take his leave. "I shall call upon you tomorrow for another tour of the south bedroom as you have promised," he said, his lips twitching at Julianna's outraged expression.

Mr. Wilmot's side whiskers fairly quivered in the silence that followed Lord Fairmont's departure. "I hope you will not think it interfering if I offer a bit of advice, Mrs. Pickering."

Julianna forced herself to relax. She was not so much concerned over Lord Fairmont's impudence as what she had inadvertently revealed to him. "I am sure your advice will always be welcome, Mr. Wilmot," she replied mechanically.

Mr. Wilmot inclined his head and settled his bulk more comfortably in the straight-backed chair. "It will not do to encourage Lord Fairmont, for while I realize his departing remark must be of the most innocent, there are others who will not be so discerning. Lord Fairmont has a reputation, deservedly so, I might add."

"Must be thinking of his father," Colonel Cramden leaned forward, raising his voice to be heard over the music of a country dance. "He was the one with the reputation. Did his best to gamble away the family fortune. Mortgaged half the estate to get the ready, I understand. Good thing he couldn't break the entail."

"I will allow that the son may have followed in his father's footsteps," Mr. Wilmot agreed with a superior smile, "but his reputation as a rake and libertine is his own. And to make such remarks to Mrs. Pickering as he has done, is surely beyond the bounds of what is proper."

Lady Eleanor, who had been momentarily occupied in carefully observing the dress of one of the dancers and planning how she might copy it at a fraction of the cost and with better regard to line and color, spoke up at last. "Nonsense. You make a hen out of what is no more than a chick."

"I beg your pardon." Mr. Wilmot's measured words belied his bulging eyes and gingery side whiskers which stood erect like the quills of a porcupine.

"Apology accepted," Lady Eleanor said promptly. "Though it would be good to remember that he who lies with dogs rises up with fleas, and no matter what you may say, there's many a woman would be more than happy to show Lord Fairmont their south bedrooms had they the chance. Good fortune has knocked upon Mrs. Pickering's door is all, and if she knows what's good for her, she'll open it wide."

Chapter Six

Julianna was up betimes the next morning. She had promised Paul a walk in Sydney Gardens to view the canals, and she wanted to be sure she was back in time to meet with Lord Fairmont. Julianna smiled as she pulled her hair back into its usual knot. She intended to have Hawkins send for Mr. Wibberting to clean the chimneys first thing. Lord Fairmont would arrive to find that a tour of the south bedroom was totally unnecessary, and, she inserted bone pins to hold her hair securely, in a few days Lord Fairmont would receive a bill for having the chimney cleaned.

Julianna's smile wavered slightly as she glanced in the mirror. The looser coiffure Lady Eleanor had achieved for her last night had been more flattering. Julianna put up her hands to take out the pins again. But no, she would never be able to duplicate the effect herself, and besides, she certainly wasn't going to make an effort to look attractive for Lord Fairmont, was she? No. Of course not. Besides, Lord Fairmont had promised to call before and had not. Who was to say he would keep his promise this time?

Nevertheless, Julianna chose a most becoming gown of peach jaconet with Brussels lace to wear to the park and pinned the small gold watch that had belonged to her mother on the bodice so she would not be late returning with Paul.

A feeling of exhilaration filled her as she ran lightly down the main staircase. Lord Fairmont had seemed so different last night. She paused for a moment, remembering his moving recitation from *Isabella*. He had not seemed the polished, cynical aristocrat at all but a man of emotion and feeling, quite unlike Lady Davina's description.

Still, had she not often seen Lord Ramsden charming and gracious when he wished to disarm someone into lending money or lure some innocent into a card game? How could she be sure Lord Fairmont was a man of honor and not merely the same sort of glib deceiver? With a frown drawing her brows together, Julianna slowly continued her descent of the stairs, her hand trailing the newly polished surface of the oak handrail.

"Well, it is quite true Mrs. Gardning has burnt the toast again," Lady Eleanor said looking up as Julianna entered the small breakfast room. "But that is hardly cause for such a look. I have found it to be quite edible if one but uses enough marmalade."

Julianna reached for the rack of toast and began to scrape off the burnt portion. "It is not the toast, Lady Eleanor, I have grown used to that."

Lady Eleanor nodded and sipped her coffee. "We shall soon be unable to eat anything that has not been reduced to cinders. But it may be for the best. When I spoke to Mrs. Randolph at the Pump Room the other day, she informed me that we were really quite lucky in our cook, for charcoal is an aid to digestion."

"Ah, you always know how to make me smile," Julianna said as she poured some coffee for herself. "And we are blessed to have such a cook, are we?"

"So it seems." Lady Eleanor spread marmalade lavishly on a piece of toast and took a dainty bite. "But if your frown was not because of Mrs. Gardning, what was the cause?"

Julianna finished her toast and brushed the crumbs from her fingers before answering. For some reason, she did not feel like discussing Lord Fairmont with her stepaunt that morning. "Oh, I was just wondering if we could afford tickets to see Mrs. Siddons if I sold Mama's garnets," she prevaricated.

"Hmmm." Lady Eleanor gave Julianna a skeptical look and seemed about to pursue the topic when a loud series of bangs suddenly sounded and Kitty emerged from the backstairs with Paul.

The little boy could barely contain his excitement, hopping about and racing at once to tug at Julianna's hand. "Go now," he demanded, his big blue eyes showing a determination that would brook no delay.

"Yes, Pog, I shall be finished in a moment." Julianna gave the wriggling body a quick hug and turned to address the nursemaid. "I will take Paul to Sydney Gardens and be back in a few hours. I believe Miss Partridge has some sewing for you to do while we are gone."

Kitty bobbed a quick curtsy. "Yes, mum. Miss Partridge is goin' to teach me how to do some fancy French stitches and all."

"Now, Jules. Go now!" Paul demanded again, doing his best to pull Julianna to the door.

"Pog you must not pull so," Julianna remonstrated. "You are not a badly trained dog being taken for a walk, you know."

Paul giggled. "Me dog," he said, quite liking the idea and beginning to bark vociferously.

"Paul, stop that!" Julianna protested when Paul

would have begun crawling about the floor on all fours.

"Woof," Paul replied, grinning up at her and displaying a formidable pair of dimples. Julianna shook her head, exchanging a look with Lady Eleanor that clearly said, "Badly spoiled, but what can one do?"

"Here." Lady Eleanor settled Paul in a chair and handed him a piece of toast. "Crumble some bread to feed the ducks, though I should not be surprised if they refused to eat it, as dry as it is." Lady Eleanor sighed and gave Julianna a rueful look. "I sometimes think my brother was right and I am no more capable of managing a household than of driving a pony cart."

"Brownie." Paul looked up from his toast crumbs, blue eyes filling with tears. Brownie was the old pony that lived on the home farm at Graxton Manor. He and Paul had been great friends.

Julianna rose quickly and held out a napkin to Paul. "You have crumbled quite enough bread for the ducks," she said. "Clean your hands now, if you please, and we will put the bread in a bit of paper for us to take to the Gardens."

Paul sniffed audibly but obeyed, though his earlier eager cheerfulness was no longer in evidence.

"I am sure Humbert would like some of those crumbs," Julianna said, doing her best to alleviate Paul's tears and her own guilt. "We shall stop to see him before we leave." Smoothing one hand over Paul's tousled curls, Julianna stood for a moment looking down at him as he obediently brushed crumbs from his hands. She knew Paul missed the country, but there was little she could do about it. And wasn't it far better for him to shed a few tears over a missed pet now, than grow into a hardened gamester under the tutelage of his father?

With a sigh, she rang for Hawkins to give him his instructions regarding the chimney sweep, took a final sip of coffee, and went to fetch the pelisse she had left by the mahogany sideboard.

A few minutes later Julianna emerged from the house, one hand clutching her reticule and a bit of wrapped bread, the other holding tightly to Paul who seemed to have regained his earlier high spirits as he woofed rather loudly at a cat sunning itself in a doorway. Soon they were walking leisurely across Pulteney Bridge and its shops, past Laura Place, and down Great Pulteney Street to the hexagonal expanse of Sydney Gardens.

It was a fair way to walk for a little boy, but Paul seemed always full of energy and would have run ahead had Julianna not been there to restrain him. Julianna, used to long rambles in the country where there was little else to do, quite enjoyed herself, for it was a fine, sunny day despite the chill wind and still early enough so that the streets were not as crowded with visitors as they would be later.

On the way, Julianna asked Paul his sums, much as her father had quizzed her when she was a child. "If we had three more mice besides Humbert, how many mice would we have?"

"Lots." Paul grinned up at her.

Julianna shook her head but could not forbear to smile. When she was not much older than Paul, she had been doing long division problems with ease and enjoying the challenge. Paul was much more like Lady Eleanor, whose chatter he seemed to emulate. In fact, Julianna would not be surprised to hear Paul spouting one of Lady Eleanor's penny wisdoms before long.

"Bridge first, Jules," Paul insisted as they entered the

Gardens, tugging her in the direction of one of the cast-iron bridges that crossed over the recently completed canal.

Together they peered over the side, Julianna looking over the railing, Paul poking his head through two of the cast-iron railing supports. Though there was little traffic on the canal at the moment, Julianna had read that goods could be transported all the way from London to Bristol in just four days.

Paul was more interested in some ducks that came swimming by than in the miracles of transportation, however. He took great delight in throwing them pieces of bread, squealing with glee whenever one of the birds caught his doughy offering. When the bread was gone, however, the ducks continued on their way, and though Julianna tried to interest Paul in counting some pieces of wood that drifted by, he soon grew bored.

Giving up for the moment on teaching Paul his sums, Julianna allowed the little boy to run ahead down one of the many pleasure paths while she followed at a more leisurely pace. With his blond curls blowing in the wind, his cheeks pink from exertion, he made a charming picture. A bewhiskered gentleman walking in their direction even stopped to stare, Julianna noted with watchful pride. A moment later the same man took out a pair of wire-rimmed spectacles, perched them crookedly on his nose, removed a notebook from his pocket, and, eyes still on Paul, began to make a quick sketch of the scene.

Alarm bells sounded in Julianna's head. It was all well and good to have someone admire Paul, but who was this man who felt free to draw Paul's likeness? And what was his motive? Did he merely admire Pog's youthful charm or . . .

"Paul!" Julianna called, doing her best to keep the panic from her voice.

Glancing up from the anthill he was poking with a stick, Paul grinned mischievously at Julianna and then began to run away across the grass, his sturdy legs pumping rapidly.

"Paul, come back at once!" Julianna demanded, fear lending an edge to her voice. What if the man had been sent by Lord Ramsden? What if—Julianna's breath came in short gasps as she gave chase, the strings of her reticule swinging cuttingly back and forth on her wrist, her bonnet sliding down her back.

"Paul." She caught him up at last, hugging him tightly to her breast as she knelt on the grass rocking breathlessly back and forth.

"Again!" Paul demanded, squirming away. "Do again!"

"No, Paul." Julianna allowed him to slip out of her arms but held him fast by the shoulders. "No, Paul," she repeated, forcing him to look at her. "You must not run away from me. When I call you must come. Do you understand?"

Paul responded by curling his arms about her neck and giving her a noisy kiss. Julianna kissed the top of his curly head in return and stood, holding tightly to his hand. The bewhiskered gentleman was no longer standing beside the path. He was, in fact, nowhere to be seen. It is almost as if I conjured him whole from my imagination, Julianna thought. Perhaps I did. Perhaps the man merely stopped to jot down a name in his notebook. Julianna allowed Paul to free his hand as she straightened her bonnet and retied the ribbons. Had she panicked without cause?

"Look, Jules," Paul announced happily, showing Julianna a pebble he had just found in the pathway.

Julianna took a deep breath. She must not frighten Paul. "It is very pretty," she acknowledged, carefully inspecting the undistinguished bit of stone. "Are you going to add it to your collection?"

The little boy frowned, considering the matter. "No," he said finally, breaking into a dimpled smile again. "For you, Jules. A present."

"Thank you, Paul. I shall treasure it always."

Paul nodded. "Keep in box?"

"Of course," Julianna agreed. The big mahogany box in Julianna's bedroom containing the remaining pieces of her mother's jewelry was associated in Paul's eyes with the place one kept one's most treasured possessions. And so it contained a snail shell and a dragonfly wing, as well as a set of garnets and a sapphire necklace.

Paul trotted away again in search of more treasures, while Julianna bit down hard on her tongue to keep from calling him back to her side. She must not allow herself to become overpossessive or frighten Paul with her own fanciful imaginings. Still, Julianna found it no easy thing to do. Lord Ramsden was not a man who lost easily.

For all the sun was warm, Julianna found herself shivering. If only she could enjoy some of Lady Eleanor's insouciance. Julianna sighed and forced herself to think of less worrisome things. Such as seeing the great Mrs. Siddons perform. I shall sell the garnets and ask Hawkins to procure tickets, she decided, no matter how foolish or impractical. Mrs. Siddons is retired and performs only at rare benefits these days. Such an opportunity may never come our way again.

For just a moment, she forgot about Lord Ramsden and indulged herself in the daydream of attending the theater dressed to the nines, with the great Sarah Sid-

93

dons performing her particular magic upon the stage. The lights of the theater would darken while those upon the stage grew brighter. There would be a hush of excitement in the air, the curtain would rise, Julianna would be conscious of nothing but the magic of the stage and the presence of the man beside her, the man with the face of an angel and the smile of a satyr. Julianna's eyes opened wide. Whatever was she thinking of? Not what but whom, she answered herself. And you know very well who the man is, your thoughts have not been far from him since last night's Assembly.

With a small, unladylike thump, Julianna sat down on a small wooden bench. Lady Davina had thought the sobriquet "The Devil" most suited to her brother, and Julianna had to agree, for the man had dwelt in her thoughts like some evil tempter.

What was it about Lord Fairmont that disturbed her so? True, he was handsome and rich, but so were other men, and she dismissed them easily enough. Lady Eleanor said he had paid Julianna marked attention. But so had Mr. Wilmot, yet Julianna found her thoughts seldom dwelling upon him. Julianna shook her head, a puzzled frown upon her brow; her reactions to Lord Fairmont were a mystery even to herself.

"I would offer a penny for your thoughts," a deep baritone voice said above her, "but they look to be worth a good deal more."

Julianna had thought herself quite alone, and for a moment a wave of breathless, drowning panic swept over her at this sudden interruption. Her eyes sought Paul, found him peacefully building a small pebble fortress, and then turned to look into the dark brown gaze of her nemesis.

"Lord Fairmont." Julianna gave a sigh of relief as

she greeted him, offering her gloved hand.

He bowed over it, returned her greeting, and asked permission to sit next to her.

"Of course." Julianna twitched her skirts aside nervously. She was grateful that the voice had not belonged to a bewhiskered gentleman with notebook in hand, but she could hardly pretend to an ease in Lord Fairmont's company. He was much too dangerous and fascinating a man for that.

"I am surprised to see you in Sydney Gardens," Julianna said, seizing upon the first innocuous topic of conversation that came to mind.

"I often walk here," he replied, looking around the park with a smile of pleasure. "And I thought that before I made my tour of inspection at Taylor Street I would take a slight detour through the Gardens since it is such a lovely day."

Julianna looked down at the pointed toes of her stout walking boots. "Actually, I have taken care of our problem with the smoking chimney myself, Lord Fairmont," she said, feeling unaccountably guilty. "It will not be necessary for you to make an inspection."

"Indeed?"

Julianna's eyes swiveled upward to his face. She was not sure if he was pleased or angry, and his expression gave nothing away.

"I know it was a bit coming of me for it is your house," she began, feeling not at all like the decisive woman she had been when giving Hawkins his instructions earlier. "But it did seem the expedient thing to do."

"Of course," Lord Fairmont agreed pleasantly. "I admire a woman of initiative."

"You do?" From Lady Davina's comments, Julianna would have said Lord Fairmont preferred the submissive female who did nothing without receiving his express permission first.

"And I also realize you felt it was a way of getting back at me for one of those wrongs women are always imagining and of piquing my curiosity at the same time."

Julianna ground her teeth. He was smiling down at her, the self-satisfied smile of a rich, handsome, aristocrat who knows he is much sought after and expects no less than that woman who will try to fix his interest.

"I assure you, Lord Fairmont, my only concern was a smoking chimney. I did not think of you at all."

"Of course," he said once again.

Julianna's eyes narrowed and grew slate gray for a moment as she struggled to keep back the words forming on her tongue. Fortunately, Paul came running up just then to inspect the new arrival.

Taking a deep, calming breath, Julianna said, "You remember Lord Fairmont, Paul?"

Paul nodded. "Lord Fairmont," he repeated obediently, before looking with undisguised curiosity at the wrapped package which Lord Fairmont carried.

"Bath buns," Lord Fairmont explained. "I promised I would bring some for Humbert next time I called."

"Good. Humbert hungry."

"I shall escort you back to Taylor Street, Mrs. Pickering," Lord Fairmont said, rising and holding out his arm.

Julianna glanced at the watch pinned to her bosom. It was much later than she had realized. Almost time for tea, in fact. Still, she disliked Lord Fairmont's casual assumption that he act as their escort. "I think we will remain a bit longer, Lord Fairmont. Paul loves the Gardens, you know. And I am a great believer in fresh air. Do not let us detain you."

96

Paul, eyes on the package Lord Fairmont held, leaned against Julianna's knee and asked, "Go now, Jules?"

"Don't you wish to look at the canal again, Paul?"

Paul shook his head. "Go now. Please, Jules?"

Growing warmer by the minute, Julianna threw a quick, annoyed glance at Lord Fairmont. He returned it with a bland one of his own. "Do you suppose you could carry this for a bit?" he asked Paul, handing him the Bath buns. "I am feeling rather fatigued, for I had quite an encounter with a pollywog this morning, you know."

"You did?" Paul's eyes grew round. "Pog?"

"Why, yes," Lord Fairmont nodded, looking down at Paul in amazement. "Do you know him?"

Paul nodded vigorously.

"Then you will be most concerned to learn of his battle this morning with a most terrible dragonfly." Lord Fairmont turned to Julianna, who still sat upon the bench, a look of outrage on her face.

"How dare you —" she began, her voice trembling.

"How dare I what?" he asked. "Offer to escort you home? Buy Bath buns for Paul?"

"Pog," she said. "Pog the pollywog is mine." The statement sounded ridiculous, she realized, like a child fighting over a toy, but she refused to withdraw it. The stories belonged to her and Paul. How dare Lord Fairmont usurp them? And more to the matter, "How did you find out about Pog?"

"I heard you relate the tale to Paul as you walked in Spring Gardens. My own mother never had the time nor the inclination to indulge my childish fantasies or to care if I fell and scraped myself. It is my experience that most women are too caught up in the social whirl to so concern themselves. Paul seemed quite taken by

97

the pollywog's adventures, and I was charmed as well."

"I see." That was perfectly possible. Julianna did her best to quiet the fear and outrage that gripped her, yet found herself quite unable to do so. Lord Fairmont had known her father. He knew about Pog. What else did he know? Julianna wondered, rising to take Paul's hand. Was she creating another fanciful foe like the bewhiskered gentleman? Or was it only common sense to be leery of such a one as Lord Fairmont. And why did she feel both fear and exhilaration in his presence?

The three of them walked slowly back down Great Pulteney Street while Lord Fairmont regaled them with the tale of Pog's latest adventure. As they passed the Guildhall, they encountered Mrs. Leacock, who greeted them with the avaricious enthusiasm of a gossip who has struck pure gold.

"How nice to see the . . . *three* of you out for a walk," she gushed. "I did not realize you were so *well*-acquainted."

"We met by chance in the park," Lord Fairmont replied calmly. "And, as we were going in the same direction, I offered to escort Mrs. Pickering home."

"I see." Mrs. Leacock nodded, looking down at Paul, who was scowling at this interruption of Pog's adventures. "How interesting."

As they detached themselves from Mrs. Leacock and continued on their way, Lord Fairmont turned to Julianna. "I am afraid we are once again a source of gossip," he observed quietly.

Julianna nodded.

"It doesn't bother you?" Lord Fairmont questioned gently.

Julianna gave a quick, elegant shrug. "I do not see that I have much choice in the matter. We have already walked past most of the town's inhabitants. To cry wolf after the sheep has been eaten, as Miss Partridge is fond of saying, would serve no purpose."

Lord Fairmont was surprised into a grin. "Trust Miss Partridge for good sense. She is your aunt, I believe?"

"My stepaunt. Paul is growing restless. Do you continue the story of Pog?"

Lord Fairmont nodded. "Of course. Do you remember where we were, Paul?"

"Pog under big rock," Paul replied eagerly. "And big fish there."

"Ah, yes, I remember. Well, Pog was a bit frightened, of course, but he knew there was one sure way to escape the dragonfly."

"What?" Paul asked breathlessly.

"To swim into the fish's mouth," said Lord Fairmont.

"Pog be eaten!" Paul cried in alarm.

"Pog? Never. 'For I could never eat Pog Pollywog,' said the fish."

Julianna looked up, her attention caught. "Why not?" she asked. "Why could the fish not eat Pog Pollywog?"

"Because if he did, Pog's adventures would be over, and I find myself growing rather fond of Pog," Lord Fairmont said.

"You . . . you do?" Julianna asked.

"Indeed," Lord Fairmont replied.

Chapter Seven

Upon arriving back at Taylor Street, Paul insisted that Lord Fairmont be shown Humbert for whom he had brought the Bath buns.

"Paul, I really don't think Lord Fairmont wants to see Humbert just now," Julianna said.

"He does. He does," Paul insisted. "Don't you, Lord Fairmont?" Paul looked up imploringly.

"Humbert lives under the cellar stairs," Julianna said, looking dubiously at Lord Fairmont's snowy white cravat and pristine coat of blue superfine.

Lord Fairmont looked down at Paul. "I would enjoy meeting Humbert," he said. "Does he take tea with his Bath buns?"

Paul snorted with laughter and shook his head. "Humbert don't drink tea."

"No? What does Humbert drink then?"

"Humbert drink . . ." Paul frowned, obviously giving the question serious consideration. "Humbert drink . . . wum toddies!"

Julianna cringed at this reminder of Lord Ramsden's influence in Paul's life, but Lord Fairmont merely smiled and said, "I think it a bit early in the day for rum toddies, myself. Shall we ask Humbert what he would like?"

100

Paul nodded, and the small party headed for the cellar steps there to await the pleasure of a small, brown mouse who refused to be coaxed out.

"There are too many people about," Julianna said. "I am sure Humbert will come out after we are gone, Paul."

Crouched beside the steps, a frown of vexation upon his face, Paul looked up, his bottom lip stuck out stubbornly. "Humbert come now!" he demanded.

"But Paul . . ." Julianna began.

"Well, Paul may stay as long as he chooses," Lord Fairmont said. "But I confess to wanting my tea. Shall we go, Mrs. Pickering?"

Paul stood up uncertainly.

"Kitty will be waiting with yours," Julianna said, quick to take advantage, "and some of those lovely Bath buns Lord Fairmont has brought."

"Come later," Paul decided.

They turned to go inside, only to encounter a person wearing the unmistakable tall black hat of the master chimney sweep heading their way, an assortment of brushes and cloths slung over his shoulders.

"Ah, you have come about the chimneys," Julianna said in a pleased voice, glad to demonstrate to Lord Fairmont that her only desire was to have the chimneys cleaned, and not, as he had suggested, to fix his interest. "Since we have guests for tea, perhaps you could begin in the upstairs bedrooms?"

The man shifted the brushes to his other shoulder and asked, "Wot's at the top?"

"Me," Paul piped up, having carefully surveyed the sweep and decided he would do for a friend.

"Well, I allus begins at the top and works down, you see. So if'n I can begin in the nursery, it'll be best."

"I help," Paul said. It was a demand not an offer.

"I think not," said Lord Fairmont.

Paul's lower lip thrust out ominously.

"You will take tea with the nursemaid and stay out of the way," Lord Fairmont continued.

"If you please, Lord Fairmont." Julianna was tight-lipped with anger at this calm assumption of authority. First Lord Fairmont usurped the story of Pog, and now he was ordering Paul about. Well, Lord Fairmont might own their house, but he did not own them. "Paul is my son, and I am the one who will order his behavior."

Lord Fairmont stepped back slightly and gestured for her to do so.

"You will take tea with Kitty and not bother Mr. Wibberting," Julianna instructed, feeling herself grow hot with annoyance. She was quite aware that her words were all but identical to Lord Fairmont's and that the wretched man was standing there looking amused. Julianna's hands clenched on her reticule.

"The butler will show you to the nursery, Mr. Wibberting," Julianna said. "And I would appreciate it if you would see that the bill is sent to Lord Fairmont."

"Beggin' your pardon, missus, but the name's Meecham, and it's him what said I should come," the sweep answered, nodding in Lord Fairmont's direction. "I does all his chimneys, allus has. But if'n you was thinkin' of hiring that Charlie Wibberting, well you goes right ahead, I says. You want rats with brushes tied to their tails runnin' around your chimneys, it's up to you."

"Rats?" Julianna asked faintly.

"Rats?" Paul echoed, fascinated.

The sweep nodded. "Fair trained 'em, I got to admit, but they don't do the job I do. I mean, I ask you, missus. If you had your choice between rats with brushes and me, which would you choose?"

There was no question in Julianna's mind. "You," she said at once. "But I don't understand Mr . . . ah . . ."

"Meecham. Aloysius Meecham at your service, missus."

"I don't understand what happened to Mr. Wibberting, Mr. Meecham. I asked our butler to send for him this morning."

Mr. Meecham shrugged. "Could be he's low on rats. They does get lost in the chimneys. That's why I don't hold on usin' 'em. You lose a brush in the chimney, it's not so bad. But you loses a rat up a chimney and—"

"Yes, yes, I'm sure," Julianna interrupted hastily. "You may proceed with your work, Mr. Meecham." Julianna turned and led the way inside, her back rigidly erect. After handing Paul over to Kitty, they preceded into the parlor where they encountered Colonel Cramden enjoying a tête-à-tête with Lady Eleanor.

At Julianna's raised eyebrow, Lady Eleanor blushed and became quite busy summoning Hawkins for more hot water.

"Well, well, it's Fairmont again, is it?" the colonel asked. "Don't see you for months, my boy, and then here we are, two days running."

"I have found life to be full of surprises," Lord Fairmont agreed, glancing in Julianna's direction. "Though sometimes what seems an unlikely occurrence is actually the inevitable result of like minds running in tandem harness." He bowed over Lady Eleanor's hand in greeting, causing that lady to utter a soft sigh and flutter her eyelashes.

"But you were speaking of horses, Lord Fairmont," Lady Eleanor prodded.

"I was?" Lord Fairmont sat down on one of the padded armchairs with piaster carving.

"Paul is quite smitten with them, you know," Lady Eleanor said. "I believe that to be true of most young boys, however."

Lord Fairmont leaned forward slightly. "I wanted a pony as a child," he said in a low tone, almost as if he spoke to himself. "In fact, I was fiercely determined to have one, but all my schemes and machinations came to nothing in the end."

Julianna looked at him in some surprise. She would have thought Lord Fairmont to have been petted and spoiled as a child. Certainly with his good looks he must have been an adorable little boy. And his parents rich enough to give him anything he wanted.

"I was sent away to school quite young," he continued. "My mother always said there was no place for an animal in London."

"Thought your family had estates in Somerset," Colonel Cramden said, frowning slightly. "Surely you spent time there between terms?"

"My mother didn't care for the country." Lord Fairmont relaxed against the oval back of the chair, and Julianna noted that his hands had been clenched upon the carved arm supports. "I was going to call my pony Brutus, Miss Partridge, and I did. Only the pony was a horse and I a man grown by the time I had my chance."

"Life is not always as we would have it," Lady Eleanor observed. "But then, it is not so bad either, for you have your Brutus in tandem harness now, do you not?"

Lord Fairmont smiled. "Brutus is not a carriage horse," he said, "and would be most indignant if he heard you naming him one. When I spoke of tandem

104

harness, I was referring to people who think alike, who have similar attitudes." His eyes moved from Lady Eleanor to Julianna. "Such a state must surely be the prerequisite to happiness in marriage."

"You deem it more important than romantic love?" Lady Eleanor asked, sitting at attention as the conversation turned to one of her favorite subjects.

"Irrefutably so," Lord Fairmont said. "One need look no farther than Byron's unhappy marriage to see that one's tastes and outlook on life must be in agreement to form a lasting union."

"But surely the most unhappy are those who wed where there is neither love nor similarity of interest, but merely a concern for property," Julianna protested, thinking of her mother and Lord Ramsden.

Lord Fairmont frowned slightly. "Perhaps," he said. "Though they, at least, suffer no later disillusionment."

"But you do agree that romantic love exists?" Lady Eleanor prodded.

"Indubitably." Lord Fairmont's frown changed to a lazy smile. "It is a very enjoyable state but one not to be considered within the bounds of matrimony."

Lady Eleanor gave a little gasp and raised her eyebrows, looking quite pleasantly shocked.

Colonel Cramden reached over and rapped Lord Fairmont on the knuckles with his cane. "Here, here, my boy. Can't go about saying such things in the homes of respectable gentlewomen. Whatever will Miss Partridge and Mrs. Pickering think?"

Lord Fairmont looked from one lady to the other, his dark eyes hooded. "They will think whatever they please. Ladies do so in any case."

Hawkins entered at that moment with hot water and a fresh plate of cakes, leaving Julianna free to contemplate Lord Fairmont's remarks as Lady

Eleanor measured tea from the fruitwood tea caddy and set it to brew.

So Lord Fairmont did not believe love a prerequisite for marriage? Well, neither did Julianna, nor did many of their class when it came to that, and most wedded couples seemed to rub along together fairly well without it. Certainly few had so stormy a relationship as did Lord Byron and Annabella Milbanke or the Regent and Princess Caroline.

"And you, Mrs. Pickering?" Lord Fairmont broke into her thoughts. "What is your view of love?"

It was a question many a female might have answered with a simpering inanity, but Julianna considered it seriously. "I think I do not like love very much." Her gray eyes focused not on Lord Fairmont but on the rose-colored garlands of petit point in the rug at her feet. "Love steals one's soul," she said softly, "and makes even the strong vulnerable."

"Your marriage to Mr. Pickering then, was not one of romantic attachment?" Colonel Cramden asked.

"No." Julianna shook her head and looked up, her eyes locking with the dark brown ones of Lord Fairmont. "It was not a romantic attachment."

Colonel Cramden smoothed his moustache. "Shouldn't have asked in any case," he mumbled. "None of my business."

"It is quite all right," Julianna reassured him. "My past is hardly a reprehensible one, and I do not mind discussing it."

"Still, I did not mean to pry, Mrs. Pickering. It is just that it was fresh to mind, since Miss Partridge was speaking of your husband's most untimely death in that earthquake before your arrival. Sad affair." He shook his head. "Treacherous things, earthquakes. It is fortunate that you and the boy were not with him at the time."

"Indeed." Julianna agreed, keeping her eyes focused on her teacup.

"Where did this earthquake occur?" Lord Fairmont asked. "It must have been of some magnitude, and yet I do not recall having read about any such in England."

Lady Eleanor studied the plate of teacakes. "Ah, but it was not the earthquake," she replied, selecting a piece of iced gingerbread. "It was the landslide afterwards."

"The landslide . . . I see." Lord Fairmont nodded reflectively.

"It took days to dig poor Parnell out," Lady Eleanor elaborated with a certain relish. "And when they did, there was no recognizing the poor man."

"A pity." Lord Fairmont sipped his tea.

"But fortunate that no one else was injured," Colonel Cramden said again. "And now, I hope you will not think me quite rag-mannered, but I had hoped to catch a glimpse of your son, Mrs. Pickering. I brought him a small present, you see."

"Why, how kind," Julianna said, grateful for any excuse to steer the conversation away from her husband's increasingly complicated demise. "I shall have Kitty fetch Paul from the nursery."

Paul arrived, his eyes going immediately to the plate of cakes and his body soon following.

"Paul!" Two female voices protested as Paul quickly crammed a piece of gingerbread into his mouth before anyone could forbid him the treat.

"You must always ask first," Julianna chided. "Now make your bow to Colonel Cramden."

Paul turned reluctantly away from the tea tray and

made a credible bow to Colonel Cramden.

"And Lord Fairmont."

Paul did as he was bid and then smiled up at Lord Fairmont. "Gingerbread?" he asked, poking a piece with one finger and looking the picture of a young child who had not eaten in days.

"You have had your tea," Julianna said as firmly as she could.

Paul's angelic blue eyes grew stormy. "Gingerbread!" He stamped one foot and glared at Julianna.

"Here, Paul. You haven't seen the present I brought you yet." Colonel Cramden intervened quickly, thrusting a small package at Paul whose face miraculously cleared.

"Present?" he asked, tearing at the paper with abandon. "Present for Pog." He ripped off the top of the box to reveal three lead soldiers, uniforms painted to resemble those of His Majesty's army. "Look, Jules." Paul trotted over to Julianna with his box of soldiers.

"You are too kind," Lady Eleanor said, beaming up at the colonel.

"No, no. I just thought . . . my little grandson collects them, you know. So I thought perhaps your Paul might enjoy them as well."

After a certain amount of prodding, Paul thanked the colonel for his gift. He then carefully lined up his new soldiers in a protective stance in front of the fireplace and returned to gaze wistfully at the gingerbread. Lady Eleanor, quick to take a hint, offered the plate of cakes around once more.

"You must give my compliments to your cook, Miss Partridge. These cakes are among the best I've tasted." Colonel Cramden underlined the compliment by biting into his third. Lady Eleanor smiled and gave Paul the piece of gingerbread he had been coveting.

Lord Fairmont, Julianna noted, refused the teacakes. No doubt that was how he maintained his splendid physique. Julianna glanced obliquely at the fitted coat of blue superfine and the beige pantaloons which clung to Lord Fairmont's muscular legs. Suddenly encountering his eyes, she blushed furiously and became intent on examining the garlands in the carpet once again. The wretched man did that deliberately, she thought. He knew I was admiring his—

"You look a bit flushed, Mrs. Pickering," the wretched man commented, "yet the weather is unseasonably cool and a fire has not been lit. Are you feeling feverish?"

Julianna turned to glare at him, her gray eyes burning like magnificent dark opals.

"Do you suppose you are coming down with a cold?" Lady Eleanor asked hopefully. "Mrs. Randolph gave me a receipt for some herbal tea which she assures me can be used to treat anything from insect bites to the ague. I have been wanting to try it," she explained to the colonel, "but unfortunately everyone has remained wonderfully healthy."

"I feel fine," Julianna replied, still glaring at Lord Fairmont, who was returning her look with a bland one of his own. "I assure you—"

A sudden loud noise brought everyone's head round. Paul, crouched on all fours, was barking quite vociferously at the fireplace. Kitty came quickly forward to scoop up her charge.

"I'm that sorry, mum," she said, trying to control Paul's wriggling body. "I don't know what's got into him today." Giving a mighty jerk, Paul struggled free of Kitty's grasp and began barking at the fireplace again.

Lord Fairmont rose leisurely, picked Paul up by his

collar, administered a quick but solid whack to his backside, and put him down again. "Now, young man," he said, looking down at Paul who was so surprised at being spanked he forgot to cry. "Just what do you think you are doing?"

"On the contrary, Lord Fairmont, what do you think you are doing?" Julianna demanded, her voice shaking in outrage as she pulled Paul into her arms.

"What obviously should have been done some time ago. The child is badly spoiled and in need of discipline."

That this was quite true did nothing to lessen Julianna's fury. "You have no right," she began, spitting out the words between clenched teeth. "Paul may misbehave. He may, indeed, be indulged too much — spoiled, if you will, but love — "

"Indulgence is not love," Lord Fairmont interrupted swiftly. "Only a ninnyhammer would equate the two."

Colonel Cramden thumped his cane on the floor. "That remark is uncalled for, Fairmont. Mrs. Pickering is in the right of it. You've no call to go disciplining her child, needed or not."

Lady Eleanor who had risen to her feet along with Julianna, nodded in agreement. "In any case, love is rarely wise." She turned to Paul. "At what were you barking, Pog, dear?"

"Rats."

"Rats?" Lady Eleanor repeated faintly.

"He means the rats in the chimney," Julianna said impatiently, still glowering at Lord Fairmont.

"You have rats in your chimney?" the colonel asked, eyeing the marble edifice with some concern as Lady Eleanor stepped quickly back.

"Of course not," Julianna replied with some asperity. "It is that Mr. Meecham Lord Fairmont hired to clean the chimneys who put the idea into Paul's head."

"Thank heavens," Lady Eleanor said, subsiding once more onto the settee.

"And I don't believe for a minute that Mr. Wibberting ties brushes to the tails of trained rats."

"Does sound a bit difficult," Colonel Cramden observed, absently reaching for another cake. "Though one never knows about these things."

Julianna looked down at Paul, who seemed none the worse for being manhandled by Lord Fairmont. "There are no rats in the chimneys, Paul," she said. "Do you understand?"

Though he wore a look of keen disappointment, Paul nodded.

"Good. Now, would you like another piece of gingerbread before Kitty takes you back to the nursery?"

Paul turned and looked to Lord Fairmont for permission, which so incensed Julianna that she cut a piece twice the usual size and handed it to the boy. Before anyone could change their minds about this largesse, Paul crammed it into his mouth.

"I shall have my physician send round something for the child's stomach in an hour or so," Lord Fairmont said. "Though if you usually indulge the boy to this extent you may already have something to hand."

Julianna's fingers tightened around the serving fork she held, but she forced herself to remain calm. The colonel was making noises about leaving, so her ordeal would soon be over.

A few minutes later, the colonel picked up his cane and rose to bid the ladies farewell. Lord Fairmont followed but made no move to leave himself. Surely he did not still expect to be shown around the house? Julianna, driven to rudeness, held out his hat and walking stick and looked pointedly at the door Hawkins was just closing behind the colonel.

"Now you may give me my tour," Lord Fairmont said, strolling over to the stairs, "and point out what is in need of repair. I do not usually act my own agent, but in this case, I will." He turned, eyebrows raised as Julianna remained by the door holding his hat and walking stick. "The butler will take care of those things, Mrs. Pickering. Come along now. I have other engagements this afternoon."

Julianna's only movement was to stick out her chin and glare at him.

"Ah, still you hesitate, afraid to make a claim upon my time." Lord Fairmont nodded. "You need not, you know. For while it is true that not everyone is the conscientious landlord I am, I believe a man has a moral responsibility in this respect."

"It is too bad you did not feel that moral responsibility when you caused Lord Carlborne to hang himself," Julianna replied bitingly.

"Julianna!" Lady Eleanor gasped.

"That was uncalled for, Mrs. Pickering." Lord Fairmont's voice was cold, his mocking look replaced by the hard arrogance with which Julianna had already become familiar. "I can see from whom Paul has his manners. Perhaps you would care to show me around, Miss Partridge?"

Lady Eleanor came forward at once. "I should be only too happy. There is the sash in the parlor window that needs replacing and the door of the nursery which is warped and does not close properly. We had meant to speak to your agent, Mr. Basset, but it will be so much better if you see the problems yourself." She ushered Lord Fairmont up the stairs, giving Julianna a look of concern from the corner of her eyes.

I don't care, Julianna thought. Perhaps it was

wrong of me to mention the marquis's death, but surely it was also wrong of Lord Fairmont to have acted as he did. I do not equate love with indulgence. Paul has not had an easy time of it, and while I may give in to his whims more than is good for him, I do not—

"Just this one more to do, missus, and I'll be through," Mr. Meecham announced, tramping into the parlor and Julianna's thoughts. "I'm that sorry though about the boy. Lord Fairmont said as how he was carrying on somethin' fierce about them rats. Didn't mean to scare him none. I was just passin' the time, so to speak."

"No harm done, Mr. Meecham. I shall busy myself elsewhere so you may get on with your job." Julianna quit the parlor a frown upon her face. So Lord Fairmont had spoken to the sweep about Paul, had he? That must count as a kindness, she supposed, though Julianna could not but wonder at Lord Fairmont's concern for a child he barely knew. Was his interest merely that of a childless man charmed by a small boy's endearing looks and impish manner? Or was there some other reason?

Julianna remembered the way Lord Fairmont had towered over her during their quarrel, the strength and intensity that lay beneath his gentlemanly facade. Admittedly, the man both intrigued and frightened her. I am like the moth dancing before the deadly heat of the candle flame, Julianna thought with a shudder. Picking up the book she had recently acquired from the circulating library, Julianna walked slowly down the hallway. Perhaps reading about the problems of the fictional heroine would give her the perspective to puzzle out her own.

Thus it was that Lady Eleanor found Julianna some

time later sitting on the window seat in the little back parlor, knees drawn up in a most unladylike posture, deep in the pages of *The Castle of Otranto*.

Lady Eleanor sat down in one of the chintz-covered chairs, a smile on her face like a kitten who has just discovered the cream bowl. She cleared her throat, made sure she had Julianna's attention, and then announced, "Lord Fairmont is such an excellent young man."

Julianna looked back at her novel.

"He was most concerned to find that you had been using that small room off the stairs. No more than a storage room he called it and told Hawkins to move your things to the other bedroom at once."

"What?" Julianna sat up and shut her book with a snap. "Surely it is for me to say which room I prefer."

"But you know you have been complaining about how difficult it is to sleep with a window on the street and no place for half your things. I should think you would be pleased, Julianna. Do not say you intended to remain now the chimney in the south bedroom no longer smokes."

"Of course not, it is just that . . ." Julianna paused to take a deep breath. "I am sorry. I do not know why I am acting so churlish about it."

"It is because you wanted to take Lord Fairmont about yourself, but that gingery hair of yours would not let you. It is like the cow who kicks over the milking stool and later regrets it." Lady Eleanor nodded wisely. "And what woman would not wish to spend time in Lord Fairmont's company? I imagine our capturing him for tea will have half the ladies in Bath looking daggers at us."

Julianna moved to the matching chair on the other side of the newly cleaned fireplace. "We hardly *captured* him, Lady Eleanor, and I do not like the idea of being in any way beholden to Lord Fairmont."

"You are upset with the way he disciplined Paul," Lady Eleanor said, "but you must admit that is something we should have done long ago. Paul is much too coming at times."

"This from you, Lady Eleanor?" Julianna asked, raising her eyebrows.

"Yes," Lady Eleanor said unequivocally. "Lord Fairmont seems very good with children. Unusual in a man. Most are content to see their offspring no more than once a day, and that is too often for some. I was quite brassy, in fact, and asked Lord Fairmont why he had never married and started a family of his own."

"And you accuse Paul of being much too coming?"

"Awful of me, I know," Lady Eleanor agreed. "For a moment I was afraid he would not answer, such a look as he had on his face. But then he smiled, and do you know what he said?"

"What?" Julianna pounced on the question.

"He said I was quite right, and that he had waited much too long as it was to settle down, but that he meant to rectify the matter shortly. Now what do you think of that?"

Julianna shrugged, feigning disinterest. "It is of no matter to me, but I do wonder. . . . Do you remember I spoke to you before about a broken engagement? His sister, Lady Davina, intimated that he now dislikes women, holds them in contempt, in fact." Julianna waited, hoping Lady Eleanor would rise to the bait.

"I have seen no evidence of this." Lady Eleanor snapped at the lure. "Lord Fairmont has always seemed most gentlemanly in his behavior towards those of our sex, though this afternoon . . ." Lady

Eleanor frowned. "Still, they say a quarrel is only the renewal of love, and I would think the woman who brings him up to scratch would be fortunate indeed."

"Did he . . ." Julianna hesitated, not knowing how to phrase the question uppermost in her mind. "Do you think he has already chosen the lady?" she asked at last.

Lady Eleanor smiled. "As to that, I cannot say. He mentioned no names, but I had the feeling he has someone definitely in mind."

Julianna found herself quickly reviewing the suitable women she knew in Bath. But, of course, the lady could be someone Lord Fairmont had met in London. Whomever she was, she would certainly not be a . . . a ninnyhammer, but beautiful and accomplished and of impeccable lineage, Julianna thought, a cloud of gloom seeming to settle over her. Though if even half of what Lady Davina said was true, the woman who became wife to the autocratic Lord Fairmont would not have an easy time of it.

"I do not envy her in the least," Julianna said, more forcibly than necessary.

Lady Eleanor did not reply, but her smile widened into something resembling a grin. "Not even when I tell you Lord Fairmont has invited us to an evening at the theater?"

"What?" Julianna could not believe she had heard right. "Lord Fairmont has invited us to the theater?"

Lady Eleanor nodded.

"To see Mrs. Siddons?"

Lady Eleanor nodded again. "He said he had a box and thought we might enjoy it. He intends to invite the colonel as well. I told him we would be most happy to attend. I think he would make amends for your quarrel."

A great wave of excitement rushed over Julianna. "Oh, Lady Eleanor, this is above everything!"

"Then I have not sunk myself beneath reproach by accepting for both of us without first consulting you?"

Julianna looked into the teasing blue eyes of her step aunt and could not keep from jumping from her chair and giving that lady a quick hug. "What a complete hand you are, Lady Eleanor. As if you did not know I have been scheming for ways we might afford to attend without outrunning the constable and have even thought of selling Mama's garnets."

"Ah, no, you will need those, Julianna. For I intend that we shall look all the crack. We may not be diamonds of the first water, but we are not antidotes either. And I mean to give the old hens of Bath something to really cackle about."

Chapter Eight

The thought of actually seeing Sarah Siddons in her celebrated role as Lady Macbeth had Julianna in a high state of anticipatory fidgets. If Lord Fairmont meant the invitation as an apology for his treatment of Paul, Julianna would graciously accept. It seemed impossible to her that her dream of just a few days ago would really come true: she would be attending the Royal Theatre, and she would be dressed to the nines, thanks to Lady Eleanor.

Not only had her stepaunt spent the following days busily creating gowns for them, but Lady Eleanor had also insisted that they employ a lady's maid for the evening. "For it will not be a great expense, Julianna, and you did win quite a tidy sum at the Winslow's supper party."

To Lady Eleanor's obvious surprise, Julianna had agreed to this suggestion at once.

"And the fact that we will be escorted by Lord Fairmont has nothing to do with it," Julianna had said firmly. She then spent the intervening days wondering exactly what that gentleman would say when he saw her in the gown of Lady Eleanor's design. There had not been time to sew something new, so Lady Eleanor had contented herself with pulling apart the bodice of

Julianna's old white satin evening dress, stitching on new lace and some tiny seed pearls, and cutting the décolletage to within an inch of decency.

At the first fitting Julianna had blushed, tugged at the bodice, and declared that she could never go out in public wearing so little.

"Nonsense," Lady Eleanor had declared. "It is merely what is fashionable. Such a neckline would be considered modest in London, and I am sure I have seen Lady Davina wearing gowns with a much lower décolletage."

That might very well be, Julianna acknowledged now as she studied herself uncertainly in the cloudy cheval glass. "But I am neither Lady Davina nor in London, and I am not at all sure that this style is suited to my figure." Much too tall and too thin. Lord Ramsden's words echoed through her mind. The figure of a schoolboy.

Julianna sighed and let her shoulders slump for a moment. She would never be a beauty. Not even Eweing, the lady's maid they had hired for the evening could change that, but — Julianna lifted her chin and straightened her shoulders — she was still Julianna Seaton. She would carry herself proudly and enjoy her evening. And if Lord Fairmont, rake and libertine that he was, chose not to find her attractive, it would not matter in the least.

Not in the least, Julianna repeated firmly. Turning from the glass, she took out a key and unlocked one of the drawers of the dressing table. From there she took the small mahogany box which contained what remained of her mother's jewelry as well as Paul's pebbles and other treasures. At least she had not had to sell the garnets in order to purchase theater tickets, she told herself, fastening the earrings and turning her head from side to side to study her reflection.

"If you will kindly sit down, madam."

Julianna turned to find Eweing, the lady's maid, frowning at her from the doorway.

"If you will but sit down, we will fasten the necklace. That is what we are paid for."

Julianna, feeling unaccountably guilty, sat down on the small stool in front of the dressing table. For though Eweing was a good four inches shorter than Julianna and unprepossessing in appearance, there was something about her that had Julianna obeying at once.

"Miss Partridge needed our help with her gown and hair, but that did not mean we were finished with you," Eweing said grimly. "Garnets are not the stone for you. Sapphires or emeralds would be much better."

"I do have some sapphires but—"

"Next time, wear them," Eweing commanded. "White isn't the best color for you, either. We told Miss Partridge, and she quite agrees. Since there's nothing we can do about it tonight, however, a touch of rouge might help."

"Paint?" Julianna queried, looking a bit shocked. In her limited experience it was only actresses or women of another sort altogether who used paint.

"Sometimes nature needs a bit of help," Eweing replied. She cast a critical glance at Julianna's face. "You have a good skin, I'll give you that." And without further ado, Eweing began to wield the rouge brush.

Julianna did not dare to move except upon command and so had no idea how she looked until Eweing stepped back and with an approving nod, said, "Makes all the difference in the world."

Julianna gazed into the mirror, the candles on each side casting a soft glow over her features. The fine white skin that went with her red hair was still there but lightly tinted so that she seemed lit from within. Even her luminous, light gray eyes seemed to sparkle and deepen in intensity.

"Oh, Eweing," Julianna murmured, quite unable to look away from her reflection, "I look . . . I look . . ."

"Of course, you do," Eweing agreed. "We have yet to fail in making even the drabbest of females look presentable. It is all in knowing what to do."

"Oh, Eweing," Julianna said again, turning to face the lady's maid who was looking grimly pleased with her handiwork. "I just wish we could afford to hire you permanently."

Eweing nodded. "We are at loose ends at the moment and might consider taking you on. As an investment."

"An investment?"

"We have discussed it with Miss Partridge, but do not get your hopes up. We shall have to think about it."

Julianna nodded, wondering if she had missed part of the conversation while she had been absorbed in her own reflection. With a slight shrug, she stood and gave a final twitch to the skirt of her gown before turning to pick up her gloves. Then, feeling a bit as if she had drunk several glasses of the bubbly which Lord Ramsden was so fond of, Julianna took one final look in the mirror. "I look all the crack," Julianna whispered to herself. "I really do." Between Eweing and Lady Eleanor, a miracle had been performed. There was no other word for it.

"Lady Eleanor." Julianna greeted her stepaunt as they met in the upstairs hallway, and waited with a small anticipatory smile for Lady Eleanor's reaction to the new, fashionable Julianna.

"Oh, my dear, you look lovely." Lady Eleanor embraced Julianna. "As I knew you would. That Eweing is a treasure."

Julianna nodded. "As are you. The colonel will be quite bowled over, I am sure."

Lady Eleanor blushed, though Julianna's words were no more than the truth. Dressed in a lime green sarcenet gown trimmed with silver cording and designed by the wearer to hide a tendency to plumpness, Lady Eleanor looked quite elegant and much younger than her years.

"Aren't you afraid the colonel will think he is robbing the cradle?" Julianna teased.

"What a farradiddle," Lady Eleanor said. "Though not an unwelcome one, I will admit. And I cannot wait to see Lord Fairmont's reaction when he sees you."

Flustered, Julianna put one hand to her throat. "I . . . Eweing says garnets are not my stone, nor white my color."

Lady Eleanor nodded. "And she is in the right of it. Next time, we shall get the saphires out, though, the garnets look much better than I expected."

"I am glad I did not have to sell them," Julianna admitted. "Though it may prove necessary later."

"Not if you play your cards right tonight, my dear."

"Whatever do you mean? We are going to the theater not a card party." Julianna fiddled nervously with the pearl buttons on her long white evening gloves.

"There is no need to play the innocent with me, Julianna. You know exactly what I mean. Lord Fairmont has developed a *tendre* for you."

"What a . . . what a whisker," Julianna said, blushing slightly beneath the rouge. "Sometimes I think you must have windmills in your head, Lady Eleanor."

Lady Eleanor replied with a raised eyebrow and a disbelieving look.

"Lord Fairmont would never look at someone like me." Julianna's voice was a combination of defiance and wistfulness. "You have said yourself that he is one of the most eligible men in England."

"And apparently one of the most discerning," Lady Eleanor said firmly. "A man does not distinguish a woman by inviting her to the theater unless he is interested."

"The invitation was to make amends for his treatment of Paul, that is all," Julianna said, starting towards the stairs. She had no wish to continue a conversation that was beginning to make her distinctly uncomfortable.

"Certainly you will not continue to deny that you find Lord Fairmont attractive."

"Since you will not allow it, it would be foolish of me," Julianna replied lightly. "And I will admit to the truth of Lord Fairmont's attraction. But just because he has invited us to the theater does not mean he has developed a partiality. Nor that I would wish for such a thing. You forget the impossibility of our situation."

Lady Eleanor said nothing, merely smiling in a self-satisfied way that set Julianna's teeth on edge at the same time it caused a giddy, soaring sensation of forbidden hope to lodge within her breast. Still, Julianna was no foolish schoolgirl. And though she could not deny Lord Fairmont's obvious appeal, she was not such a widgeon as to overlook his faults.

And Julianna did not think it an error of judgment to say these were numerous indeed. While it might be true that Paul had deserved the treatment Lord Fairmont had meted out and the incident best forgot, there was no denying the man was an imperious, high-handed, domineering womanizer, whose reputation as a notorious rake was as well-known as his libertine habits. Lord Fairmont had not only caused Lord Carlborne to hang himself over a gambling debt but had ruthlessly married his sister to a fortune-hunting friend. No wonder his betrothed had felt the scandal of a broken engagement preferable to wedlock. Julianna silently repeated the litany of Lord Fairmont's faults as she descended the stairs beside Lady Eleanor.

It did little good. The minute Julianna saw Lord Fairmont waiting for them in the doorway of the parlor, so tall and handsome in his black evening clothes, his strong chin resting atop the intricate folds of his immaculate cravat, her heart gave a little lurch, turned over, and came to rest at his highly polished evening pumps. No use telling herself she was a clunch, a green girl with no sense, a nodcock who allowed a handsome face and rake's experienced charm to bring her to point non plus, her heart was quite badly dipped, and Julianna was not sure it would recover.

Lord Fairmont stepped forward, his golden hair glinting in the light of the candles in their brass wall sconces. "Miss Partridge." He bowed over Lady Eleanor's gloved hand. "And Mrs. Pickering." Julianna's hand was raised to his lips and held just a fraction longer than necessary, turning the common greeting into something approaching a caress.

Lady Eleanor watched the proceedings with an indulgent I-told-you-so smile and did her best to become invisible.

Julianna, looking into Lord Fairmont's dark brown eyes and feeling the warm pressure of his fingers upon her gloved ones, commanded herself to stop being foolish and to start breathing again. He is only a man, she told herself sternly. Though he may look like a

Greek god, he is a man. Stop making a cake of yourself. You cannot permit yourself to care for him. Remember how arrogant he is, how high-handed. Think of the way he treated Paul. But instead Julianna found herself returning his smile and remembering only his kindness.

"You are looking quite lovely," Lord Fairmont murmured in a voice meant for her ears alone.

"Horsies!"

Three pairs of eyes turned to the top of the stairs where Paul stood, curls tousled, blue eyes alight with anticipation.

"Me see horsies," Paul said, happily running down the stairs, nightshirt billowing out behind.

"Paul, what are you doing here? You should be in bed. Where is Kitty?" Julianna, who had been caught in the rosy haze of romance only a moment ago, was now caught in the harsh reality of motherhood.

Paul, after casting Julianna a look of acute dislike, ignored her, and went to tug at Lord Fairmont's immaculate coattails. "Me see horsies," he demanded once again.

Lord Fairmont glanced at the two women, shrugged, and said, "I don't see why not. The evening is mild, and if we wrap him in a shawl, he shouldn't take a chill."

Julianna was tempted to ask if this would not be an example of a ninnyhammer's indulgence but wisely kept such churlish thoughts to herself.

"Paul does like animals," Lady Eleanor said, looking down at Paul, who was viewing all this adult conversation with outthrust lip. "And I know he misses Brownie, the pony he left behind in the country."

Lord Fairmont smiled charmingly at Lady Eleanor. "Then Paul must, indeed, see the horses. You have been living in the countryside around Bath until recently?"

"No, we —"

"I will ring for Hawkins to fetch a shawl," Julianna interrupted with a warning glance at Lady Eleanor. Not for a moment would she consider leaving her stepaunt alone with Lord Fairmont. He was much too clever at manipulating a conversation to his own ends.

"You rang, missus?" Mrs. Gardning appeared in the hall, looking annoyed at being disturbed.

"I rang for Hawkins," Julianna replied. "Where is he?"

"Had to step out for a minute. What is it you want?"

Julianna frowned. The housekeeper-cook was being inexcusably insolent. "I want you to fetch a shawl from my room, Mrs. Gardning."

Without a word, the housekeeper turned away, leaving Julianna feeling acutely embarrassed that Lord Fairmont should have witnessed such a scene. He will think I cannot handle the servants along with everything else, she thought, the silvery glow of the evening beginning to slowly tarnish.

Paul, whose patience with these adult delays had come to an end, tugged urgently at Lord Fairmont's coat again. "We go now!" He backed away slightly as he encountered Lord Fairmont's stern gaze but refused to be put off. "Go now. Please. Horsies be sleeping soon."

"My horses are allowed to stay up quite late to meet little boys," Lord Fairmont replied. "Now unhand my coattails and behave, or you shall not see them after all."

A few minutes later, Paul, wrapped in a paisley shawl much to his annoyance, was taken out to see the matched pair that drew Lord Fairmont's carriage. Even Lady Eleanor, who considered horses great, nervous beasts who were best avoided, admired the pair's sleek appearance which denoted the care obviously lavished upon them.

After Paul had been pried away and given into the care of Kitty, who had arrived on the scene full of apologies, the two ladies were handed into the carriage.

"It was kind of you to show Paul your horses," Julianna remarked as she settled herself against the plush squabs.

"I have strong views about raising children," Lord Fairmont admitted from the seat opposite. "Which is why I am afraid I was a bit high-handed in my treatment of Paul the other day. I realize that most in our class believe children should be reared by servants and considered only when it is time to arrange a marriage that will be advantageous to the family. I disagree, though that is how I was raised."

"I see." Julianna nodded in the darkness of the carriage, the picture of a small boy, not unlike Paul, vivid in her mind.

"Yes," Lord Fairmont said quietly. "I think you do. I have little affection for my family, Mrs. Pickering. When my father died I shed not a tear, my only concern being for the estate which he had encumbered with gambling debts. I would not have any child feel for me what I feel . . . felt for my father."

An uneasy, reflective silence fell in the dark interior of the carriage, both Lord Fairmont and Julianna occupied with their own thoughts. Lady Eleanor looked from one to the other, smiled and nodded, the gesture all but invisible in the darkness. "Does Colonel Cramden not join us?" she asked, breaking into the lengthening silence.

Lord Fairmont turned and blinked, as if surprised to find her there. "He will meet us at the theater. He said he preferred to walk since he will be spending the rest of the evening in inactivity."

"Yes. I have noticed that if he sits too long, his leg becomes stiff," Lady Eleanor said, not stopping to consider the impropriety of a maiden lady remarking on a gentleman's limbs. Fortunately no one seemed to notice, and it was not very many minutes later that the carriage drew up at their destination.

"Does the rest of your party join us in the theater?" Julianna asked, as they alighted in the Sawclose.

Lord Fairmont leaned forward, his hair glinting in the light cast by the carriage lanterns. "I invited only you and Miss Partridge in addition to Colonel Cramden," he replied. "And had propriety allowed, I would have invited only you." His voice was a warm, intimate murmur, and Julianna, looking up into the dark eyes so intent upon her own, could think of no reply. Like a tongue-tied schoolgirl, she lowered her head and quickly followed Lady Eleanor through a series of rooms to the box which Lord Fairmont had hired.

The new theater in Beaufort Square had been designed to impress, and Julianna could not help but think it accomplished this admirably. Her gray eyes silvery with excitement, Julianna looked around the sumptuous interior. Three tiers of seats supported by cast-iron pillars gave it a lofty appearance, while the walls, covered with stamped cloth that matched the covering of the seats, and the gilt latticework surrounding the boxes added to its magnificence. Julianna gazed upward at the five allegorical scenes painted on the ceiling and connected by plaster

MORE PASSION AND ADVENTURE AWAIT... YOUR TRIP TO A BIG ADVENTUROUS WORLD BEGINS WHEN YOU ACCEPT YOUR FIRST 4 NOVELS ABSOLUTELY *FREE*
(AN $18.00 VALUE)

Accept your Free gift and start to experience more of the passion and adventure you like in a historical romance novel. Each Zebra novel is filled with proud men, spirited women and tempestuous love that you'll remember long after you turn the last page.

Zebra Historical Romances are the finest novels of their kind. They are written by authors who really know how to weave tales of romance and adventure in the historical settings you love. You'll feel like you've actually gone back in time with the thrilling stories that each Zebra novel offers.

GET YOUR FREE GIFT WITH THE START OF YOUR HOME SUBSCRIPTION

Our readers tell us that these books sell out very fast in book stores and often they miss the newest titles. So Zebra has made arrangements for you to receive the four newest novels published each month.

You'll be guaranteed that you'll never miss a title, and home delivery is so convenient. And to show you just how easy it is to get Zebra Historical Romances, we'll send you your first 4 books absolutely **FREE**! Our gift to you just for trying our home subscription service.

BIG SAVINGS AND FREE HOME DELIVERY

Each month, you'll receive the four newest titles as soon as they are published. You'll probably receive them even before the bookstores do. What's more, you may preview these exciting novels free for 10 days. If you like them as much as we think you will, just pay the low preferred subscriber's price of just $3.75 each. *You'll save $3.00 each month off the publisher's price.* AND, your savings are even greater because there are never any shipping, handling or other hidden charges—FREE Home Delivery. Of course you can return any shipment within 10 days for full credit, no questions asked. There is no minimum number of books you must buy.

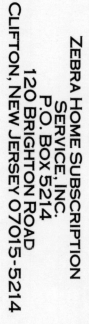

wreaths of flowers. She sighed, feeling pleasantly overwhelmed by the sheer splendor of it all.

Lady Eleanor fingered the draperies at each side of the box with a professional air and frowned slightly. The cloth was green velvet edged with gold, quite attractive under ordinary circumstances but not when one was wearing lime green sarcenet. Julianna's white satin might not be the most flattering color, but at least she could sit near the front of the box without fear of offending.

"Ah, you are before me." Colonel Cramden entered the box, a pleased smile turning up the ends of his moustache. "I must say I am really looking forward to this evening. Good of you to include me, Fairmont."

"I imagine you would have found a way to obtain tickets by means fair or foul in any case, Colonel."

Colonel Cramden nodded. "Wouldn't miss seeing Mrs. Siddons for the world, though tickets are reportedly as scarce as hen's teeth. Did see one fellow hawking some outside the entrance tonight, however. Reminded me of that fellow who acts as butler for you, Miss Partridge. That's the way to make some easy money, I should think. Buy the tickets at the regular price and then sell them to some desperate soul at twice that. Should think the man would realize a handsome profit."

"Indeed," Julianna agreed, "for I understand seats are selling for outrageous prices. I had all but given up hope of being able to attend."

Colonel Cramden nodded and settled himself comfortably in one of the chairs, propping his cane against the wall. "Remember seeing Siddons perform Lady Macbeth some fifteen years ago when we were both in our prime. Be interesting to see how she has fared. Though it can't be easy coming out of retirement like this to perform at benefits once or twice a year."

"Were you in the audience the night that young boy joined her on stage?" Lord Fairmont asked.

Colonel Cramden shook his head. "Heard about it though." He turned to address the ladies. "It seems it was very hot, and they sent this boy to fetch something for Mrs. Siddons to drink. When he returned, he asked where she was and having her pointed out on stage, he simply walked out and joined her there. She was in the middle of her sleeping scene and could not get him to leave. I understand the audience was in a regular uproar over the whole thing."

"Let us hope nothing of that sort happens tonight," Lady Eleanor said, "for we have been so looking forward to the performance. It was as Lady Macbeth that Mrs. Siddons gave her final performance before retiring, was it not, Lord Fairmont?"

Lord Fairmont did not reply, and the others noticed that his attention had become riveted on one of the boxes opposite.

"I see Lady Davina is also in attendance," the colonel said.

"Yes." The words were spoken between lips tightly compressed. "And I strictly forbade her to go out this evening."

The unfairness of this quite incensed Julianna. "How could you?" she demanded. "Mrs. Siddons performs so infrequently that each occasion must be deemed a gift not to be overlooked. To be angry because Lady Davina wishes to attend, to forbid her to do so, is unforgivable."

"Lady Davina does not attend tonight to see Mrs. Siddons perform but to be seen herself. Preferably by me, I imagine." Lord Fairmont's voice and eyes were hard.

130

"Still, it does seem a bit much, Fairmont," the colonel ventured. "I mean, don't see that your sister's attending can do any harm."

"She was quite ill this morning." Lord Fairmont turned his attention to his guests once more. "I am sorry. You are not to blame for my sister's behavior. It is just that I promised Grey, that is, her husband Edgar Greyling, that I would see she did not endanger her health this time."

"Ah, yes. Heard your sister was increasing again," Colonel Cramden said. "That's why you're in Bath, is it, rather than London?"

Lord Fairmont nodded. "My sister has already had one child stillborn and almost died in the birthing. The doctor insists that she live quietly and get as much rest as possible. Though Davina looks quite healthy, she is not as robust as she appears. And she does her best to flaunt both the doctor and myself at every turn. Unfortunately, Davina is encouraged in this by my mother. I had hoped she would be a calming influence, but I should have known better. My mother cares for no one but herself, and I am afraid she sets the example Davina follows. Still, I will not allow my sister to endanger her life again through her own foolish behavior."

An uncomfortable silence followed this revelation, as each in turn thought over what had been said. Then the lights dimmed and the performance began, and Lady Davina was forgotten.

Chapter Nine

As far as Julianna was concerned, the performance of Sarah Siddons that night would remain in her memory as one of the high points of her life. Lady Davina, Lord Fairmont, worry over Lord Ramsden discovering their whereabouts: all were forgot and the knots in which her emotions seemed so often tied were unraveled by the magic presence of Sarah Siddons on the stage.

From the first entrance of the great actress, when the audience crowding the theater erupted into spontaneous applause and shouts, to Mrs. Siddons's last speech, Julianna was enthralled. It seemed almost a sacrilege to withdraw to one of the retiring rooms for refreshment during the intermission. And for the most part Julianna sat quietly, sipping the tea Lord Fairmont provided while taking little part in the talk that swirled around her. She was still caught up in the dark tragedy of the stage.

In Lady Macbeth's last scene, Mrs. Siddons's tragic cry of "Out, damned spot! Out, I say!" had Julianna twisting her own hands. When the actress spoke her final words, "What's done cannot be undone. To bed, to bed, to bed!" there was such applause, such shouts, that the other actors could barely be heard. But Julianna sat silently, her gray eyes misty with tears. So intensely had she become involved in the terrible happenings on stage that it was some time before she could bring herself back to reality and join in the accolades heaped upon Mrs. Siddons.

Later, as the last words of the play were spoken and the final applause had died down, Lord Fairmont turned to Julianna and spoke quietly in her ear. "I need not ask if you enjoyed yourself, I see."

"No. Oh, no." Julianna's voice was hushed, her face unsmiling, but her eyes shone with the wonder of it all. "It was . . . it was the most marvelous thing."

Lord Fairmont smiled, a smile quite unlike any she had seen on his face before. It was not the curving of the lips that came automatically to the face of an accomplished rake, nor the polite stretching of the mouth which society deemed correct. No, this was a smile that told of a secret shared, a secret that would be quite defiled if one attempted to express it in words.

"I am glad," Lord Fairmont said simply, and then turned away to address Lady Eleanor.

Colonel Cramden rose stiffly to his feet and leaned heavily upon his cane. "Well, Mrs. Siddons is not quite as I remembered, her voice is not as strong, nor her carriage as majestic, but still her acting in the night scene was quite admirable. Especially when one considers that she is so seldom upon the stage these days."

"But . . . but did you not think she was quite magnificent?" Julianna asked.

"Ah, were I seeing Mrs. Siddons for the first time, I would indeed think so," he replied kindly. "But I remember her performance of twenty years ago . . ." He paused and his brown eyes grew clouded for a moment. "I saw her once play Juliet and ever after fancied myself in love. I could never understand why she preferred that Romeo chap, you know. But then . . . old memories play tricks . . ." He looked up and smiled at Julianna and suddenly tapped his cane smartly on the floor. "And you are quite right. Mrs. Siddons was magnificent tonight as always."

The noise and bustle of the departing theatergoers had begun to diminish, and Lord Fairmont suggested that they take their departure as well. Julianna rose with reluctance, taking one last look around the theater.

"We will come again," Lord Fairmont said. "Though I cannot promise another night such as this."

With a sigh, Julianna followed Lady Eleanor through the now deserted anterooms to the waiting carriage. It had begun to rain, a soft drizzle that served to dampen Julianna's spirits as well as her gown. She was feeling unaccountably low now that her magical evening was almost over.

Colonel Cramden joined them in the carriage, the two men sitting opposite the ladies. The interior was dim, lit only by the outside carriage lamps, and slightly chilly. Julianna shivered as the carriage started toward Taylor Street.

"When I was a girl, we used to engage in amateur theatricals," Lady Eleanor said, breaking the silence that seemed to wrap itself around her companions. "I made a great many of the costumes, and one of my best friends from the village, Amy Gillthorpe, who became Amy Fothering, helped me rehearse my lines. It was such fun. Once we even attempted *Richard III*. Rather ambitious of us, I know, but it was not badly done."

"Who played Richard?" Lord Fairmont asked. He

was sitting back in the carriage, idly observing Julianna's profile as she gazed out at the darkened streets.

"My brother. He was quite good, but then the part suited him."

"Your brother is a hunchback?" Colonel Cramden leaned forward to inquire.

"What? Oh, no . . . no. It is just that he is like Richard III in personality."

"Hardly complimentary," Lord Fairmont said. "Is your brother still alive?"

"Unfortunately, yes," Julianna broke in, turning her head to stare challengingly across the dimness at Lord Fairmont. Talk of Lord Ramsden had brought her back to the harsh reality of her situation. Lady Macbeth was dead, life went on, what was done could not be undone. Nothing had changed, though for a brief, magical moment it might have seemed that way.

Now Lord Fairmont's questions, casual as they might have been, sounded dangerously prying to her ears. And though Julianna might admit that her breath all but stopped when Lord Fairmont looked at her in a certain way, and that she might, indeed, have misjudged him . . . she could not allow herself to trust him.

No, the lesson her stepfather had taught when Julianna first offered her childish devotion had been well-learned. Never trust a man. Especially when that man is capable of breaking your heart.

The carriage arrived in Taylor Street and, after the steps had been let down, Lord Fairmont assisted Lady Eleanor and Julianna to alight. Hawkins opened the door for them, and the ladies turned to bid Lord Fairmont and Colonel Cramden good night.

"I shall call tomorrow, if I may?" the colonel inquired of Lady Eleanor. She blushed and nodded and mentally inventoried her gowns, wondering which she should wear.

"I am afraid I shall be out of town for a few days," Lord Fairmont excused himself. "But I hope to call upon you when I return. There is a private matter of some importance I would like to discuss." He looked at Julianna as he said this, indicating in all but words that the private matter concerned her.

Julianna swallowed nervously but forced a calmness to her features that was quite at odds with the romantic notions that galloped through her mind in the direction of her heart. "We shall look forward to seeing you," she replied politely, and then thanked him for the evening.

"The pleasure was mine," he assured her as he took his leave.

As soon as the door was closed, Lady Eleanor turned and gave Julianna a quick embrace. "He means to make you an offer," she exclaimed. "Oh, Julianna, I am so happy for you. All our problems will be solved. And what a match! This will certainly put a flea in my brother's ear."

"I haven't the slightest idea what you are talking about," Julianna replied mendaciously. "Lord Fairmont was merely informing us that he would be gone for a few days but would pay us a courtesy call when he returned."

"Pish-tish. When a man tells a maiden lady that he has a private matter of some importance to discuss with her, it can mean only one thing." Lady Eleanor took up her candle and began to mount the stairs.

"You are being quite nonsensical," Julianna said, following her stepaunt's bustling figure. "Lord Fairmont means to warn me against gambling with his sister again, that is all."

Lady Eleanor continued up the stairs not deigning to answer.

Julianna tried again. "Lord Fairmont might indulge in a flirtation, but he would never consider marriage to someone with so little to recommend her." Julianna stopped at the top of the stairs. "Would he?" she whispered, staring into the flickering yellow flame of her candle, as hope battled with fear.

"Julianna?" Lady Eleanor waited beside the opened door of Julianna's bedchamber. "It is not I who is being nonsensical," she said, shooing Julianna inside. Lighting the candles that stood on the marble top of the mahogany dressing table, Lady Eleanor pushed Julianna in front of the cheval glass and stood back.

"It is never wise to count one's chickens before the eggs are laid," she said. "But my pate is not as addled as some might think."

"Lady Eleanor, I never meant—"

"I know exactly what you meant. You are afraid that if you admit to the truth of something, you will put a curse on it and it will not be. Such superstitious thinking comes from having Lord Ramsden for a stepfather. But you do not wear your clothes inside out for luck as he sometimes does, do you?"

"No, of course not."

"Nor are you foolish enough to turn around twice and spit before sitting down to a table of cards."

"I would never be invited back." Julianna smiled.

"Well, then, why do you fear to admit your partiality for Lord Fairmont and his for you?"

"Because it is not true. It cannot be true," Julianna protested.

"Ah, but you were not sitting towards the back of the box so you would not clash with the draperies." Lady Eleanor nodded wisely. "And so you were not in a position to observe that Lord Fairmont watched you more than the great Mrs. Siddons tonight."

"He did? Really?"

Lady Eleanor nodded again. "I will not argue Lord Fairmont's partiality, however. You will have proof of that, I am sure, soon enough. What I will argue is your disparagement of yourself. You seem to think you are not worthy of Lord Fairmont, which, if we are to speak of untruths, must certainly count as falsehood."

Julianna looked at her image in the mirror and frowned. She saw very little that was pleasing or, at least, very little that would be pleasing to one of the most eligible bachelors in the kingdom.

"You are loyal, intelligent, kind . . ."

"Men look for such qualities in their dogs or horses, Lady Eleanor," Julianna protested, "not in the women they would marry."

". . . good with children . . ."

"Lord Fairmont can afford to hire a loyal, kind nursemaid."

". . . and though you may not be a diamond of the first water, you have a certain elegance few women can achieve."

"I do?" Julianna blinked at her image. It was the same as always. Nothing had changed. "I am too tall and too thin. My hair is an ugly shade of red and board straight. My eyes—"

"You quote my brother," Lady Eleanor interrupted. "The only thing wrong with your eyes is that they are too honest. They made Ramsden squirm every time you looked at him direct. And your hair is a lovely shade of auburn as well as being wonderfully thick. With Eweing to dress it, it will soon be fashionable as well."

138

Julianna turned from the glass to clasp her step-aunt's hand, a worried frown furrowing her brow. "I wish we could afford to hire Eweing, Lady Eleanor, truly I do, but you know we cannot. Though we may seem flush in the pocket after my good fortune at the Winslows, most of that must be used to pay the tradesmen's bills. And we really should begin to put something aside for emergencies."

"Eweing will cost us nothing." Lady Eleanor smiled. "I have no doubt she will request an interview tomorrow for the purpose of telling us that she has decided to accept the position of lady's maid . . . as an investment."

Julianna sat down on the dressing-table stool and glanced up at her stepaunt uncertainly. "Eweing did mention something about an investment, but I had no idea what she was talking about."

"It is very simple." Lady Eleanor took a seat on the fourposter and prepared to explain. "I told Eweing that Lord Fairmont was showing an interest in you, and if she would help us bring him up to scratch, she might have a place in your household once you are married. Eweing invests a few weeks of her time, and she may reap the benefits of employment in an earl's household."

"Lady Eleanor, you did not!" Julianna was on her feet, an embarrassed flush staining her cheeks.

"Certainly, I did. Eweing has no blunt to gamble with, only her talents as a lady's maid. She was quite willing to give it a shot, I assure you."

Julianna had always been fond of her step aunt, but she viewed her now with undisguised dislike. "Better she should have put her blunt, excuse me, her talents on you. It is far more likely that you will ensnare the colonel than that such as Lord Fairmont would look twice at a country nobody like me."

"He already has," Lady Eleanor said complacently. "And as for the colonel, it is true I have hopes of him, but it would not be a brilliant match. Not like yours with Lord Fairmont."

"Lady Eleanor, I have told you that this . . . this partiality for me you think to see in Lord Fairmont is no more reality than . . . than Lord Carlborne's specter roaming the halls."

The candles flickered on her words, and Julianna felt a sudden chill, but she ignored it as well as Lady Eleanor's raised eyebrows.

"Well, I do not say you are wrong, Julianna. About the specter, I mean. For I have never understood why Lord Carlborne should haunt us. And I daresay the sudden breeze is no more than a draft from the door which has drifted open." Lady Eleanor gave Julianna a look of calm sensibility.

Julianna went to the door and kicked it shut, the calm facade on which she prided herself quite lost at the moment.

"And we quite stray from the point, in any case," Lady Eleanor continued, coming to her feet and turning Julianna to the mirror once more. "I was telling you that you must not confuse what my brother says with fact. Now, your hair, with Eweing's ministrations, can be made to look quite lovely."

Julianna nodded grudgingly, but it was quite true. The loose waves softened the sharp angles of her face in a most attractive manner.

"As for your height and figure, there is nothing amiss there either. Lord Fairmont is taller than most men, and some good loving and a few children will take care of your lack of curves."

"Lady Eleanor!"

"I know I have shocked you, Julianna. Maiden ladies are not supposed to know of such things, but I assure you I was young once too. And in love, I might add. Ramsden would not give his consent, of course, for the small annuity Papa left me would have passed into my husband's control. And to my everlasting regret, I allowed myself to be ruled by Ramsden and by propriety rather than make a runaway match. Ah, but how I wish now I had grabbed for my happiness, Julianna." Their eyes met for a moment in the glass before Lady Eleanor looked away. "I will this time, however. You may bet on that, my dear, for it is a sure thing."

Julianna turned, taking the shorter woman into her embrace. "I did not know, Lady Eleanor. I suspected, there was some talk among the servants at Graxton Manor, but I did not know that Lord Ramsden had so abused you. I am sorry, my very dear stepaunt, but you are quite right, and I will bet on what I know to be a sure thing—Colonel Cramden's growing fondness for you."

Lady Eleanor nodded and returned Julianna's embrace before stepping back and sitting down on the fourposter once more. There were tears in her eyes, and Julianna offered the handkerchief from her reticule.

Dabbing at her eyes, Lady Eleanor said, "You may be right and I shall be given a second chance at happiness. I pray that may be so. But I shall be content if I know that Paul is safe and you have had the courage not to act the hen-wit as I did. For if Lord Fairmont fancies you over those insipid beauties the Ton is forever parading about, he shows good sense, and you had best show some, too."

Julianna smiled, though her smile was not a happy

one. "You are prejudiced in my favor, Lady Eleanor. But even you must admit I have become an ape-leader. If I am so desirable, why has no man before made a push to secure my affections?"

"The cupboard door was closed. No one could see the wares," Lady Eleanor said irrepressibly and watched with pleased affection the genuine smile that now enlivened Julianna's face. "But we have made good our escape from Graxton Manor, and there is no reason for you to remain on the shelf with the door closed any longer. Besides, think of the security it would give Paul to have someone like Lord Fairmont as his steppapa."

"Paul already has a father. We forget that. And however much you might imagine Lord Fairmont to fancy me, what do you think he would say when he found I had lied about Paul? That I have, in fact, been lying from the moment we met?"

Lady Eleanor bit her lip and frowned, turning the matter over in her head. "Well, it certainly cannot be denied that lies like chickens often come home to roost. Still, perhaps Lord Fairmont would understand if you were to tell him the truth?"

Julianna looked up from the seed pearl she had been worrying on the bodice of her gown. "I do not think I could chance telling him. I am not a gambler at heart, you know, and I would be risking Paul's happiness as well as our own. I will admit that I find Lord Fairmont attractive, but I am not sure that I trust him."

"Experience and my brother have taught you to be wary of men, I think," Lady Eleanor said sadly.

Julianna nodded. "And to tell Lord Fairmont the truth of Paul's identity and why we are here would be to give him a power over us I would rather no man ever possessed again."

"Do you really think he would go to Ramsden with this knowledge?"

Julianna shrugged, looked down at the slightly threadbare carpet at her feet, took a brief turn about the room, and finally said, "I do not know. I am wary of his charm and his questions. And though my heart may urge me to trust him, my head says to remember that gossip is rarely made up out of whole cloth."

"The gabblemongers will always find a man as wealthy and attractive as Lord Fairmont a prime object of their tongues. Colonel Cramden counts him as friend, and that is enough for me."

"Were I the only one concerned I might follow my heart though I fear it would surely be broken. But there is Paul to consider."

Lady Eleanor sighed. "Ah, Julianna, you know how much I love Paul. But I would not have you throw away your happiness for the child. Nor, despite what you think, do I believe your mother would have wanted such a thing."

"My mother—" Julianna began and stopped. For all she had loved her mother dearly, there had been times when Julianna had felt more the parent than the child.

"Your mother was a charming woman but not a strong one," Lady Eleanor said. "She made a push to marry your father, but once he was gone she retreated into herself. I remember when you first came to Graxton Manor, a frightened ten-year-old child dressed in expensive silks and satins with lace and fussy furbelows."

"All provided by my maternal grandparents," Julianna said with a small smile. She sat down on the fourposter beside Lady Eleanor, her hand absently tracing the carved leaves in the mahogany wood.

"Though I do believe that was the last time I wore such things."

Lady Eleanor pursed her mouth in a moue of disgust. "Not necessarily by choice. Once my brother got his hands on your mother's fortune, it went quickly enough. Your grandparents must have had more money than sense."

"So Mother always said. They forbade her to marry Papa whom she loved and then, after his death, insisted that she marry Lord Ramsden for whom she could not care. But their grandson shall have a title, which is what they wanted, may God rest their souls." For a moment Julianna's eyes took on a blank opaque look as she stared, unseeing, at the faded blue flowers on the room's papered walls. "To my thinking, a happy childhood is worth more than a dukedom. Or an earldom," she added, remembering Lord Fairmont's words concerning his own boyhood days.

The two ladies continued to sit silently for some time side by side on the blue coverlet, their thoughts occupied with memories of the past and fears and hopes for the future. Though only a few hours had elapsed since Mrs. Siddons had taken her last bows, the tragedy of Lady Macbeth which had so enthralled them, seemed as faded as the carpet beneath their feet.

"Ah, well," Julianna said at last, shaking off the mood that enveloped them and seemed to smother their earlier happiness. "To quote Lady Macbeth, 'What is done cannot be undone. To bed.'"

Lady Eleanor nodded and rose to her feet. "Let us throw off our melancholy mood, my dear. The chickens do not worry about the fox until he enters the henhouse, and we must seek to emulate them."

"I shall do my best. And until Eweing decides

144

whether I am worth the gamble, I will endeavor to help you out of your gown," Julianna said. "And offer you my heartfelt apology as well."

"Apology?" Lady Eleanor craned her neck to look at Julianna who was carefully undoing the myriad small fastenings at the back of the sarcenet gown.

Julianna, tongue between her teeth, finished her task before replying. "I do owe you an apology, you know. For I said I no longer wore silks and satins nor lace and fussy furbelows, while here I stand clothed in that which clearly gives a lie to my words. At least what there is of it," she continued irrepressibly, indicating the abbreviated bodice. "Are you sure this is not the reason Lord Fairmont looked at me more than Mrs. Siddons this evening? Perhaps he wanted to be ready should I take too deep a breath and my gown fall at my feet."

"I have no doubt the dress was one of the reasons Lord Fairmont looked at you," Lady Eleanor agreed smugly. "A few fine feathers scattered about so the fox does not mistake the henhouse never goes amiss."

"So I am the hen and Lord Fairmont the fox?"

"Or vice versa." Lady Eleanor smiled and began to unhook Julianna's white satin gown.

Later, as Julianna snuggled beneath the blue coverlet, her tired thoughts whirling about in her head, she thought again of Lady Eleanor's words. "But how absurd," she murmured. "The hen does not try to attract the fox, for the fox would surely ravish her." Julianna's eyes opened wide for a moment, then with a quick giggle she turned her head into the feather pillow and did her best to dream of handsome blond foxes for the remainder of the night.

Chapter Ten

Since the house on Taylor Street had been hired furnished, there was little Julianna could say when a cart arrived from Lord Fairmont the next morning containing a new dressing table, chairs, and fresh hangings for the south bedroom.

"What did I tell you?" asked Lady Eleanor with an air of complacency. "Lord Fairmont is definitely interested. Why else do such a thing?"

"Perhaps he means to up our rent," Julianna replied as she watched the men unload the cart and carry the furnishings upstairs. "And however kind you may think Lord Fairmont, he is also inexcusably highhanded. Just because he is . . . is swimming in lard, he thinks he can ride roughshod over everyone else. Well, it will not do, Lady Eleanor. It simply will not do."

"But I should think you would be pleased. Look what a lovely shade of yellow the hangings are." Lady Eleanor observed them with a professional eye as they were carried past. "Lord Fairmont must have gone to a deal of trouble choosing them, and how percipient of him when yellow is your favorite color and flattering besides."

"I doubt Lord Fairmont had the choosing of them,"

Julianna replied, torn between pleasure at the sight of the new furnishings and anger at Lord Fairmont's presumption. "He probably ordered Mr. Basset to see to it without a moment's inconvenience to himself."

"That's as may be," Lady Eleanor said, "though it is hardly wise to blacken the kettle when you must needs find yourself polishing it again. And I am surprised to find you so out of charity with Lord Fairmont after his kindness in inviting us to the theater last night."

Julianna looked away, pretending to watch the carter's men, too shamefaced to admit the truth of Lady Eleanor's words. It was just that after a night spent dreaming of handsome blond foxes invited into the henhouse by unsuspecting chickens, she needed to armor herself against the reality of the day in any way she could.

"You had best sort out your feelings before Lord Fairmont returns to have that private discussion with you," Lady Eleanor advised.

Julianna blushed. "He . . . he probably wants to inquire if the new furnishings are suitable. And in any case, my feelings do not enter into this. It is Lord Fairmont's house, he may do what he likes with it." He already seemed to be doing what he liked with her heart. Julianna turned to mount the stairs. "I think I shall see what the new furnishings look like. Do you come with me, Lady Eleanor?"

Before Lady Eleanor could reply, Hawkins, nimbly sidestepping one of the carter's men, crossed the hall to her side. "Pardon, milady, but Mrs. Gardning has informed me that someone named Eweing has arrived at the servants' entrance and refuses to leave. Was you expecting someone?" He gave them a look of questioning reproof.

"Ah, yes, Hawkins, indeed we were." Lady Eleanor

smiled at Julianna in quiet triumph. "Eweing is to be the new lady's maid. Have Mrs. Gardning show her to a room, and then return to supervise the carter's men. Oh, and Hawkins, inform Mrs. Gardning that there will be guests for tea."

"You need not crow," Julianna said after Hawkins had taken his departure. "Even though you were right and Eweing has decided to invest in us as you predicted."

"Eweing has decided to invest in you," Lady Eleanor corrected.

"Well, I am very much afraid she will soon find herself bottoms up," Julianna replied, continuing up the stairs.

At least the south bedroom now looked cheerful. The yellow silk had been hung about the fourposter, and the carter's men were busily engaged in removing the old furnishings.

"Oh, you might leave the hangings," Julianna said from the doorway. These could be easily cleaned, and while the dark blue velvet might not have been the happiest choice for a bedchamber, there was no saying but that Lady Eleanor might be able to fashion something quite elegant from it.

Stepping into the bedroom, Julianna looked around in amazement. It was something wonderful the difference the new furnishings made. Two lady's chairs covered in the same yellow silk as the bedhangings had been placed near the fireplace and draped over the backs waiting to be hung were panels of flowered silk for the windows with just a touch of the same yellow. The dressing table, of a light walnut inlaid with a darker wood, was much larger than the old one, and Julianna began quickly to transfer her bottles and hairbrushes to its polished surface.

When she was finished, Julianna stepped back and looked around the room once more. It was really quite splendid, she had to admit. And even if Lord Fairmont's agent did have the choosing of it, the thought and kindness had been Lord Fairmont's own. With a small sigh, Julianna turned and descended the stairs to the parlor where she sat down thoughtfully on the settee. Lady Eleanor was quite right and she must sort out her feelings before she met with Lord Fairmont again.

This proved impossible to do, however, for Lord Fairmont was like some multifaceted gem showing first one edge and then the other, but never the whole. To allow herself to love such a man could prove fatal and yet . . . if only she could be sure Lord Fairmont could be trusted! Julianna's glance encountered the predatory eyes of the owl gleaming from the clouded glass of the curio cabinet, and she gave a small shiver. Perhaps the wisest thing was to trust no one at all.

After their life of moldering isolation at Graxton Manor, it was most gratifying to see the number of invitations which Hawkins brought to the parlor when the morning's post arrived. Gratifying and surprising as well, for one of the invitations proved to be from Lady Fairmont. How odd, Julianna thought, for I would not have thought she was aware of our existence, and we have never been formally introduced. Lady Eleanor, entering the parlor and being informed of the matter, pounced upon the engraved invitation with glee.

"It is at Lord Fairmont's prompting, there can be no doubt," she said happily. "We must begin thinking of what to wear at once, for you must look your best, Julianna, though I am sure Lord Fairmont is not the sort to allow his family to influence him. Still, I think that sea green muslin with the dropped waist would be a good choice. It is most becoming, and you look quite elegant in it. I shall go and consult with Eweing. What a shame the soiree is in two days and we have not time to make something new." Like one of the winds that swept across the high streets of Bath, Lady Eleanor was out the door before Julianna had a chance to voice her own preference in the matter.

The following days were a flurry of fittings and consultations and pinnings with Julianna feeling quite disgustingly like a dressmaker's dummy. When Lady Eleanor was not poking her with pins, Eweing was plaiting and combing and curling her hair, frowning over various styles and whispering with Lady Eleanor but rarely consulting Julianna.

"It is all quite ridiculous," Julianna told Paul, when she had been able to escape with him for a few hours to one of the parks. "I do not know why Lady Eleanor makes such a fuss, for Lord Fairmont informed us that he was going out of town and will probably not even be present at his mother's soiree. And I do not believe for a minute that it was at his instigation we were invited. Surely it is more likely Lady Davina, who insisted she be given a chance to gamble with me again."

Such sensible thoughts were quite wasted on Lady Eleanor, however.

"You must on no account listen to Mrs. Pickering," she informed Eweing. "She is disappointed because Lord Fairmont will not be present and does not understand the importance of impressing a man's parent."

Eweing, in the middle of wielding the curling tongs,

clicked her tongue in disgust. "If madam is going to move her head about in that manner, she will have to find someone else to dress her hair."

Julianna held her head as still as possible, but her thoughts were quite another matter, for they went buzzing about like so many bees around a hive. What would Lord Fairmont's mother be like? Her son had certainly painted an unflattering picture. Was Lady Fairmont a selfish creature who cared only for her own pleasures as he had intimated? Juliannna thought of the plump woman with orange hair she had observed some weeks ago, face flushed as she played yet another hand of piquet. Compulsive, Lord Fairmont had said of his sister. Was it true of his mother as well?

The day of the soiree arrived and found Lady Eleanor and Julianna in front of the chevel glass in the south bedroom making the last-minute adjustments every woman finds necessary. Lady Eleanor wore pink satin with a blond lace fall and a pink satin toque upon her head. Julianna, dressed in pale blue *gros de Naples,* the sea green muslin having been deemed not fine enough, wore artificial flowers in her hair which matched those ornamenting the hem of her gown. Lady Eleanor pronounced them both quite splendid.

"Madam will do." Eweing nodded.

"Thank you, Eweing," Julianna responded, feeling just a bit nervous about the evening ahead. "I shall just look in on Paul for a moment before we go."

Lady Eleanor insisted on accompanying her, and so it was that both ladies, dressed in their evening finery, climbed the creaking stairs to the nursery to look in on the sleeping figure of the little boy.

One hand curled into a fist beneath his cheek, Paul's flushed cheeks and blond ringlets made him

151

look like one of Botticelli's cherubs. The painted head of a toy soldier peeked from beneath the blanket ready to do battle while Kitty snored softly from one corner of the room where she slept on a trundle bed.

"Paul looks so angelic," Lady Eleanor whispered, shielding the light from the candle with one hand as they looked down on the little boy. "One would never suspect the amount of mischief he can get into."

"Appearances are often deceiving," Julianna agreed, closing the door softly as they left the nursery and thinking of the image that had been reflected in her cheval glass that evening. For did she not look as assured and worldly-wise as any woman of the Ton, while inside she quivered like an eel in aspic? I would as lief be home reading one of Mrs. Burney's novels, Julianna thought, as attending a soiree given by the mother of an earl.

Lady Eleanor was all agog, however, telling Julianna over and over how lucky they were to have been singled out so by the countess. "Most women would give their eye teeth to attend one of Lady Fairmont's soirees," she said as they bounced along in the hackney they had hired. "I cannot wait to crow about this evening to Mrs. Leacock tomorrow at the Pump Room, for it is certain she has never been so honored."

Despite her brave words, Lady Eleanor grew silent as the hackney stopped in front of an imposing mansion of sparkling Bath stone and a footman sprang forward to let down the steps. "Oh, my," she gasped softly as she stepped onto the freshly swept pavement and took in the four seemingly identical footmen in blue livery holding torches aloft to light the way.

"I suppose they must be alive?" Lady Eleanor whispered as they prepared to walk between them.

"I would not care to wager on it," Julianna replied, noting that the men did not blink nor even seem to breathe.

Holding their beaded evening bags tightly and trying to walk as if they were used to passing between human sconces every night of their lives, the two entered the mansion through an imposing Palladian portal. Inside were more footmen, this time holding candelabra and lighting the grand staircase that led to the first floor and the receiving line, which was dominated by a plump woman with orange hair wearing an elaborate headdress of *crêpe lisse* and diamonds, and a gown of puce satin that looked as if it would surely burst its seams at any moment.

The dowager countess gave Julianna two fingers and stared at her blankly, clearly having no idea who she was. "Mrs. Pickering," Lady Davina spoke from her mother's side. "I am so glad you could come, for my brother is not in town, and so we shall be able to have cards."

Julianna felt a strange disappointment at these words. She had known that Lord Fairmont would not be present, had she not? And that the invitation had been sent at Lady Davina's instigation was certainly no surprise. So why this sinking feeling, this feeling that whatever magic the evening might have held had quite disappeared?

"It is as I said," Lady Eleanor whispered, coming up to Julianna a moment later. "The countess has no idea who we are. I am quite sure the invitation was at Lord Fairmont's insistence."

"I think it was Lady Davina that would have us attend," Julianna disagreed. "She means to match her gambling skills with mine again."

Lady Eleanor's blue eyes lit up hopefully. "There is

153

some very fine Urling's point lace in one of the shops which would look wonderfully well on that zephyrine silk which I have been eyeing this past week or more. What good fortune!"

"Do not spend my winnings so soon," Julianna warned, "for I have quite decided not to gamble with Lady Davina."

"But my dear—no, I shall say nothing. It is because Lord Fairmont disapproves, is it not?"

Julianna flushed and looked away. "It does not seem right to accept a man's friendship and then serve him so."

"I quite agree." Lady Eleanor patted Julianna's gloved hand and then added irrepressibly, "Sometimes it is better to hatch the egg than to have it for breakfast."

Lady Fairmont's soiree was an exclusive affair, not more than fifty or so had been honored by an invitation, and Julianna overheard the dowager countess complaining that Bath Society was not what it had been in her youth. "Nothing but retired officers and jumped-up merchants. I do wish Fairmont would allow us to return to London."

In vain did Lady Eleanor search for one of those retired officers, but Colonel Cramden was nowhere to be found.

"Perhaps the colonel had a prior commitment?" Julianna suggested.

"More likely he did not receive an invitation," Lady Eleanor replied with a worried frown. "I wondered that he did not offer to accompany us. Though I am surprised Lord Fairmont did not add the colonel's name to the list of those invited."

"I am sure there is some good reason for his absence," Julianna replied soothingly. "Now, why do you not have another lobster puff and enjoy yourself so you may tell the colonel about the soiree when next he calls."

Lady Eleanor nodded and smiled, but it was clear that she was not enjoying herself half so well as if the colonel had been present. Julianna was not in the best of spirits herself. Being in Lord Fairmont's home, seeing the luxury he took for granted, made her more aware than ever of the difference between them. Standing on the edge of the crowd for a moment, Julianna glanced up at the sparkling chandeliers which poured brilliant drops of rainbow light about the room, noted the silk-hung walls, the costly gilt-edged mirrors, the enormous bouquets of flowers which filled the room with a sweet scent.

Ah, no, Julianna thought, the kaleidoscope of colors from the women's dresses beginning to blur as her eyes filled with tears, Lady Eleanor is quite wrong. Lord Fairmont can have no interest in me. He is merely being kind to someone he perceives as a poor widow.

"I have been looking everywhere for you, Mrs. Pickering." Lady Davina, sounding almost accusing, descended upon Julianna. "It is a sad crush in here. Let us go into the small parlor where the card tables have been set up. I would challenge you to a game of piquet." Lady Davina's face was flushed, her eyes glittering dangerously as if she had a fever.

"Are you feeling quite the thing?" Julianna asked, remembering that Lady Davina was in a delicate condition.

Lady Davina frowned. "I am bored almost to death if that is what you mean. Come, you must and shall save me." Lady Davina turned, the elaborate hem of her white satin gown brushing the floor, the pearls which decorated the flounces gleaming dully.

Julianna followed as Lady Davina made her way through the crowd. She would suggest that they play for matchsticks or penny points. Lord Fairmont would surely understand when she explained that his sister did not look in a mood to be crossed.

The small parlor was an oasis of quiet activity: the low buzz of voices as bids were made, cards picked up and discarded. The Dowager Lady Fairmont was there as well, easily recognizable by her orange hair and elaborate headdress. Apparently her role of hostess ended when she had greeted her guests, since she did not look up as they entered the room.

"Here we are." Lady Davina's frown turned to a smile as she seated herself at a small corner table and gestured to one of the footmen for cards and wine. "Now," she paused, and Julianna noted that she seemed oddly short of breath, a circumstance which was explained when Julianna observed that Lady Davina's waist was quite as narrow as her own. Tight lacing, Julianna thought, remembering Lady Eleanor warning against such a thing when her mother was expecting Paul.

"Now we shall enjoy a cozy game of piquet, shall we?" Lady Davina continued as she reached for her wine glass.

"Lady Davina," Julianna began cautiously, "I am afraid I did promise Lord Fairmont that I would not gamble with you again."

"But he is not here and so shall not know. Do you cut the cards?"

Julianna's hands remained in her lap. "That makes no difference to me. I made your brother a promise."

"And so you promised me," Lady Davina snapped. "You promised to be my friend. And now you are not."

"Lady Davina." Julianna reached one gloved hand across the small table. "I do not think a true friend would encourage you to gamble."

Lady Davina's blue eyes flared. "A true friend?" She shook off Julianna's hand. "It seems I have no friends, for if you were one you would realize I am moped to death and must do something or lose my mind." Her small, rosebud lips began to tremble, her eyes to fill with tears. "And I do not think you refuse to play with me because of friendship, but because my brother has . . . has bullied you into saying you would not. I told you he would do this; he does not wish me to have friends or enjoy myself."

"I think your brother is merely concerned," Julianna replied, realizing as she said the words just how much her opinion of Lord Fairmont had changed. "But let us not brangle over his motives. If you wish to play a hand of piquet, we shall do so. But only at a penny a point."

The smile which had begun to curl Lady Davina's lips stopped mid-curve. "Ah, you are bamming me," she said, the smile continuing into a most charming dimple. "We shall play for pound points as usual."

"Lady Davina . . ."

"Else there is no reason to play." The words were as steely as Lady Davina's blue eyes.

The swish of satin was heard, and both ladies looked up to see the dowager countess descending on them.

"You shall change partners with me, Davina," her mother commanded. "Mr. Beldene has been telling me about our guest's prowess at cards, and I wish to try my hand."

Lady Davina looked up at Mr. Beldene, who was young and rather handsome and smiling suggestively as he looked at the very abbreviated bodice of her gown. "An excellent suggestion, Mother," she agreed, rising and giving her hand to the gentleman.

Mr. Beldene paused to greet Julianna. "I believe I saw you walking with Lord Fairmont the other day," he said. "You had a young boy with you."

"My son Paul."

"Ah, indeed. I did wonder, such a happy . . . family picture as you presented. I was telling our hostess about your husband's most untimely death at the hand of a marauding band of Red Indians while in service in the Colonies. Most sad."

"Did they attack the carriage before or after the earthquake and landslide?" a deep voice inquired.

Four sets of eyes swiveled around to the newcomer, but he looked only at Julianna.

"Really, Fairmont, why must you always turn up when you aren't wanted," his mother demanded peevishly. "Now do go away, I wish to try my luck with Mrs . . . ah . . ."

"Mrs. Pickering, Mother," Lord Fairmont supplied. "It was her husband, Parnell Pickering, who was killed by the Red Indians."

"Mrs. Pickering? I don't believe we've met. Fairmont, what are you doing back so soon? I thought we would be free of your presence for some days more."

Her son merely smiled and said, "Naturally I concluded my business as quickly as possible so that I might rejoin you before the family estates were gambled away entirely."

"Really, Fairmont! That is most unfair."

Lord Fairmont ignored this comment and took the seat Lady Davina had recently surrendered. "See to your guests, Mother. I all play a game of cards with Mrs. Pickering myself. Now, shall it be piquet or two-handed whist?" he inquired as the dowager countess stalked away.

"I . . . Lady . . . Miss Partridge will be wondering where I am." Julianna half-rose from her chair.

Lord Fairmont put a restraining hand upon her gloved arm. "Colonel Cramden has but lately arrived. She will be well occupied." He gathered up the cards and gestured to the footman for another glass of wine.

"I was about to leave, Lord Fairmont," Julianna insisted, though she made no move to do so. No man had a right to be so handsome and charming and to smile so.

"Piquet?" he asked, placing the cards on the table and waiting for Julianna to make the cut.

For a moment she avoided the pack of waiting cards, her eyes on his. She knew it was merely candle-light reflected in those brown depths; Lord Fairmont's eyes did not glow with a special warmth when they looked at her, and yet . . .

"The cards, Mrs. Pickering," Lord Fairmont prompted gently.

Julianna blinked and tore her eyes away from his. I must think of Lord Fairmont as simply another card player, she told herself. One who is hopefully more skilled than his sister. She cut the cards. An ace of spades.

Lord Fairmont reached for the pack. He cut the cards in turn. A queen of hearts.

"So you are the dealer," he said, pushing the deck across the small table to Julianna.

Julianna nodded. "I did tell Lady Davina that I would play only for penny points," she said, her voice giving no evidence of the surging exhilaration that was slowly filling her. Lord Fairmont would be a challenge. She was beginning to look forward to matching her skills with his.

"Penny points?" he chuckled. "I can imagine Davina's reaction to that, and I am afraid I must agree."

"But . . ." Julianna looked up from the cards, ". . . but I thought you would approve."

"Oh, I do—when you are playing with Davina. But I would have more of a challenge. What do you say we play for kisses instead?"

Julianna cleared her throat. "I beg your pardon?" She could not have heard correctly. A peer of the realm did not suddenly make improper suggestions to a guest.

"Not a kiss a point," Lord Fairmont continued, his brow wrinkled as if in serious thought, "that would be excessive considering the circumstances. Let us say a kiss a game, to be paid by the loser in the privacy of the library."

"Lord Fairmont!" Julianna whispered, looking around to see if anyone could hear their scandalous conversation.

"You may claim the same from me, if you wish," he said, magnanimously. "Or if that is not to your liking, at least *not yet* to your liking, I shall wager to give Paul a pony should you win the game."

"We have no—"

"And I shall make provision for the pony's stabling and endeavor to teach Paul to ride myself."

"He is too young."

"Many a boy has learned to ride before he could walk."

"Really, Lord Fairmont, you go too far."

"Are you afraid to accept the challenge?

Julianna hesitated, not knowing what to say, the flush that burned her cheeks surely obvious to anyone who looked in their direction.

"Deal the cards, Mrs. Pickering," Lord Fairmont instructed, a smile spreading slowly across his face.

"Very well," Julianna agreed. Perhaps Lord Fairmont meant only to unnerve her with the impropriety of his wager. She had seen her stepfather use the same tactic often enough to break another player's concentration. Lord Fairmont would find such an obvious strategy did not work with Julianna Seaton. With calm deliberation, she picked up the deck and dealt out twelve cards, two at a time.

Julianna turned the first card face up. It was the ace of hearts. The trump suit. "My point, I believe." She put up a white marker.

Each had six white and four red markers with which to keep score. Six white equaled one red. Lord Fairmont called points and, having the higher cards, put up a white marker in turn.

The sequence was called.

Lord Fairmont had the king, queen and jack of hearts. He put up a red marker and three white ones.

Julianna had four of a kind in the trump suit. She put up a red marker and four white ones.

The cards were shuffled and dealt again. Lord Fairmont won the next two tricks, forcing Julianna to take down her white counters. Julianna claimed the next trick.

The score mounted.

Julianna's demeanor remained calm, but the exhilaration of a challenging game with a skilled opponent filled her. Lord Fairmont scored an imperial with the diamond suit. What were the chances of his having four of a kind as well?

"Some more wine, Mrs. Pickering?"

"No, thank you." Julianna's voice was cool. "I rarely

drink anything stronger than water when I play. My trick, I believe."

Lord Fairmont nodded, smiling lazily across at her, his cards held carelessly in one hand. "I have heard of your remarkable ability at cards, the way you seem able to remember every suit played, your skill at calculating the odds. Which makes it surprising that you lost a not-inconsiderable sum to Mrs. Mickleberry the other day. The old lady must be sharper than she appears."

"I lost only a few pounds," Julianna corrected. "And Mrs. Mickleberry is certainly not the half-wit gossips would paint her."

"No," Lord Fairmont agreed. "She is a sweet lady who must pinch every penny and who you all but coerced into playing piquet with you."

Julianna fidgeted with her cards and refused to look at him.

"And the few pounds you lost enabled her to eat the first decent meal in weeks. I am afraid you are not a true gambler at heart, Mrs. Pickering."

"So my step—so I have been told," Julianna said and placed her cards on the table. "My trick, Lord Fairmont."

He smiled. "I did not previously know of Mrs. Mickleberry's unfortunate circumstances. I shall direct Mr. Basset to see what can be done to help her."

"That is kind of you." Julianna fingered her white marker nervously. Must Lord Fairmont be kind and generous on top of everything else? And how had he found out about Mrs. Mickleberry? Julianna had not even mentioned the matter to Lady Eleanor.

"We are quite evenly matched, Mrs. Pickering. It is rare to find a player of such skill in Bath these days. Was it your father taught you to play?"

Julianna looked at him sharply. "Do most fathers instruct their daughters in games of chance, Lord Fairmont?"

"Ah, then it must have been poor Percival Pickering, your late, lamented husband."

"Yes." Julianna concentrated on arranging the cards she held by suit. "Yes, of course."

"Or was it Parnell, his twin brother?"

A chill swept suddenly over Julianna as she saw the trap Lord Fairmont had carefully sprung. She reached absently for her wineglass, sipping at its contents while her mind sought for an answer. "You speak in riddles," she said at last. "My husband had no brother. His name was Parnell Percival Pickering. Because his father's name was also Parnell, he was often called Percival." She set down her wineglass, but her fingers remained curled about its crystal stem as her eyes challenged Lord Fairmont across the card table.

"Indeed?" Lord Fairmont's eyebrows rose. "My name is Gabriel Damien Sinclair. Which name do you prefer?"

"We are not on a first-name basis, Lord Fairmont."

"Ah, but I would so like to be . . . Julianna."

Julianna! The crystal stem of the wineglass snapped in her fingers. He had called her Julianna!

"You have cut yourself." Lord Fairmont took her hand and rose, pulling her up with him. A footman rushed over to mop up the spilled wine as Lord Fairmont walked quickly from the room his hand firmly about her wrist. A short corridor led to a pair of carved doors. Lord Fairmont pushed them open and pulled Julianna inside.

The room was dark, lit only by a small fire and a pair of branched candelabra that gleamed upon the mantel, their silver surfaces reflecting the flames below.

Lord Fairmont released Julianna and turned to close the doors, the sound of the latch echoing in the silence of the waiting room.

"I —" Julianna turned, swallowing nervously as she looked first at the closed doors and then at the shadowed form of Lord Fairmont as he leaned back against them. "This is most improper, Lord Fairmont," she whispered. "My — my reputation . . ."

"My reputation, Iago, ah, yes, my reputation," he quoted softly, pushing away from the doors and advancing into the room.

Julianna backed away, stumbling into a leather upholstered chair.

Lord Fairmont stopped and held out his hand. "Let me see how badly you have cut yourself, Julianna."

Like an obedient child, Julianna placed her hand in his. He turned it over, touched the place on her thumb where the wine glass had cut her glove. A small drop of blood stained the white fabric with crimson.

His dark eyes lifted to hers for a moment before he slowly began to slide the long glove from her arm.

"Lord . . . Lord Fairmont." Was she protesting? Supplicating? The pain in her thumb throbbed, her heart beat in unsteady rhythm. Julianna closed her eyes, her senses concentrated on the feel of Lord Fairmont's fingers as they slid slowly down the soft skin of her inner arm.

"Julianna."

"Why . . . why do you call me that?" she asked, opening eyes that had darkened to a smoky gray. "My name is Penelope. Penelope Pickering."

Discarding her glove, he cupped her hand in the warm, intimate embrace of his own. "I prefer Julianna," he replied softly, looking down at her hand

164

which felt strangely naked and vulnerable beneath his gaze.

He bent his head, touching his tongue, warm and moist, to the drop of blood that welled upon her thumb. Julianna's breath caught in a soft gasp of distress and delight.

"Ah, Julianna." He turned her hand over and pressed his lips to her fingers. "We did not finish the game; I have not won. I know I have no right to claim my kiss, but . . ." He raised his head, his eyes black opaque pools. "I find I cannot help myself."

His movements were slow, deliberate, inevitable, as he drew her into his embrace, brushing her lips with the breath of a kiss.

"On the contrary, Lord Fairmont," Julianna whispered, raising her mouth once more to his. "I think the game is most certainly yours."

Chapter Eleven

Julianna sat at the breakfast table, slowly crumbling bits of toast while Lady Eleanor interrogated her.

"But what happened after you left the cardroom with Lord Fairmont?" Lady Eleanor asked for the fourth time. "Everyone was quite agog to know. Mr. Wilmot swears he saw you fling your wineglass at Lord Fairmont, but Mrs. Fisher claims that it was Lady Fairmont who tried to stab you with a pen knife. I said you had one of your megrims—not that I have ever known you to have one—and it was that which caused you to spill the wine. Not that I believe it, of course, but I have always felt it is better to speak first and think afterwards. Still, you would tell me the truth of it. A trouble told is a trouble halved, Julianna. And something must have happened, for there is your best gown with a wine stain no amount of sponging will remove and you with blood dripping from your finger."

"Hardly dripping," Julianna countered, looking down at her thumb which still sported the bandage Lord Fairmont had tied around it last night. "And while it is kind of you to ask, it hurts but a little and will soon heal, I should think."

"Julianna!" Lady Eleanor tried to look indignant but since she had just taken a bite of toast spread with a goodly amount of marmalade and must swallow or choke, the effect was quite spoiled. "Julianna," she repeated when she was able. "You know I don't give a fig for your finger. That is, I am sure I am happy you are not seriously injured but—"

"I dropped my wineglass, Lady Eleanor. That is all. I was unforgivably clumsy, and I am sorry my lovely gown was ruined."

"Perhaps Lord Fairmont will buy you a new one."

"Lady Eleanor . . ."

"What time does he call?"

"How did you know Lord Fairmont meant to do so?"

"Because he will want to inquire how your finger is faring, of course," Lady Eleanor said at her most innocent. "Besides, you have changed your gown three times in the past hour and driven Eweing to distraction by insisting that she recomb your hair twice. This from a woman who never used to care what she wore and felt a simple hairstyle suited her best. It is plain to anyone with half an eye for such things that Lord Fairmont means to call and make you an offer."

"Do you think so?" Julianna asked, anxiously smoothing the bandage on her thumb. "He did say he wanted to see me privately but . . . but what if he only means to discuss the window sash or some such thing?"

After he had kissed her, Lord Fairmont had quickly put her to one side and gone to open one of the library windows. She had stood there like some witless widgeon knocked all cock-a-hoop by his embrace while he had stood by the open window calmly explaining that heat was bad for the book bindings. Were those the words of a man about to offer for a woman, the words of a man in love?

Julianna frowned and began to worry the bandage with her teeth. How could she have responded so wantonly to his kiss? She should have screamed in outrage or at least pretended to a maidenly swoon. I have probably given him a disgust of me, she thought. For once he had neatly finished dressing her finger, Lord Fairmont had suggested that he call Miss Partridge, saying he thought it best if Julianna left as soon as possible. She had wanted to protest, to say her thumb hurt only a little, but then Julianna had caught sight of herself in one of the library mirrors—hair disheveled, the bodice of her gown gaping, her cheeks as flushed as an opera dancer's. No wonder Lord Fairmont had wanted nothing more than to usher her from his house as quickly as possible.

"Perhaps Lord Fairmont will not call at all," she said now in a small voice.

"Nonsense," Lady Eleanor chided. "A man such as Lord Fairmont does not closet himself with a respectable female nor ask to speak to her privately unless he means to make her an offer. I am sure even his mother and Lady Davina expect to soon be welcoming you into the family. And when Lord Fairmont does propose, you must tell him the truth."

"I am not sure . . . that is, of course, you are right." But it was quite possible Lord Fairmont already knew the truth. He had called her Julianna. She had forgotten that. Had he deliberately kissed her hoping that in her confusion she would forget? Julianna stopped worrying the bandage with her teeth and reached for another piece of toast. What

168

did it all mean? And what should she do about it?

"If . . . if Ramsden knew the truth about us, we would be risking everything, you know," Julianna said, eyes on the bread she was shredding. "What if he proved to be acquainted with Ramsden and informed him of our whereabouts?"

Lady Eleanor sipped her coffee, her eyes on Julianna's bent head. "Do you truly believe Lord Fairmont is the sort of man to do that?"

Julianna shrugged in pretended nonchalance. "When I am with Lord Fairmont, when I see the patience he shows in dealing with Pog, I think not. But then I remember he forced his sister into an unhappy marriage and caused Lord Carlborne to hang himself, and then I think perhaps I do not know Lord Fairmont at all."

Lady Eleanor snatched the last piece of toast from the silver rack before Julianna could reduce it to crumbs. "It is my belief that Lord Fairmont may not be as much to blame for these things as we think," she said, scraping off the burnt portion of the toast with her knife. "According to the colonel, Carlborne was a rackety sort given to high dramatics. It is quite possible Lord Fairmont merely meant to teach the young man a lesson and would have forgiven the debt in time. As for Lady Davina's forced marriage . . . Well, we have only that young lady's word for what took place. And from what Eweing has told me—"

"Eweing? But what does she know of the matter?"

"Eweing was formerly employed as maid to Lady Davina. And summarily dismissed when she dared to suggest that tight lacing was not in the best interest

169

of Lady Davina's unborn child. She says the other servants have nothing but praise for Lord Fairmont and heartily dislike the caprices of his mother and sister. Pass the marmalade, if you please."

Julianna brushed crumbs from her fingers and did as she was bid. It was quite possible that what Lady Eleanor said was true. But there still remained the fact that Lord Fairmont had called her Julianna. Had he merely deduced it from the fact that Paul called her Jules? Was that probable? "Then you think that should Lord Fairmont offer for me I should trust him and tell him the truth about our situation?"

Lady Eleanor spread marmalade copiously on her toast. "The mill doesn't grind with water that is already past. I think you should forget the gossip about Lord Fairmont and do what you feel, Julianna. What your heart urges, not what your mind deduces."

"But my mother—"

"Your mother followed her heart and married your father and was happy. It can never be wrong to marry where there is love. It is true that in some arranged marriages the couples rub along together quite well. But I would rather sit on the shelf with the cupboard door closed," Lady Eleanor smiled and paused to pat Julianna's hand, "then have such a marriage."

"I must think what is the best, the logical thing, for me to do," Julianna said.

Lady Eleanor swallowed a bite of toast and licked the marmalade from her fingers. "I am afraid there is often nothing logical about love"

Julianna remembered the feel of Lord Fairmont's lips as they brushed against hers, the scent . . . the taste . . . the warmth of him.

"But sometimes for a lucky few, logic and love combine."

"Yes," Julianna whispered. "For a lucky few."

Julianna sat on a small straight-backed chair and looked nervously out the parlor window at the grassy square of Taylor Street. Her fingers twisted in her lap as if intent on strangling each other, her thoughts as entangled as her fingers despite her talk with Lady Eleanor. Rising with some agitation to her feet, Julianna paced back and forth upon the Oriental carpet.

There were so many things to be considered: Paul, Lord Ramsden, their precarious situation. What did Lord Fairmont know? And, assuming the worst, assuming he had somehow found out the truth, would he speak of it to anyone else? Stealing away with Paul as she had was no light thing. People had been transported, thrown in prison for less.

Julianna stopped before the window and looked down at the grassy square where the leaves of the trees moving in the wind threw speckled shadows across the pavement. Mr. Potter from one of the adjoining houses minced up the street, his shirt points high, his form corseted to fashionable slimness; a servant polished the brass knocker on one of the houses across the square, but Julianna saw none of this, so completely did Lord Fairmont fill her mind and inward vision.

"Gabriel Damien Sinclair," she whispered to the faint image of herself reflected in the window glass. Was he angel or devil? Julianna turned back to the room, encountering the yellow glare of the stuffed owl in its glass case. A swift shiver coursed down her spine. What was the probability of Lord Fairmont having found out the truth? And if he had? To love meant to trust. Did she trust Lord Fairmont? More importantly, did she love him?

Hawkins knocked on the door. "A gentleman to see you," he announced and, while Julianna's breath was still caught in her throat, ushered in Mr. Wilmot.

Julianna did her best to hide her disappointment, but the smile she gave Mr. Wilmot was a forced one.

"I know it is much too early for a social call," he excused himself, shaking his head at his own audacity. "But I was passing and wanted to give you this book." Mr. Wilmot presented Julianna with a small elegantly bound book of tanned leather edged with gold.

"How kind." Julianna inclined her head. "I shall ring for refreshments."

"No, no, dear lady. I think I know better than to impose on your hospitality when it is not even your at-home day. Though I would not say no to some of those delicious cakes your cook makes so well and perhaps a glass of wine?" He sat down on the settee and smiled at her, showing a row of crooked teeth.

Julianna turned to the butler. "Some wine and cakes for Mr. Wilmot, Hawkins," she ordered. "And please apprise Miss Partridge that we have a visitor."

"You remember my mentioning the volume of poetry by Lord Fitzhugh to you the other day?" Mr. Wilmot prodded. "I knew you would be anxious for a copy and thought I would save you a trip to the circulating library."

"Thank you."

"Wonderful versification, you'll find." He nodded

towards the book Julianna had placed on the occasional table.

"I'm sure."

"And what did you think of our Siddons the other night?" he inquired, one hand smoothing the dashing scarlet waistcoat he wore.

Julianna smiled politely, though the trip to the theater seemed now to have happened eons ago. "I quite enjoyed myself. I had not been to the theater before."

"No? Then how fortunate that you were able to attend with Lord Fairmont, who I understand to be quite knowledgeable in these things. Though I was surprised to find his party to be so small and, shall we say, intimate? Was someone suddenly taken ill at the last moment and unable to attend?"

"I have no idea," Julianna replied and wished with all her heart that Lady Eleanor would soon arrive.

"I believe Mrs. Leacock also encountered you and Lord Fairmont out for a stroll with your son?"

"The earl and I met by chance when Paul and I were returning from the park," Julianna said, wondering why she felt a need to defend her behavior.

Mr. Wilmot smiled, his side whiskers bristling upwards as he did so. "I am quite fond of children also. It was always a sorrow to me that my late wife and I had no little ones to call our own and gladden our hearts. Perhaps I might meet Paul some time?"

Since Paul was, at that very moment, languishing in the nursery because he had snatched three macaroons from the tray meant for tea, upset a bowl of buttermilk, and soiled his clothes beyond redemption by attempting to coax Humbert from beneath the cellar steps, Julianna answered Mr. Wilmot's question with a noncommittal smile.

"Of course, the child will soon be going away to school, I imagine."

"Paul is not yet two, Mr. Wilmot."

Mr. Wilmot gave her a superior look. "It is never too soon for a child to begin his lessons. And most authorities feel it is fatal for a boy to remain too long with his mother. The discipline of strangers is essential to develop a boy's character."

"You are no doubt right," Julianna agreed, her voice glacial. "And now that Paul has learned to walk, it is time I considered sending him away."

"A wise decision." Mr. Wilmot beamed at her approvingly. "And if I might offer a further bit of advice? It would be best to keep him from association with Lord Fairmont. Especially after what happened last night."

Julianna did not reply. Mr. Wilmot had revealed his hand, and it was obvious that his reason for calling was to find further gossip on which he could dine out. Julianna was determined not to provide it.

"I was not in the cardroom at the time, but I understand you threw a glass of wine at Fairmont when he made an insulting remark?" Mr. Wilmot leaned forward, ears all but flapping.

"Ah, Mr. Wilmot." Lady Eleanor swept into the room. "How nice to see you again."

"Yes." Mr. Wilmot did not bother to hide his disappointment at this untimely intervention. "I wished to deliver a small volume of poetry I thought Mrs. Pickering might enjoy."

"How kind."

Hawkins arrived with refreshments, and Lady Eleanor offered Mr. Wilmot some wine before handing round a plate of cakes. "Did you enjoy the performance the other night?"

Mr. Wilmot selected one of the macaroons that had escaped Paul's onslaught and nodded. "I have been inquiring of Mrs. Pickering exactly what happened. I was, unfortunately, not in the cardroom at the time, you see, and—"

"The performance at the theater, Mr. Wilmot," Lady Eleanor corrected, her smile small but grimly polite.

"Ah, yes, indeed. I found it quite moving, especially when Lady Macbeth was washing her hands. I am a great believer in cleanliness, you know."

"She should have tried borax mixed with alcohol," Lady Eleanor said. "I have found that it will remove almost any stain not of long standing."

"Indeed?" Mr. Wilmot seemed much struck by this. "Even wine stains?" he asked coyly.

Julianna rose to her feet. "I am afraid we have a previous engagement in a few minutes," she said coldly, despite her flaming cheeks. "It was so nice of you to call."

Admitting defeat, Mr. Wilmot rose to take his leave.

"At least he has no further gossip to grind in his mill," Julianna said when the door had closed on their unwanted guest.

"Silence is often a woman's best gown," Lady Eleanor agreed. "But when there is enough water, the wheel will turn whether there is anything to grind or not."

"I am quite aware that I am become a source of gossip, Lady Eleanor," Julianna began stiffly, "but I am not yet ready to discuss what occurred last night." She had no wish to worry Lady Eleanor with supposition, and as for what had passed between her and Lord Fairmont in the library. . . .

"Never mind, my dear," Lady Eleanor said. "You will tell me when you are ready. Now I must fetch my pelisse. Colonel Cramden has promised to take Paul and me on an excursion to Prior Park, for I have no wish to play gooseberry when Lord Fairmont calls. Just remember to follow your heart, Julianna. I would not have you live a life of regret as I have. And keep in mind that reformed rakes often make the very best husbands, my brother excepted, of course. The eggs have been broken, the omelet made, and there is nothing left to do but remain contentedly at home to eat it."

Julianna gave her stepaunt a hug. "Thank you," she whispered. "I shall remember that."

After Lady Eleanor and Paul had left with the colonel, Julianna went upstairs to check her appearance in the cheval glass that stood to one side of her dressing table. Replacing one of the pins in her hair and shaking out her skirts, Julianna took a deep breath and let it out in a sigh. Should she have worn the dark blue muslin with ruffed collar rather than the pale canary ornamented with white lutestring? Lord Fairmont had shown a preference for yellow. But still . . . Julianna fidgeted with a bit of lace and frowned at her reflection. With Eweing off on errands there was little she could do about changing gowns now, she told her image firmly, and in any case, she would better spend her time deciding what she should say to Lord Fairmont.

Would he propose? And what would she say if he did? She had never meant to marry, had never meant to give her trust to a man again, but there was something about Lord Fairmont . . . Gabriel. Julianna smiled at herself in the mirror, trying to ignore the small, sharp stab of fear that told her love could make even the logical heart of a mathematician's daughter behave foolishly.

The knocker on the outside door sounded loudly, turning Julianna's insides to blancmange as she realized Lord Fairmont must have arrived. She stepped out of the room and ran lightly down the stairs. Perhaps she should wait for Hawkins, in fact, Julianna knew she should, but she was no longer interested in propriety where Lord Fairmont was concerned.

Julianna threw open the door, a smile of greeting upon her face.

"It's about time." Lady Davina entered in an impatient swish of silk. "I dislike being kept waiting on doorsteps."

"L-Lady Davina?"

Lady Davina turned, and Julianna could see that beneath the fashionable bonnet of *gros de Naples*, traces of tears were visible on Lady Davina's flushed cheeks.

"Is—is something wrong?"

"Of course, something is wrong," Lady Davina said on a half sob. "And it is—it is all my wretched brother's fault!"

Though the lutestring trimming her dress seemed suddenly composed of steel bands designed to crush the heart within her breast, Julianna remained calm. "Let us go into the parlor," she suggested. "And you may tell me what has happened."

One arm around Lady Davina's shoulders, Julianna ushered her across the hall, noting for the first time the slight figure dressed in serviceable gray that

177

hovered just within the door.

"You have brought your maid?" Julianna asked.

Lady Davina nodded. "I was so shaken by what happened, I could barely stand. I could think of nothing but of coming to you, begging your support." Blue eyes brimming with tears were raised to Julianna's face. "Oh, do say you will stand my friend as you have promised, Mrs. Pickering."

"Of course." Julianna patted Lady Davina's shoulder reassuringly and swallowed the deep sense of foreboding lodged within her throat. "You must remain calm and tell me what has happened to upset you so."

"It is Fairmont. He has always been cruel and uncaring, but I never thought he would go this far." Lady Davina searched in her reticule for a handkerchief to stem the tears that coursed down her cheeks.

"Has he refused to pay your gambling debts?" Julianna prompted, thinking it more than likely some trifle that loomed large only in Lady Davina's mind.

"It is much, much worse," Lady Davina cried tragically, carefully dabbing at her cheeks. "Fairmont has . . . has beaten me."

"What!" Julianna stared, unable to believe Lady Davina's words.

Lady Davina untied the ribbons of her bonnet. "Oh, I knew you would not believe me. But see —" She removed the headdress, the feathered trim trembling as she did so. A large red welt disfigured Lady Davina's temple.

"Lord Fairmont did this?"

"And more," Lady Davina said. "My back and side are a mass of bruises."

Julianna shook her head. It could not be. The

178

man she had come to know would not so use a woman.

"You doubt me," Lady Davina accused. "I knew you would. You are like all the other women who flock around Fairmont because he is rich and you think his cruel character matters not. But my maid has seen how I have suffered. It was she who put cold compresses upon my back. She will stand as witness if you doubt my word."

"But Lady Davina, I cannot believe—" Julianna pressed her lips together and forced herself to speak calmly. "I cannot believe your brother would do this."

"Stanford."

The maid rose from the straight-backed chair near the door. "Yes, milady?"

"Is my back not terribly bruised?"

"Yes, milady."

"And was not my brother the cause?"

"Yes, milady."

Julianna closed her eyes, her hands clenched upon the gilded arms of the chair in which she sat. Had it happened again? Was Lord Fairmont no better than Lord Ramsden? Was her love and trust to be betrayed, to be flung aside like a worthless vowel? Lady Davina's voice came to her as if from a far distance.

"Why do you think Clothinda fled from him, preferring scandal to marriage? I warned you what my brother was like."

And I chose not to heed it, Julianna thought. I allowed myself to be dazzled by his looks and charm like any chit from the schoolroom. "I shall—I shall fetch a restorative," she mumbled, fleeing from the room.

For once Julianna was glad that Hawkins was derelict in his duties. She stood for a moment in the dining room, fumbling with the keys that would unlock the small bottle of medicinal brandy kept in the sideboard. Many men considered women chattel, she knew, their sisters no more than property to be sold to the highest bidder. But Lord Fairmont, despite his sometimes high-handed, autocratic ways, had not seemed that sort of man. Julianna remembered the patience he had shown with Paul, the way he had lifted the small boy up to be introduced to his carriage horses, the story he had made up concerning Pog which had so incensed her at the time. Her lips curved into a tender smile. Surely a man who would admit to a growing fondness for a little boy could not brutally beat his sister for no reason. Especially when Lady Davina was in a delicate condition and had been entrusted to his care.

Julianna poured a small glass of brandy for Lady Davina and carried it back to the parlor.

"Why did Lord Fairmont beat you?" she asked, watching Lady Davina's face carefully as she handed her the brandy.

Lady Davina took a small sip, shuddering slightly as she swallowed. "My brother expects complete and instant obedience," she answered. "Surely you have seen that?"

Julianna nodded slowly, remembering the way Lord Fairmont had disciplined Paul. At the time she had been outraged, but gradually she had come to think a measure of discipline would be good for the boy. That Lord Fairmont, in fact, would be good for the boy.

"When . . . when I did not do exactly as he wished," Lady Davina continued, her voice quavering, "when I asked to be allowed one small pleasure, a harmless amusement . . ."

Gambling, Julianna thought. Lady Davina has been gambling for high stakes again. But surely that is no reason for Lord Fairmont to treat her so.

"What is it exactly that you want of me?" she asked.

Lady Davina put down the glass of brandy and looked up at Julianna, the tousled golden curls and pale skin contrasting with the deep red welt that stood like an accusing exclamation point upon her brow. "I would beg sanctuary from my brother," she said, "until I can obtain a private carriage to take me to my grandmother. It will only be for a few hours, but Fairmont was . . . was in such a temper, I almost feared for my life."

"And the life of your child."

"What? Oh, yes. Of course. My child."

"I have heard that you have already miscarried once. I cannot believe that Lord Fairmont would—"

"I can show you the marks, if you like."

Julianna shook her head. "No, I . . . Yes. Yes, Lady Davina, I should like to see the bruises. It is not that I doubt you, but it is a serious charge that you make against your brother."

"I would like to lie down, in any case," Lady Davina said, rising unsteadily to her feet. "I am not feeling quite the thing."

Julianna conducted Lady Davina and her maid upstairs to the south bedroom, the cheerful yellow hangings and charming furnishings now seeming no more than a sign of Lord Fairmont's duplicity. Had she not compared his character to a multifaceted gem? Ah, and she had been right. For Lord Fairmont was like some jewel that sparkled and charmed in the sunlight but turned dull and ugly in the darkness. Perhaps there was some excuse for his behavior. Julianna knew Lady Davina was not as innocent as she seemed. Yet what excuse could there really be? And could Julianna ever trust such a man with Paul?

Turning to her wardrobe, she took out a cashemire wrapping dress which Lady Davina might wear while she rested. Stanford undid the small hooks at the back of the figured silk gown and pulled the fabric aside so that Lady Davina's back was exposed.

Bile rose in Julianna's throat as she viewed the darkening bruises disfiguring the pale skin. Lady Davina might be impulsive and headstrong, but she could have done nothing to warrant such harsh treatment. "Could your . . . could your mother do nothing to stop him?" Julianna asked.

"He has threatened to cut off her allowance if she interferes."

"Even so . . ." Julianna shook her head. How could any woman stand by and see another used so?

"Promise me you will tell no one I am here," Lady Davina urged. "Not even Miss Partridge. I shall be safely on my way to my grandmother's estate in a few hours."

"Your grandmother does not fear Lord Fairmont's wrath?"

Lady Davina smiled for the first time since she had entered the house on Taylor Street. "My grandmother fears no one. Least of all Fairmont." She stepped out of the silk gown and allowed Stanford to help her into the cashemire wrapper. "If you could see about hiring a private carriage for me, however, I should be grateful. And do you mind paying for it as

182

well?" It was the innocent question of a woman who had never had to worry about money in her life.

"Of course," Julianna agreed. It would necessitate selling her mother's garnet set, private carriages did not come cheaply, but Julianna could hardly refuse. She closed the door to the south bedroom and stood a moment in the hallway. She would send Hawkins to sell the garnets and hire the carriage, provided she could find him. Then Julianna very much thought she would go to her old bedroom and indulge in a hearty bout of tears.

How could she have been so mistaken in Lord Fairmont? How could she have contemplated marriage to such a man? Well, I must consider myself fortunate that Lady Davina came to me for help, Julianna decided. Otherwise I should never have known what a villain Lord Fairmont really is.

Eweing bustled into the north bedroom, hands on hips. "The door of Madam's bedroom is locked," she accused. "And whyever is Madam looking as hagged as makes no matter? It is a good thing we finished our errands early. Madam's hair looks as though she had been pulled through a hedgerow."

"I am sorry to so sabotage your investment, Eweing."

"We still have time to repair the damage, if Madam will just remove herself to her bedroom. Of course a smile on Madam's face would not come amiss either. And we will definitely need the rouge pot. No question about that." Eweing crossed the hall to the south bedroom and stood waiting by the door. "Well? What are we waiting for? Even a miracle takes time."

Julianna did not move from her stance by the window overlooking the street. "Has Hawkins returned yet?"

Eweing shrugged. "We didn't see him in the kitchen. Mrs. Gardning was there, though, boiling the life out of a leg of mutton. Tea and milk toast, that's what we mean to have for our supper."

"Please see that Hawkins reports to me as soon as he returns."

"Fine. Now we had better set about repairing the damage before Lord Fairmont comes. Miss Partridge told us she was as sure he was going to pop the question as she was that chickens need plucking. Not but that Mrs. Gardning might try roasting them with the feathers on."

Julianna permitted herself a small smile, though it was more a mechanical movement of the lips than anything else.

"Is something wrong, Mrs. Pickering?" Eweing moved back into the room and came to stand in front of Julianna.

"I am very much afraid your investment has gone bottoms up," Julianna replied, not turning from the window.

"That's as may be, but —"

"Excuse me, Madam." Hawkins stood in the open doorway. "I thought you would like to know as soon as I returned." He handed her a small package. "The carriage shall be here promptly at the hour requested."

Julianna took the package and nodded her dismissal before turning back to the window once more. The square of greenery below wavered and blurred as she gazed at it. I am crying again, she thought, putting up a hand to surreptiously wipe away a tear. I must not. I must not hold onto the hope that something will happen to reveal that it has all been some horrible mistake. What mistake could there be? Lady Davina's bruises are real enough, her fear of Lord Fairmont almost palpable. The only mistake was when I gave him my love and trust.

The clock on the mantel chimed the hour. It was almost time. Lord Fairmont would be arriving soon.

"Mrs. Pickering?"

Julianna blinked. Eweing still stood there, a look of concern on her face.

"Something is wrong here," Eweing said. "Something that has Madam fairly moped to death. Shall we fetch Miss Partridge?"

"No." Julianna shook her head. "She has not yet returned from Prior Park, and there is nothing she could do in any case." There was nothing anyone could do. "I shall be fine, Eweing."

The sound of the door knocker echoing down the hallway brought Julianna's head round. Though she had not seen him arrive, Julianna was certain that this time it was, indeed, Lord Fairmont come to call.

Chapter Twelve

Julianna descended the stairs. Her hair had been recombed, all traces of tears wiped from a face which felt like a stone mask that would crack at any moment. Lord Fairmont awaited her in the parlor, standing expectantly just inside the doorway. A few hours earlier Julianna would have imagined that his eyes lit with pleasure when they saw her, and the very thought would have been a pleasure to her as well. Now, Julianna entered the room with her granite mask firmly in place, her great gray eyes glinting with silvery tears she refused to shed.

"Lord Fairmont." Julianna nodded, not offering her hand, and preceded to a damask chair to one side of the fireplace. The room felt cold, and Julianna shivered slightly, wishing she had remembered to bring a shawl.

Lord Fairmont remained near the door, frowning slightly. "Is something wrong?" he asked at last, advancing into the room. "You seem quite unlike yourself."

"On the contrary, Lord Fairmont. I am quite myself this morning. Last night," Julianna paused as the memory passed like a pain through her body, "I behaved rather badly. Please accept my apologies if I

186

embarrassed you. My only excuse is that I do not often drink wine."

"In that case, I can only hope that you indulge more often." Lord Fairmont took a seat opposite. "And how is your finger?"

"It was a small cut." She shrugged away his concern.

"Julianna—"

"I would prefer that you not address me by that name," Julianna said coldly. "To those outside the family I am Mrs. Pickering."

"And what if I said I did not wish to remain outside the family?"

Julianna pressed her lips together. How dare he! How dare he sit and bandy words with her after using his sister so cruelly. He was Lord Ramsden all over again. "I would suggest you had little choice in the matter," she replied. Any tears of regret that still remained dried up as quickly as did love and hope within her breast. "Would you care for some refreshment, Lord Fairmont?"

"I prefer those outside the family to call me Gabriel," he answered. "And no, I will not indulge, but I would suggest that a glass of wine might improve your pallor and disposition. Though I cannot promise to play the gentleman should you decide to . . . embarrass me again."

"Lord Fairmont—"

"Gabriel."

"Lord Fairmont," Julianna repeated firmly. She would not allow him to put her to the blush. "You said you wished to speak to me privately. I would appreciate it if you would do so and then leave."

His eyes narrowed, and for a moment Julianna was afraid she would be given proof of that same violence to which Lady Davina had been subjected "Women are given to odd humors," he said instead, rising to his feet and pacing to the empty fireplace. One hand resting on the mantelpiece, he turned. "I am willing to indulge you for now, Julianna. But do not try me too far."

"It is not my intention to try you at all," Julianna replied. She, too, rose to her feet. It was better to be standing, facing him.

"You were willing enough last night," he reminded her. Though he seemed relaxed, leaning casually against the marble mantelpiece, Julianna noted that his hand was clenched into a fist. This was not a man used to losing. This was a man who had proven himself to be both unscrupulous and dangerous.

"What is it you wished to say to me, Lord Fairmont?"

"Sit down, Julianna." He did not move; he expected to be obeyed.

"I prefer to stand." Julianna looked him in the eye, refusing to be cowed into meek obedience, though now more than ever his use of her name sent a tremor of foreboding rippling down her spine.

"Sit!" Lord Fairmont ordered once again, his voice harsh as he pushed away from the fireplace and advanced on her.

"And what will you do if I refuse?" Julianna questioned, her voice falsely sweet. "Beat me?"

He smiled, his lips a cruel slash across a face an angel might have envied. "Would you enjoy that, Julianna?" he asked.

Julianna sat, her face as scarlet as the roses in the carpet at her feet.

"Thank you." The words were a polite mockery. "I do not know what has happened since last night to make you so quarrelsome, but I will tell you plainly that you will cease to vent your spleen on me and behave yourself. Do you understand?"

Julianna said nothing, her eyes on the rounded toes of her blue kid slippers. She heard his sigh, the creak of leather as he settled in the chair opposite her once again.

"Come, Julianna. We are not off to a propitious start, but you can have little doubt as to the reason I asked for private audience with you today."

Julianna gave an unconvincing shrug. "The window sash that sticks? Or perhaps you wished to ascertain if the new furnishings you provided were to my liking? You need not have bothered, they are quite lovely. I meant to pen a note of thanks this afternoon."

"I thought the color would suit you well." His brown eyes regarded her with some concern.

"And how is Lady Davina?" she asked, reminding herself that the man who sat there so handsome and charming had brutally used his sister only a few hours before.

"Davina has hopefully learned her lesson and will thwart me no longer," he replied. "But why do we speak of her?"

"Why indeed, Lord Fairmont? She is but a thorn in your side that you would pluck out as soon as possible and . . . and throw to the wolves. Is that not correct?"

"I doubt that most wolves would be interested in your mixed metaphor, Mrs. Pickering," he replied. "But to answer what I believe to be your question, no, I have never made any pretense of a fondness for Davina. And probably because of this, I have indulged her whims more than is good for her. Still, I have taken pains to rectify the matter. Now, may we please cease to speak of my sister?"

Julianna gave him a short nod. The pains had not been his but Lady Davina's. She folded her hands together in her lap, her posture as straight and unyielding as a stick.

Lord Fairmont took note of this and with a puzzled frown upon his face said, "I would ask you once again if something is wrong, Julianna — sorry, Mrs. Pickering, and if there is anything I might do to rectify the matter. I would hope that we are well enough acquainted for me to claim your trust."

Ah, so he would claim her trust? Did he think her some thick-headed chit he could easily charm with his handsome face and false sincerity? Some green girl with more hair than wit? He knew no more of trust than did Lord Ramsden. Less. Odds were there was some purpose behind that look of concern upon his face, though she was not yet sure what it might be.

She studied the tips of her slippers again. Would he offer some excuse for his treatment of his sister if she asked? Lord Ramsden had always been ready enough to excuse his own behavior no matter who might suffer from it.

"Mrs. Pickering."

Raising her head in automatic reply, Julianna found herself looking into Lord Fairmont's eyes, cold and blank and obsidian, seeming to reflect her own despair.

"Mrs. Pickering, as you are no doubt aware, I have come to ask for your hand in marriage."

Was it possible that her heart could still leap with happiness at these words? That for one brief instant, she could contemplate uniting herself with this man and consigning her conscience, her obligations, and her damned logical, mathematical mind to the very devil?

"You have been a widow now for some two years, I believe?" Lord Fairmont continued.

Julianna nodded.

"Though you seldom speak of the late, no doubt much-lamented, Parnell Percival Pickering who died so tragically in so many ways," Lord Fairmont paused and Julianna looked up at him sharply, but his face was as remote as any effigy on a tomb, "I think I am not wrong in assuming you are over your loss and would consider marriage again. Thankfully, you are no longer a young girl who would expect romance and pledges of undying love, but a mature woman who can appreciate the practical advantages of marriage to a man such as myself."

Julianna's hands clenched in her lap as she fought back a reply. What practical advantages could outweigh the cruelty of a man who would beat his sister and she with child?

"I can assure you that my estates are now quite in order and I would be able to provide for you handsomely. Though I expect we shall have children of our own, an exercise I have determined you would not be adverse to."

Julianna's eyes all but started from her head. An exercise to which she would not be adverse? Was that what last night had been about? To find out how she felt about . . . about . . . The blush burned in Julianna's cheeks as she glared at Lord Fairmont, noting the small self-satisfied smile with which he regarded her.

"I shall, in any case, see that Paul is taken care of." The smile disappeared as Lord Fairmont spoke again. "Though Paul could not, of course, inherit the estates. Miss Partridge, unless I much mistake the matter, will soon be Colonel Cramden's responsibility. The banns for our wedding could be read in the Abbey Sunday next."

"Excuse me, Lord Fairmont." Julianna spoke at last. "But why do you wish to marry me, of all people?"

He shrugged, his broad shoulders evident beneath the blue superfine of his coat. "You have doubtless heard of my ill-fated betrothal to Clothinda Dewlap, now Clothinda Eppinhay. I do not care to go through that again. Your circumstances are such that I know you will not cry off the engagement."

"What—what do you mean?"

"What do you think I mean . . . Mrs. Pickering?" he countered.

Never had Julianna felt more like a mouse confronted by a hungry tomcat. "And if I refuse?"

"I would suggest that you reconsider."

Julianna took a sharp breath. Lord Fairmont did not wish to marry her out of love or regard, but because of the power he had to keep her in her place. He was Lord Ramsden all over again. Lord Ramsden using her love for Paul to make her do his bidding.

Julianna shook her head. There was no question. She would take her chances that Lord Fairmont would not reveal whatever knowledge he possessed. Julianna would never give a man such power over her again. And yet, despite all she knew to his discredit, some part of her would say yes, Julianna thought, even as her lips moved and she answered, "No, Lord Fairmont. I have no wish to marry you."

"I see." Lord Fairmont took a quick turn about the

192

room, stopping to stare out at the square below as Julianna had done some hours earlier. At last he turned. "I will not pressure you, but I do not believe you have fully considered the matter. You are in an unenviable state, my dear. Trying to raise a child, to eke out a living on what? Your savings? The small amounts you may win from time to time at cards?"

"There . . . there is my inheritance from my husband," Julianna prevaricated.

Lord Fairmont gave her a look of patent disbelief. "Give me credit for some intelligence." He all but sneered the words. "No, my dear, you will very soon be at wit's end, trying to pinch your purse just a bit tighter each month to pay your bills. How long can you go on hoping your winnings at cards will pay for the few luxuries you and Miss Partridge allow yourselves? And would you subject Paul to this, when I stand ready to offer so much more and the protection of my name as well?"

For a moment Julianna was almost tempted to change her mind, though it had nothing to do with veiled threats or indisputable logic and everything to do with the state of her heart. She closed her eyes, shutting out the sight of the man who, despite everything, had come to mean so much to her. Still, there had been no word of love, no gesture to show Julianna she was anything more than a brood mare to him. And I must not forget Lady Davina, Julianna thought, the words whispering inside her head, warning her, arming her against the lure cast by Lord Fairmont's charm and the remembered warmth of his embrace.

Julianna opened her eyes and searched his face, looking for some sign that this was more than a business transaction to him, some sign that would tell her this was a man she could trust. "Lady Davina," she began, knowing that she must in all fairness give him a chance to explain.

"I do not wish to discuss Davina," Lord Fairmont said brusquely. "I have made you an offer you would be a fool to refuse. What is your answer?"

"That I must be a fool," Julianna replied. Though it was not because she refused his offer but because she so longed to accept it that she deemed herself one.

"Would you prefer me to make protestations of undying devotion, Julianna?" he asked, all pretense of patience gone. "Throw myself on my knees before you?" Taking her by the arms, he pulled her roughly from the damask chair. "How long do you think that sort of emotion lasts? Clothinda spoke of love, of how she cared for nothing but me. And all her poetic assurances were gone the instant she learned of my father's gambling debts." Lord Fairmont thrust Julianna sharply aside.

Julianna stumbled and would have fallen had she not grasped the back of the chair.

"Women! A pox on you all. A man's trust and care are not enough. Why did I ever think you different?"

"Lord Fairmont, please!" Julianna recoiled from his anger. Had she ever thought him incapable of Lady Davina's accusations, she did not now.

"It was seeing you with Paul," he said, the anger suddenly draining from his voice, leaving it flat and emotionless. "That first day in the park when I saw the two of you together, saw the concern with which you dried Paul's tears, the tenderness and love you had for him, the love that had always been lacking in my own life, the love I had always wanted . . . and I thought, here at last is someone unlike the spoiled society women who cannot see beyond a man's fortune and pedigree. Here is a woman of true warmth and trust and generosity. Even if I was no longer capable of the love I had squandered on Clothinda, I knew you were the one I wanted to bear my children, to spend my life beside."

"Lord Fairmont . . ."

"I disapproved of your gambling, of course. It had destroyed my family, and I would not have a wife who was so addicted. But then I realized you gambled not out of any true love of card play but only out of necessity, and I determined to ask for your hand in marriage."

"Please . . ." Julianna held up her hands to ward off the sharp pain his words inflicted.

"Do not worry, my dear. I shall not badger you to change your mind. I accept your decision and shall not bother you again." He walked over to Julianna and took her gloved hand, raising it to his lips. "Goodbye, Julianna." She felt the warm pressure of his mouth on her fingertips for an instant and then he was gone.

Julianna hurried to the window and looked out. There was still time. She could raise the sash, call to him, tell him that she had changed her mind . . . but no. He had accepted her decision. And she must remember what he had done to Lady Davina, what he was capable of doing. Lord Fairmont's tall figure came into sight a moment later, and Julianna watched as he stopped to don his hat before striding quickly out of sight.

Well, and so that was done. A lucky escape, in fact. Julianna sat down on the small rosewood settee. There was no reason to feel as if a small part of her had shriveled and died. Had Lord Fairmont not given proof of the violence that lurked beneath his gentleman's facade? Not given proof that what the rumormongers said of him was true? And as if that were not enough, he had told her in plain words that he did not love her, was incapable of the emotion.

Marriage without love was no more than a sham. Like the castle of that name built by Mr. Allen, such a marriage was a mere facade without substance or foundation. Her mother had shown her that. Julianna fingered the carved-leaf design surrounding the padded arm of the settee. It would be time to dress soon. Lady Eleanor and Paul would be returning. Life would go on. She had done the right, the only thing under the circumstances.

"Has my brother gone?" Lady Davina entered the room cautiously and looked around. "What did he want? Did he come about me? I hope you did not tell him I was here?"

"Of course not." Julianna shook her head. "I promised that I would not."

"Good. I am sure he does not yet know that I am missing and thinks I still cower in my room. Does my brother often call upon you? You must not think he means anything by it, you know. Fairmont is a terrible flirt."

Julianna turned away. "Would you care for some refreshments, Lady Davina?"

"If you please. I confess to being quite famished. After the accident my only thought was to escape Fairmont's wrath, and I have had nothing since breakfast."

"Accident?" Julianna turned from the bellpull. "What accident might that be?"

Lady Davina did not answer but looked accusingly at the ribboned carving that edged the chair in which

196

she sat. "May I request a cushion for my back, Mrs. Pickering? Stanford would dose me with laudanum but I refused and now regret it."

A commotion could be heard in the hallway announcing the arrival of Lady Eleanor and Paul. "If you will excuse me for a moment." Julianna started toward the door, only to have it open as she reached it.

"Hawkins said you were in the parlor, Julianna, and I could not wait to hear—oh, Lady Davina. How unexpected."

"Horsie." Paul pranced into the room, holding a small carved horse in front of him. "Look, Jules. Look what Colonel Cramden gave me."

"Colonel Cramden bought it from a street vendor for Paul," Lady Eleanor explained as Paul galloped about the room clutching his new wooden friend and making whinnying noises. "Such a dear man."

Lady Davina, lips pressed tightly together, glared as Paul cantered around her chair. "For heaven's sake, send the boy to the nursery!" she demanded. "Children do not belong in drawing rooms. Where is his nursemaid?"

A sudden silence descended. Paul stopped and looked uncertainly from Lady Davina to Julianna.

"Go away, I said." Lady Davina made dismissing motions with her hands.

"Paul, why don't you go to the kitchen and find Kitty," Julianna said, urging Paul to the door. "Tell Mrs. Gardning that you are to be allowed a piece of iced gingerbread. I will be along in a few minutes to hear about your day, and we shall see if we can persuade Mrs. Gardning to part with some cheese for Humbert."

Julianna watched Paul trot happily down the hall

and then turned from the door, the smile fading from her lips. "I realize you are not feeling quite the thing, Lady Davina," she said, "but I would remind you that this is Paul's home and you, not he, are a guest in it."

Lady Davina's eyes filled with tears. "Oh, please do not be angry with me, dear Mrs. Pickering. I have very delicate nerves, and it has been a most trying day."

"I should think it has," Lady Eleanor agreed. "I imagine Lord Fairmont gave you a rare scolding."

"Worse than that," Julianna said softly. "Lady Davina's back is a mass of ugly bruises. I would not have thought him capable of such action."

"Well, I would." Lady Eleanor plumped herself down in the damask chair. "Nasty brutes, horses. I've always said it doesn't pay to trust a horse's hoof or a dog's tooth. Why, I'd as lief be a chicken facing a fox as climb onto one of those animals. Not but that Brownie wasn't an amiable sort. But there, one exception only proves the rule."

Julianna looked puzzled. "I do not see what that has to do with Lord Fairmont's brutal treatment of Lady Davina."

"I think, perhaps, I should go to my room," Lady Davina declared suddenly. "I believe I feel a spasm coming on."

"Your room?" Lady Eleanor demanded, the flowers in the bonnet she had not yet removed waving wildly about. "What do you mean, your room?"

"I have offered Lady Davina temporary sanctuary from Lord Fairmont," Julianna explained calmly.

Lady Eleanor eyed their diminutive guest shrewdly for a moment. "I think I smell a rat, and I don't mean Humbert. Supposing you explain exactly what is going on here."

"Lord Fairmont has given his sister a terrible beating; her back is bruised beyond belief."

"And you think Lord Fairmont did this?" Lady Eleanor gave Julianna a searching look.

"Well, I . . . I did not at first, but then Lady Davina—"

"Lady Davina fell from her horse this morning," Lady Eleanor stated in a no-nonsense voice. "Gossip has it that she was out riding in the park against Lord Fairmont's express orders. That's where her bruises came from. Lord Fairmont's not the sort to raise his hand to a woman. Surely you know that, Julianna?"

"I . . . Lady Davina, is this true? Are your—"

"Do you suggest that I lied?" Lady Davina rose to her feet and winced, tears starting to her eyes. "Oh, now see what you have done! My back is on fire again. Ring for Stanford at once."

"That will not be necessary." Lord Fairmont spoke quietly from the doorway where he had entered unnoticed by the three women. "No one answered my knock, and the door was on the latch so I decided to announce myself," he explained. "I have come to fetch you home, Davina."

Lady Davina tilted her chin. "I have no intention of going with you, Fairmont. Mrs. Pickering has ordered a private carriage for me, and I shall be leaving on an extended visit to the country."

"Indeed?" Lord Fairmont asked with raised eyebrows. "And here I would have said you had every intention of going direct to London. How little I know you, sister."

"Lady Davina intends to visit her grandmother," Julianna broke in nervously. "Surely there is nothing wrong in that."

Lord Fairmont gave Julianna a look of polite inquiry. "Davina intends to visit our grandmother who has been dead these seven years and more? Well, she should certainly find it peaceful."

"Beast!" Lady Davina hissed the epithet.

"Do not try me too far," Lord Fairmont warned, all pretense of politeness gone. "I returned home only to hear of your accident and to find that you had disappeared. Fortunately, you have the brain of a peagoose and were easily traced, having employed my own coachman to fetch you here. Did you think he would not tell me, Davina?"

"I gave the brute half a crown!" Lady Davina cried, incensed by the injustice of it all.

Lord Fairmont gave his sister a look of disgust. "I pay my servants well and see that they are treated fairly. They are more loyal than my own family as I have reason to know. How could you so endanger your own life and the life of the child you carry?"

"Pooh! You exaggerate. It was to be no more than a gentle gallop around the park. If that dog had not darted out, you would never have known."

"Davina! The doctor forbade anything but the most gentle of exercise. Do you forget that you almost died last time? If it were not for the fact that Grey is returning home next week, I swear I would—"

"Grey is coming home?" Lady Davina's face lit with pleasure. "How can you be sure? I have had no word."

"I received a letter from him this morning and one awaits you as well. Had you not been so busy flaunting my wishes, you would have had it by now. I am afraid I did Grey no favor when I gave in to your demands that you be allowed to marry. I should have let you pout and starve yourself. For all you thought yourself in love, you were much too young."

"Mama married when she was only sixteen," Lady Davina protested.

"That is certainly no recommendation for early marriage," Lord Fairmont said. "Though I should think even a child would understand that what you did this morning was madness. Have you no sense, Davina? Risking your life and the life of your babe?"

Davina wrinkled her nose at him. "Do not try to depress me with your might-have-beens, Fairmont. I am too happy now that Grey is returning. He will allow me to do just as I please. I shall make him take me to London. We shall have such a time! Where is Stanford? Honestly, the woman is never about when I need her. Is your carriage outside, Fairmont? I would go home directly to read Grey's letter."

Julianna watched in bewilderment as Lady Davina all but danced from the room, calling loudly for Stanford as she did so. What had happened to the woman who had been forced to marry, who had been starved into submission? Had all of that been no more than fabrication on Lady Davina's part, as well?

"And now, if I might have a word with you privately, Mrs. Pickering?" Lord Fairmont turned to Julianna.

"Well, I must change my gown in any case," Lady Eleanor said, bustling to the door that Lord Fairmont was holding open and cravenly leaving Julianna to her fate.

Lord Fairmont shut the door firmly and stood, one hand on the doorknob, regarding her. Julianna swallowed and risked a nervous sidelong glance at his face. It did not reassure her.

"Lord Fairmont," she began as he continued to stand like some portent of doom by the door. "I . . . I swear I did not know—"

"Did not know that my sister was in your house? Davina has many vices, but I had not thought breaking into people's homes was one of them. I hope you have thought to count the silver."

"Is it necessary to speak to me in that way? I admit I was wrong, should never have believed your sister—"

"And what exactly did you believe, Mrs. Pickering?" he asked, moving away from the door at last. "What touching story did my dear sister impart this time? I have no doubt I figured badly in it. I always do."

"You did not—"

"Ah, but of course I did. You need not spare my feelings. I asked Davina to obey Dr. Phillips's orders to rest and not ride until after her child was born. So, of course, I am branded a villain. I do not blame Davina. She only follows where my mother leads. And while my mother has always regarded me with indifference, she has come to loathe me since my father's death."

His eyes narrowed for a moment as he looked unseeingly across the room, and Julianna held her breath, waiting for him to continue.

"Do you have any idea what it is like to suddenly discover that your inheritance is gone, Mrs. Pickering?" he asked, his eyes focusing on her at last. "To find that the estate that has been in your family since Charles I has been mortgaged to fuel your family's gambling fever? When my father died, I found there was nothing left but debts. I tried to make my

202

mother understand that she must retrench. Of course, she laughed and refused to even consider it. Why should she, when her own son did not, she asked, and called me a selfish wastrel. Which I suppose I must have seemed," he said, giving a careless shrug. "For do you know how I managed to save the estate and provide for my loving family?" He looked at Julianna and smiled.

"Ah, you will appreciate the irony of this, my dear. You see, I gambled. Oh, I always had. What young man of our class does not? But now I played for serious stakes. And one day, when my mother had pawned one more family heirloom, when one more mortgage payment was due upon the estate, I refused a young man's request that his debt be forgiven. I could not wait, you see. Payment on the estate was overdue. And so Lord Carlborne went home and hanged himself."

Julianna closed her eyes and sank down upon the settee. She wanted to cover her ears, wanted Lord Fairmont to stop and yet . . . and yet . . . she opened her eyes. He stood, staring down into the empty fireplace. And Julianna wanted to gather him into her arms as she would Paul and tell him that everything would be all right. Though she knew it was too late, much too late for that.

"People talk about Carlborne haunting this house." Lord Fairmont looked around the room and gave a mirthless laugh. "He does not haunt the house," his voice lowered to a harsh whisper, "he haunts me. And ever shall."

"Lord Fairmont." Julianna put out one hand in a pleading gesture "I did not know. How could I?"

"How could you not?" he asked in turn. "You may not have known the facts, but what have I done that you would so mistrust me? And what has Davina done to earn your trust when I have not?"

Julianna shook her head helplessly. "I do not know. Her back was badly bruised. She said you had . . . had beaten her."

"And you believed her? Believed that I not only brutally used my sister but endangered the life of her unborn child as well? What kind of monster do you think me?"

"I do not think you a monster at all. I—I love you." The words seem to spring from her mouth of their own volition, though Julianna could not deny the truth of them. It seemed impossible to her now that she had believed Lady Davina. "I love you," she repeated again, "but I am also afraid."

"Afraid? As well you should be if you think me capable of such an act. I thought you different, Julianna, but you are like every other woman who prates of love but knows not what it is. With love there must be trust, and if you had trusted me, you could never have believed Davina. Never."

Tears blurred Julianna's vision as she struggled for composure. "You do not understand," she whispered.

"I understand that Davina meant to make mischief between us because she knew I cared for you." Lord Fairmont stepped towards Julianna, his eyes intent upon her face. "And she succeeded . . . she succeeded all too well." He continued to look at her silently for the brief time it took the mantel clock to strike the hour and then he turned, striding rapidly to the door.

Hawkins stood in the hallway, a startled look upon his face. Lord Fairmont brushed past him. The outside door opened and closed, the sound of finality echoing down the silent hallway.

Julianna remained sitting numbly on the settee. I will not cry, she told herself, even as the tears began to course slowly down her cheeks. I will not cry.

"Jules?" Paul stood just inside the door clutching his toy horse, his mouth smeared with sugar icing.

Julianna forced a smile to her lips. "Yes, Paul?"

"Lord Fairmont gone?"

Julianna nodded. Paul trotted over and clambered into her lap. "Did you hurt self?" he asked, his blue eyes dark with sympathy.

Julianna hugged the little boy close, her chin resting on his golden curls. "Yes, Paul, I'm afraid I did."

Paul struggled up to plant a wet, iced kiss on Julianna's chin. "Better now?"

Despite the raw pain which still seemed to eat away at her heart, Julianna smiled. "Much better," she agreed, though she was afraid this was a hurt that would not heal . . . this was a hurt that would be with her to the end of her days.

Chapter Thirteen

"You know the old saying, Julianna. A roasted pigeon will not fly into your mouth. Or is it a leg of mutton will not walk to your table?" Lady Eleanor frowned. "Well, at any rate, you know what I mean. You must make a push to get Lord Fairmont back."

Julianna sighed and looked up from the novel she had been pretending to read. This was old ground that had been ridden over many times in the past two weeks. "I sent him a formal note of apology, Lady Eleanor. What more can I do? Would you have me twist my ankle outside his door as Miss Finley did to poor Mr. Penington?"

"There is nothing poor about Mr. Penington," Lady Eleanor corrected. "Miss Finley's mother made quite sure of that before she allowed her daughter to twist her ankle. And as I recall, Mr. Penington offered for Miss Finley within a sennight. While I do not suggest you twist your ankle, surely you could contrive for some mishap to occur?"

"Actually, I had considered such a thing." Julianna blushed and ran her fingers over the newly cut pages of her book. "Only momentarily, you understand. But it would never do. Odds are Lord Fairmont would not be at home and I should merely be hustled into a hackney by his butler or one of those stone-faced footmen."

know very well what it is, my dear. Love and a cough cannot be hid, no matter what you say. Now the colonel is calling to escort me to the Orange Grove this afternoon. I know it looks like rain, but there, it often does and never a drop falls. Do say you will join us. There is something so soothing about walking in the gardens and looking out over the Avon. And the colonel has promised we shall stop for ices afterwards."

Julianna smiled. "Almost you tempt me. But I am not quite reduced to playing gooseberry. I have several errands that must be done today. Do not worry. I shall soon put the episode with Lord Fairmont quite out of my mind."

Lady Eleanor gave her a look of patent disbelief but said only, "If you mean to go to the circulating library, I would be happy if you would return my book, *The Idiot Heiress* and bring me something new. Perhaps *The Cavern of Horrors, or Miseries of Miranda* or if that is not available the new one by Selina Davenport, *An Angel's Form and a Devil's Heart*. I understand it to be quite exciting. And if anyone should inquire, *The Idiot Heiress* was quite enjoyable. I would never have suspected that the heroine's maternal grandmother would prove to be the madhouse keeper."

"Lady Eleanor, for shame!" Julianna scolded, holding up the book she had placed upon the table. "You see I have been reading *The Idiot Heiress,* and now you have ruined the ending for me."

"Nonsense," Lady Eleanor refused to be cowed. "You know you always figure out what is going to happen while I never can. I daresay you were quite aware that Lady Azelia would marry Sir Lucius and Lady Jane drink herself to death."

"Did I not know it before, I do now," Julianna said. "I shall stop and inquire if *The Cavern of Horrors* is available."

Lady Eleanor, in the act of threading her needle, looked up and responded with a dimpled grin much like Paul's. "Good. I am sure Miranda's miseries are just the sort of thing you need to be able to place things in perspective, for I begin to think you will never be over your fit of the dismals else. Not to say you don't have good reason. But there, what is meant to be will be, and if you are born to be hanged you will never drown. I am sure we will soon have more invitations than we know what to do with, and there is no saying but that Lord Fairmont will come round in the end."

Julianna, remembering the look on Lord Fairmont's face and the way he had walked away from her, took leave to doubt this. "Do not try to cheer me with false promises," she said. "It may be true that we will not be reduced to penury, but as for Lord Fairmont, I am afraid my cupboard door has been firmly shut again. Still, as I never expected nor desired to marry, I have lost nothing. For I had quite made up my mind to refuse him in any case."

Lady Eleanor raised her eyebrows. "And you accuse me of offering Spanish coin," she chided. "Well, there may be some who would say marriage is the worst blunder a woman can make, but I would differ with them. And what has been shut can soon be opened again, you know. Now promise me that you will wear the bonnet I finished fashioning for you yesterday and allow Eweing to dress you in something more becoming than that drab muslin you are wearing. There is no saying when you might encounter Lord Fairmont. You would not want him to think you had been moping about."

Julianna agreed that it would be as well to look her best. "Not that I care about Lord Fairmont. But it does not do to look the dowd."

Some fifteen minutes later Julianna could be seen leaving the small house in Taylor Street wearing a

French walking hat ornamented with twisted ribbon and a dress of zephyrine silk, the hem of which was decorated with rosettes to match the ribbon in her bonnet. She wore Limerick gloves upon her hands and carried Lady Eleanor's copy of *The Idiot Heiress* in a string bag, for truly she did not think she cared to read it now she knew the ending.

Walking quickly past the shops on Milsom Street, Julianna cast a worried glance at the dark clouds which hung like heavy curtains shutting out the light. The buildings which shone so brightly in the sun were now a shadowed gray. It was a wretched day, but one that seemed to fit Julianna's mood, for all she tried to put on a bright face for Lady Eleanor's sake. Still, perhaps a visit to Mr. Godwin's circulating library would dispel her gloom.

Though Julianna could remember having had books such as *Robinson Crusoe* and *The Little Female Academy* as a child, and Graxton Manor had possessed a good but dusty collection of the classics before Lord Ramsden had sold them so he might wager the proceeds on a pig named Harry, it wasn't until Julianna had come to Bath that she had encountered the novels of Jane Austin and Maria Edgeworth.

Now eagerly searching the shelves of the circulating library as a hunter might search for its prey, Julianna pounced upon a copy of some poems by Mr. Shelley which she had been wanting to read—she had returned the collection lent to her by Mr. Wilmot as not being to her taste—and did her best to find something Lady Eleanor might enjoy. Books were more important than ever to the two ladies now they were spending so many evenings at home. Still, Julianna could not quite bring herself to choose the new Selina Davenport no matter that Lady Eleanor had requested it, for the title, *An Angel's Form and a Devil's Heart* re-

211

minded her too much of Lord Fairmont.

Instead, Julianna selected a novel about a wicked count and his pursuit of a beautiful ninnyhammer named Marianne, which she was confident Lady Eleanor would enjoy just as well. Then, after a quick peek out the window to see that though still cloudy, the rain had not yet commenced, Julianna sat down to spend a few minutes perusing one of the London papers.

There was little of interest Julianna had not already read in the *Bath Chronicle* and she was about to replace the paper on the table when a paragraph near the back seemed to fairly leap out and seize her by the throat:

A substantial reward has been offered by Lord Victor Ramsden, Graxton Manor, Wentfeld, for information leading to the return of his son, Paul Marnay. The boy is two years of age, with light complexion, blond hair, and blue eyes. He was unlawfully removed from his home by two women, one about forty-six with blond hair and one twenty-four with red hair.

Julianna's face blanched as white as the paper. She read the notice again. There was no mistake. Anyone who knew them would make the connection at once.

Looking quickly about to make sure she was not observed, Julianna tore the notice from the paper with shaking hands and hurried out of the circulating library. She would pack their bags, order Hawkins to fetch a carriage. They would leave at once.

But where would they go? What would they use for funds? Julianna sped across the pavement, her reticule and string bag swinging wildly back and forth along with her thoughts. Her savings were almost depleted and most of her mother's jewels sold. There was still the sapphire set, of course. She could pawn them, but what then? She must talk to Lady Eleanor . . . Lady Eleanor. She would certainly not want to leave Bath, not when it meant leaving the colonel as well.

"Oh, dear." Julianna stopped to stare unseeingly at a most hideous bonnet of chip straw in a shop window. Her gloved hands clenched and unclenched about the strings of her reticule. There is nothing for it, she decided at last. Plans must be made, Lady Eleanor told. But first . . . first she must make sure Paul was all right. That he was safely at home with Kitty.

Julianna reached Taylor Street just as the first drops of rain began to fall. She hurried forward only to be brought up short as she noticed the slight figure of a be-whiskered gentleman standing on the pavement. Beside him stood a woman wrapped in a dark cloak. It was Eweing. Julianna was sure of it. Eweing and the man Julianna had seen making a sketch of Paul in the park.

"Eweing!"

The man turned at Julianna's call, then quickly grasped the woman's arm and hurried her away.

"Eweing, wait!" Julianna started to run after them, then stopped. First she must make sure that Paul was in the house. That he was safe.

Pushing open the front door, Julianna paused only to hurl her belongings upon the hall table before lifting her skirts and hurrying up the stairs. The first floor was reached, then the second and third. Panting slightly, Julianna sped across the landing to fling open the door to the nursery.

It was deserted.

Gasping with breathless fear, Julianna ran to the barred nursery windows. What she hoped to see she could not have said. But certainly she caught no glimpse of Paul in the dark, rain-soaked square below.

"Kitty. Where is Kitty?" Julianna mumbled, returning down the stairs once more at a stumbling run.

"Was it the nursemaid you was wanting, Madam?" Hawkins asked, springing from the dark shadows of the stairs.

"Yes, have you seen her? And Paul?"

Hawkins smiled slightly and inclined his head. "I believe them to be still in the kitchen, Madam. The young master insisted on feeding that rodent of his and they was caught in the rain. Mrs. Gardning is making hot chocolate, concerned as she is that the boy don't take a chill."

"Oh. Oh, good. Thank you, Hawkins." Julianna put out one hand to steady herself on the hall table, feeling almost faint with relief. Paul was all right. She needn't have worried.

"Perhaps you would care for a cup of tea in the parlor?" Hawkins suggested in a voice of some concern. "I could light the fire if you wish."

"Some hot tea would be wonderful," Julianna agreed, "but first I would like to see Paul." With unsteady legs, Julianna walked down the hallway that led to the back of the house, her heart still pounding loudly in her ears. Paul was safe. That was all that mattered. Paul was safe . . . for now.

The kitchen was warm and cozy. Paul sat swinging his legs on one of the chairs, a mug of hot chocolate in his hands. Julianna took a deep breath. Though she wanted to run to Paul and clutch him up in her arms, feel the solidness of his small body pressed tightly against hers, she knew she must not. It would only frighten him to no purpose. And so she contented herself with ruffling his hair, damp and curling from the rain.

"Did you feed Humbert some cheese?" she asked, forcing her face into a smile.

Paul nodded and dimpled up at her, a moustache of hot chocolate ringing his mouth. He is so dear, Julianna thought. If anything were to happen to him, I think I would—

"Shall I bring Madam's tea to the parlor?" Hawkins asked.

214

Julianna nodded. Tea would be welcome now. Now that she had seen Paul. "You must come and tell me about your adventures when you have finished your chocolate," she told Paul and, dropping a swift kiss on the top of his head, turned to follow Hawkins and the tea tray.

The door to the kitchen swung closed behind her, shutting out the warmth. Julianna walked back down the hallway, the relief she had felt at seeing Paul slowly turning to a feeling of icy numbness. Once in the parlor, she collapsed onto the settee, her thoughts as frozen as the pond at the back of Graxton Manor during the cold, bleak days of winter. Julianna could not think, was incapable of deciding what her next step should be.

Mechanically, she measured the tea from the tea caddy, poured the hot water, allowed the tea leaves to brew before pouring it into a delicate china cup edged with a garland of pink rosebuds. I suppose I should send for Eweing, ask her who the gentleman was and why she did not stop when I called, Julianna thought, sipping her tea. There is probably a simple explanation and nothing at all to do with Paul. The hot tea and sudden cessation of worry for Paul's immediate safety were soothing. The chill numbness of fear began slowly to melt away.

Julianna removed her bonnet and put it to one side. And I will talk to Lady Eleanor about what is to be done as soon as she returns. Yes. Julianna sipped her tea again. That was the logical thing to do. There would be no more sudden midnight escapes. The London paper had been several days old. If anyone had been going to inform Lord Ramsden they would have done so by now, and he at their door with his dark, sardonic smile of amusement at their expense. Yes. Julianna leaned back on the settee. They were surely safe for now.

"Excuse me, Madam."

Julianna blinked. Hawkins stood stiff as a statue beside the tea tray. "You need not have remained," she said with a smile. "I assure you I am quite all right now, though I should like to see Paul again as soon as he has finished his chocolate."

"Indeed, Madam." He inclined his head. "But there is something I believe we should discuss first."

Julianna raised her eyebrows, not so much at Hawkins's words, as at the way he was looking at her. "Yes, Hawkins?" she asked sitting up. "Is there some problem?"

"I would call it more of an opportunity, Madam." Hawkins produced a small piece of paper and laid it on the tea tray beside Julianna's cup.

It was the notice Julianna had torn from the London paper.

"I saw you were a bit upset when you came in," Hawkins explained. "And I thought it might be worth my while to take a look around. It was in that string bag. Careless of you to leave it about like that."

Julianna swallowed and took a deep breath, giving herself time to anchor her mask of indifference firmly in place. "You read the notice?" she asked, looking up at him at last.

"Oh, yes." Hawkins smiled thinly. "I can read quite well. At one of my former posts the lady of the house took on the charity work of teaching me. It has proved well worth the effort, though never more so than now."

Julianna reached for her teacup and sipped its now cold contents. "I am sure an education is always worth one's time and effort, Hawkins."

"Ah, you're a cool one, Mrs. Pickering. I said as much to Mrs. Gardning, you know. She won't be as easy a nut to crack as the last one, I said."

"I am not interested in your nuts, cracked or otherwise," Julianna replied with a look of cool disdain. "My only concern is your insolence which I will not tolerate. You will get your things together and leave, Hawkins. And do not expect a reference."

Hawkins settled himself in one of the damask chairs. "Oh, I'll leave all right. But first, I believe we have some business to discuss."

"We have no—"

"Otherwise I'll be forced to go to this Lord Ramsden and tell him what I know." Hawkins smiled. "The reward would come in handy, you know, and it seems to me I'd only be besting you at your own game."

"And what might that be?" Julianna asked, playing for time, praying that some clear way out of this situation would present itself to her.

Hawkins leaned back in the chair. "It's like that notice says. You unlawfully removed the boy from his rightful home. And I'm thinking you don't look much like a relation, so I wouldn't be surprised if you didn't plan to ask for a bit of money for his return yourself."

"You are being quite ridiculous." Julianna rose from the settee. "I refuse to listen to this any longer. If you do not leave, I shall inform the authorities."

"I doubt that, Mrs. Pickering." Hawkins rose beside her. "We both know I'm right. You shouldn't have given that fancy lord of yours his walking papers. Once you was leg-shackled, he could have done the bleeding. Now it'll have to be you, and shutting me up is going to be a costly business."

Julianna walked to the door, head high, back ramrod straight.

"You see, me and Mrs. Gardning have been talking about buying an inn, but that takes a bit of blunt. Still, I'm sure you'll want to contribute." Hawkins then named a sum that stopped Julianna in her tracks. She whirled around.

"You must have windmills in your head. I could never

raise such a sum . . . even if what you said was true."

Hawkins smiled. "Oh it's true, all right, and we both know it. As for the money, all you have to do is sell some of those fancy jewels of yours. Fact is, I'll even sell them for you, like I did before. Only this time, I'll keep the money. What do you say, Mrs. Pickering?"

"I say, you are to leave this house and leave it at once!" Julianna demanded, making one last effort to gain control of the situation.

Hawkins sauntered up to her. "I'll wait until tomorrow night, Mrs. Pickering. Until tomorrow night. Then I'll see how much this Lord Ramsden is willing to pay." He stared at her for a moment before brushing past.

Lady Eleanor returned an hour later garrulously enraptured with the Orange Grove and Colonel Cramden. "For truly, Julianna, and you may say I am prejudiced if you will, but truly, he is quite the nicest man, generous and . . . handsome. Do you not think he is handsome? So commanding somehow. When he looks at me I feel all weak and . . . and fluttery. Oh, you may smile, if you wish, but one cannot love and be wise, and I would just as soon not be wise. We walked to the obelisk in the center of the garden and talked of . . . of well, commonplaces, I suppose. Only they did not seem commonplace when I was with the colonel. And there was a woman selling flowers near the Abbey. So of course, the colonel must buy me some. And when it started to rain, he was so afraid I would get wet and catch a chill. He called a hackney at once, and then he must ask me over and over if I was sure I was not too cold or too hot. Oh, Julianna," Lady Eleanor stopped for breath, "I am so happy we came to Bath. Do you know I feel as if I were in my salad days again."

"You would . . . you would not consider leaving then?"

"Leaving?" Lady Eleanor gave her an incredulous look. "Leaving when I am quite certain the colonel means to make me an offer at any moment? I may have more hair than wit, but even I am not such an addlepate. Whyever do you ask such a thing?"

Julianna shrugged her shoulders, trying for a nonchalance she was far from feeling. "I thought, perhaps, if something should happen, if Lord Ramsden learned of our whereabouts . . ."

"Has he?" Lady Eleanor gasped, all happiness gone from her face in an instant. "Has my brother found us out?" Rising quickly to her feet, she came to stand beside Julianna's chair. "I knew it was too good to be true. He will ruin everything for me again, I know he will. And I had so hoped . . . Are you sure, Julianna?" Lady Eleanor's eyes pleaded for denial, her face a haggard mask of hope and despair.

Julianna gave a quick laugh and rose to her feet beside her stepaunt. "Do not so agitate yourself," she scolded. "I meant it only as supposition." She gave Lady Eleanor a quick hug. "I am sorry I frightened you so."

"Oh, Julianna, you do not know . . ." Lady Eleanor sank down upon the settee, one hand to her breast. "I was so afraid for a moment." Searching in her reticule, Lady Eleanor took out a lace handkerchief and dabbed at her eyes. "If anything should happen to ruin my happiness now, I do not think I could bear it."

"Nothing will happen, my dear," Julianna assured her. "I shall see to it."

The rain had stopped, and the wet pavement glistened beneath her feet as Julianna walked quickly down Milsom Street. The reticule on her arm swung briskly back and forth, its jeweled contents light for all their value. Her thoughts centered on Hawkins, her lips curling as she walked.

How could they have so mistaken the man? Lady Eleanor had had the hiring of him, of course. And checking a man's references was a tiresome formality to be dispensed with in her opinion. Still, Hawkins had seemed so honest and upright and . . . and butlerish. Though now Julianna stopped to think about it, he had seldom been about when needed, yet often could be found lurking in the hallway when he had no business to be there.

I should have known, Julianna remonstrated with herself. Why is it that I trusted Hawkins, yet the one man I should have trusted I did not?

Ten minutes later, Julianna stood outside Brown and Rolinson, one of the most expensive jewelry shops in Bath, staring down at a diamond necklace in the window. If Hawkins had his way her mother's sapphires would soon be displayed there as well. Julianna clutched her reticule tightly with one hand. Her father had given the sapphires to her mother on their wedding day. It had been a gift given with much love. To sell them to feed the greed of a villain like Hawkins was unthinkable. Julianna squared her shoulders. Hawkins was but a minor player in this game of chance. He would soon find out that Julianna Seaton rarely rose from the table a loser.

"I need an inexpensive paste copy of a sapphire necklace similar to this," Julianna said to the clerk behind the counter of Brown and Rolinson. She opened her reticule and showed him her mother's necklace. "I need it immediately and will take whatever you have to hand."

Chapter Fourteen

Any elation Julianna felt over besting Hawkins at his own game was gone by the next morning, dissipated by the harsh light of reality much as the pink-gray mist that hung over the Bath hills dissolved in the glare of the early morning sun. The butler would find out that the sapphires were paste as soon as he tried to sell them. True, there was some satisfaction in the fact that the necklace had been paid for with money earmarked for Hawkins's wages, but still, all Julianna had gained was time to make plans — she had not really won the game.

"Madam did not sleep well?" Eweing asked, placing a small cornette over Julianna's hair.

"No, Madam did not," Julianna answered with some asperity. She felt, in fact, as if she had slept with a frown upon her face. It had been there when she went to bed last night and it was there this morning as she sat on a low stool allowing Eweing to dress her hair. "Where were you last night?" she asked, rubbing at the crease between her brows. "I had to undress myself, and earlier I thought I saw you out walking with a gentleman."

"That we was, Madam," Eweing surprised Julianna by admitting. "We had Miss Partridge's permission, of course. Miss Partridge thinks it very romantic."

"She does?" Julianna's eyes widened as she looked at Eweing's image in the mirror. "Do you mean . . . ?" Could Eweing, the proper lady's maid, be courting?

Eweing took a round dress of jaconet muslin from the wardrobe. "If Madam will stand?"

Julianna stood, allowing Eweing to dress her as if she had no more say in the matter than a dressmaker's dummy. "The gentleman then is . . ."

"The gentleman is an artist, Madam." Eweing shut her mouth firmly on the words, leaving Julianna in no doubt that nothing further would be forthcoming on the matter.

Dismissing Eweing, Julianna went to the bellpull to summon Hawkins. So the bewhiskered gentleman was courting Eweing? However improbable that might seem to Julianna, she had no reason not to believe it. Eweing would hardly risk being caught out in a lie which might result in dismissal. In any case, why should Eweing lie about it? Did Julianna really think the woman involved in some sordid conspiracy with Lord Ramsden to spirit Paul away? If so, Eweing had had ample opportunity in which to act and yet had not.

No, Julianna had little doubt but that Eweing and the bewhiskered gentleman were courting. And he was an artist. He had probably caught sight of Paul by chance that day in the park and decided to sketch him. There was nothing remarkable about that. Paul was a very handsome little boy. *I must stop imagining things,* Julianna told herself. *There is enough on my plate to worry about without seeing something sinister behind every chance remark or meeting.*

Hawkins, for once prompt in responding to a summons, took the velvet case which Julianna handed him and gazed avidly at its sparkling contents. "Thank you, Madam. I am glad there will be no need to report the young master's whereabouts to Lord Ramsden. Mrs. Gardning and I have become quite fond of the boy, you know."

Julianna raised one eyebrow in disbelief. "I am happy to be able to oblige you. Now you will oblige me by waiting a few days to sell the jewels. I need time to make plans and do not wish my friends to know I have been reduced to such straits."

"Of course, it does seem a shame that a young boy should be separated from his father like that," Hawkins continued as if she had not spoken.

Julianna's eyes narrowed. "What do you mean, Hawkins? Paul is no longer your concern. In fact, I think it might be best if you and Mrs. Gardning made plans of your own, plans to be packed and out of this house as soon as possible." Julianna did her best to shrivel the butler with an icy stare. It was a performance worthy of Mrs. Siddons, but unfortunately Hawkins was an unappreciative audience.

"Not very friendly like, are you, Mrs. Pickering? And here was I prepared to offer you special terms on the next installment."

"The next—"

The butler nodded. "But only half as much this time. Mrs. Gardning and I don't mean to be greedy."

"You may go, Hawkins," Julianna said firmly. "And you will not get a farthing more."

Hawkins shrugged. "Don't really matter much. With this," he held up the velvet case containing the paste necklace, "and what we'll get as reward money, Mrs. Gardning and I will be able to set up in style."

"I should turn you over to the authorities, Hawkins."

"But you won't, Mrs. Pickering, you won't," the butler assured Julianna with an oily smile. "And if you want to protect that little boy of yours, you'll come up with the money by tomorrow evening."

Well, the fox is certainly in the henhouse now, Julianna thought as she descended the staircase some few minutes later. She had thought to gain time but had not even that. Certainly they must now leave Bath. There was no question in Julianna's mind. She would not allow herself to be bested by such a slippery eel as Hawkins. But what to do about Lady Eleanor? No sooner was one problem solved than another cropped up in its place.

Feeling as if she were wearing a cap of gloom instead of the charming cornette of ribboned lace, Julianna continued into the breakfast room. Thankfully, Lady Eleanor was not yet up. Julianna needed time alone to decide what should be done. Pouring herself some coffee, lukewarm but the least of Hawkins's faults to be contemplated at the moment, Julianna sat down at the breakfast table, picked up a piece of singed toast and began to shred it upon her plate, as had become her practice when she was worried about something.

As soon as Hawkins realizes he has been duped or that I will not meet his demands, he will inform Lord Ramsden of our whereabouts. Julianna brushed crumbs from her fingers and reached for another piece of bread. Lady Eleanor will not wish to leave because of Colonel Cramden, but it is impossible that she should be left behind. Could the colonel be trusted with the details of their dilemma? Or —

"Jules, Jules!" Paul ran into the breakfast room, tears cascading down his face and dripping from his chin. "Humbert gone!" he sobbed. "Humbert ate up!"

"What?" Julianna looked from Paul's bent head, now buried in her skirts to Kitty, who stood helplessly by, ringing her hands.

"It's not my fault, mum. It's not my fault," Kitty whined, her face as contorted as Paul's. "It's that there wretched black cat. It's a mean 'un I said, soons I saw it. A real mean 'un. Always sneakin' around by the back door where it don't belong."

Julianna's head whirled as she tried to sort through this jumbled account of disaster. "Yes, well, a cat," she said. "And Humbert. I see." And suddenly she did see. "Oh, dear. Are you sure Humbert isn't just hiding, Paul?"

Paul nodded, wiping his face on her skirt. "I called an' called an' I had cheese an' . . . an' . . ." he stopped to wipe his nose with his hand ". . . an' I looked under the stairs an' . . . an' he gone, Jules. Humbert got ate!"

The fresh wail that arose from Paul had Julianna turning to her coffee cup for strength. She didn't need a missing mouse on top of everything else.

"I'm sure nothing of the kind has occurred," she said, with more resolution than she was truly feeling. "Humbert is probably just, ah, visiting his family. Yes, Humbert has decided to visit his family in the country."

"He has?" Both Paul and Kitty spoke at once and looked at Julianna hopefully.

"Yes," Julianna said firmly, as she saw Paul's woebegone expression begin to lighten. "I am sure of it."

Paul nodded and looked thoughtful. "Him come back?"

Julianna eyed the little boy cautiously. "Well, you know Paul, it's just possible that Humbert will decide to stay in the country and—"

"Him come back!" Paul demanded, thrusting out his bottom lip which was beginning to quiver again.

"Yes, yes, of course he will." Surely there is somewhere I can obtain a field mouse by tomorrow, Julianna thought. And who knows, we may all be back at Graxton Manor by then the way things are going.

To take Paul's mind off the missing Humbert, Julianna offered to take him to the Orange Grove to view the obelisk, remembering as she did so Lady Eleanor's comment about the soothing effect of the gardens and the view of the Avon. If ever Julianna needed soothing, it was today, she decided.

Changing quickly into a dress of French gray Circassian cloth, the jaconet muslin having become sadly damp and puckered (which caused Eweing to raise her eyebrows in disapproval at Madam having so little regard for her gowns), Julianna set off with Paul in the direction of New Bond Street. Though Paul had regained his high spirits, he was still a bit anxious about his pet.

"Where Humbert live?" he asked as they passed onto the High Street.

"In the country, Paul, I told you."

"Where in country?" Paul persisted. "By Pog?"

Julianna knew Paul was thinking of the pond in back of Graxton Manor where they had first encountered pollywogs and the stories about Pog had begun. "No," she said. "Not by Pog. That would be too far."

"In park?"

"Maybe in the park, Paul. I don't really know," Julianna answered absently. She was thinking of what it would be like if Lord Ramsden found them, if they really did have to return to Graxton Manor. Julianna shuddered at the thought. No. It was impossible. Quite impossible. She would do everything in her power to keep such a thing from happening.

Holding tightly to Paul's hand, Julianna walked down the path that led to the obelisk erected in honor of Prince William of Orange. Paul looked up at the monument, awed as always by its size, walked around it three times, and then pointed to the Latin inscription at its base. "Read me," he demanded.

Julianna obliged, knowing from past excursions that while Paul had no idea what the words meant, he loved the sound of them. When she had read the inscription twice, Paul nodded, stepped back, and announced that he was now going to look for Humbert.

Julianna sighed. She could understand Paul's concern, and she fervently hoped that the little mouse had not met an untimely demise beneath a cat's paw, but she was also becoming heartily sick of hearing Humbert's name. "Humbert is not here. I know that for a certainty, Paul. Now, would you like to spend a few minutes in the Abbey?"

Paul frowned and looked up at Julianna dubiously. "Humbert not here?"

"No." Julianna shook her head, doing her best to hold on to her patience and thinking that she should have brought Kitty along rather than leaving her behind to assist Eweing. "I am sure Humbert's family does not live in the Orange Grove."

Paul thought for a moment and then nodded. "We see Abbey," he said, taking Julianna's hand and tugging her forward. They walked around to the west front of the old building where Paul stood, head back, mouth open, gazing up at the turrets decorated with ladders upon which angels eternally climbed. It was a sight Lady Eleanor always found most distressing. "For I have no head for heights," she would say. "And if that is the sort of thing angels must do, then I shall never be one, I am afraid."

Hurrying Paul inside before he could demand a ladder of his own to climb, Julianna felt the peace of the old building descend upon her like a benediction. Though it was fashionable to attend daily services there, the Abbey was thankfully all but deserted at such an early hour.

They moved slowly up one of the aisles, Julianna noting with fond amusement the way the light from the large clerestory window fell softly to halo Paul's blond head, though he was hardly behaving angelically at the moment. The large monument to James Montague, Bishop of Bath and Wells, had caught Paul's attention and he was giving it a rather closer inspection than the old bishop would have approved.

At least Paul has temporarily forgotten about Humbert, Julianna thought, as she turned her own eyes upward to gaze at the fan vaulting for which the Abbey was famous. Was it too much to hope that the field mouse would return of its own volition, that it had not, indeed, fallen prey to the cat? Or must Julianna consider some way to obtain another mouse for Paul on top of everything else?

Julianna sighed. If only . . . No, I must stop such thoughts, she chided herself. Though she could not quite keep herself from wishing there were someone like Lord Fairmont to whom she could turn. He would doubtless have known just what to do about Humbert. And Hawkins, Julianna was sure, would never have dared try to blackmail Lord Fairmont.

Still, it would not do to keep dwelling on the man. That episode was finished. As dead as . . . as Bishop Montague. There could be no resurrecting a love that had never existed in the first place. No. The love had been wholly on her part, Lord Fairmont had said as much. And though the pain of his absence was still a sharp knife cutting away at her peace and happiness, Julianna told herself that time healed all wounds. Even if it took a millennium or more before a scar could form over so deep a one. Eyes misted with tears, Julianna turned to look at the lovely east window as memories flooded her being along with the soft-hued rays of light.

"Julianna."

Her name whispered eerily across the sanctuary.

She turned. That voice! It had stalked her through a thousand childhood nightmares. "Lord Ramsden." She murmured the words between the gloved fingers that covered her mouth. "Lord Ramsden." No. Surely not. Surely it was some trick of her imagination. She could see no one. No one was there.

A step. A footfall to her left. A muffled laugh. Then, for an instant, a figure was silhouetted in the light from the great window. Small. Slim. Unmistakable.

And then it was gone. Had it been the trick of an overwrought mind, a mind that had already been stretched beyond its emotional limit?

"Paul . . ." Whether a trick of her imagination or not, Julianna was suddenly anxious to quit the Abbey. "Paul?" He was no longer inspecting Bishop Montague. But he could not have wandered far.

"Paul?" Julianna called again, her voice beginning to rise. "Answer me, Paul!"

The words echoed mockingly back at her across the nave.

Julianna began to rush back down the aisle calling Paul's name. The few people walking about the Abbey turned to stare.

"For shame, running in a church like that. Only a woman of no breeding whatsoever would do such a thing."

"And shouting. She was positively shouting. Imagine making such a cake of oneself."

Julianna heard the words of censure that followed her but paid them no heed. Where was Paul? He had been there one moment and the next — Spotting a churchwarden by the door, she hurried up to him. "Have you seen a little boy? Blond hair, about two?"

"There was a little fellow here a few minutes ago, might be the one you mean. No need to worry though. Left with his father. Small man, dark hair. Didn't look much like the child. But that's what the boy called him. They was going to look for a gentleman named Humbert from the sound of it. Anything wrong, miss?"

Julianna was sitting down on a hard wooden chair in a small anteroom. A pervasive chill in the air caused her to shiver.

"Brought you some tea, miss." The churchwarden placed a mug in her hand.

"Yes. Thank you." Julianna sipped the sweetened contents automatically.

"You sure there's nothing wrong, miss?"

Everything, Julianna thought. Everything is wrong. But she said nothing, merely shaking her head. "I felt a bit faint for a moment is all. I shall be fine directly."

Julianna finished the tea, thanked the churchwarden, and walked slowly out of the Abbey. Her mind was numb. The unimaginable had happened. Lord Ramsden had found them. But how? Even had Hawkins betrayed her after reading the notice, Lord Ramsden could not have gotten to Bath so quickly. It must have been someone else. Someone else who had read the notice and decided to claim the reward. Not that it mattered. Not now. The important thing was that Lord Ramsden was in Bath. And he had Paul.

Outside the sun was a harsh glare that hurt the eyes. Julianna blinked and stood irresolutely by the Abbey doors wondering what to do. She needed time to think. Where would Lord Ramsden have taken Paul, and why? For Lord Ramsden did nothing to a purpose other than his own, and Julianna doubted that his purpose was to regain his son. No. Lord Ramsden would want money. Julianna smiled grimly as she began to walk slowly home. Your pockets can be no more to let than mine, my dear steppapa, she thought. And I did not contrive to save the sapphires from Hawkins only to meekly hand them over to you. Ah, no. I must consider what other cards remain to be played.

The small house in Taylor Street was in a turmoi, when Julianna returned, for the colonel had called, requested private audience with Lady Eleanor, and made her an offer.

"You cannot imagine, Julianna! Why, I had barely my cap on when he called—much too early, as the colonel admitted himself. But he said he had not slept but an hour for worrying over the matter, and so he would come and get it over with in all haste.

"Well, do nothing quickly but catch a flea, I told him, for truly, Julianna, I have been waiting for this moment so long, I would needs prolong it. And there is more to marriage than four bare legs in bed, after all."

Julianna, who had scarcely walked through the door before being assaulted with Lady Eleanor's verbiage, could only nod.

"But of course I accepted, only pretending reluctance at first, and then I must tell him the truth about our situation. Though some say that only children and fools tell the truth, I do not agree, for I have always maintained that as a tree falls so shall it lie." Lady Eleanor rattled on, following Julianna into the parlor.

"And, after all, how would the banns be called, I ask you? For I cannot be married as Miss Partridge. I doubt it would be legal, and in any case, the truth will out."

"Indeed, and I am very happy for you," Julianna said as Lady Eleanor paused for breath. Though she had half-thought to tell Lady Eleanor what had occurred, she found she could not bring herself to so spoil her stepaunt's happiness. And what purpose would it serve in any case? Julianna had decided on her walk home what she must do.

"Well, and so am I, Julianna—happy, I mean. The colonel means to have the banns posted at once. And

231

he was not a bit put off when I told him about Ramsden and all. 'Needs must when the devil drives,' is all he said. And he was glad that I trusted him with our secret, for he is more than fond of Paul, you know, and quite understood that we could not leave the child in my brother's care. 'I shall help in any way I can,' he said. Such a dear, dear man. You do not think this will put us in any peril, do you? With the banns being read and all? I would not want my happiness to endanger you and Paul. And the colonel did mention a special license if I thought it necessary."

Julianna patted Lady Eleanor's hand as they sat together on the settee. "I am sure you need not fear Lord Ramsden finding us out when the banns are read. Now where do you plan to be wed, and when?"

"The colonel is calling to take me out for a drive, and we mean to discuss — Oh, my goodness! Look at the time." Lady Eleanor looked at the little clock on the mantelpiece with horror. "And I really must change my dress, Julianna. I know that some would say that once the fox is caught one need not tend the snare, but I must disagree. I hope Paul will not mind if we do not take him?"

"Don't worry about Paul, my dear. Be happy. I shall take care of things here."

"Then I shall be off upstairs to change my gown," Lady Eleanor said, springing to her feet. "I think perhaps the blue walking dress with the plaited front and ornamental braiding. Has Eweing returned from her errands yet?" Lady Eleanor turned to ask from the parlor door. "Never to mind, Kitty shall assist me. And I think the cork bonnet trimmed with satin." Her voice floated back into the parlor as she mounted the stairs.

The smile Julianna had kept pasted upon her face faded quickly to be replaced by a look of resolution. Julianna had never been one to sit back and allow fate to have its way. She had decided upon a course of action, the only possible course, actually, and she would act upon it before her courage deserted her. She would go to Lord Fairmont, explain everything, and ask for his help. Surely no matter how he regarded her, he would not refuse to help Paul.

Getting to her feet, Julianna paused a moment to tuck her hair in place and straighten her skirts. She would not take the time to change her dress, she thought, turning to the door. Suddenly a brown furry comet streaked across her path. Julianna screamed and jumped back, one hand pressed to her rapidly beating heart as she gazed down at Humbert, who had stopped abruptly in the middle of the carpet and now stood paralyzed with fear before the glass case that contained the stuffed owl.

Well. Julianna took a deep breath. Well. That was one problem solved. Humbert had not met an untimely demise beneath the paws of the black cat but had simply decided to move inside and grace the parlor with his presence.

Taking the elegant chip straw bonnet she had been wearing, Julianna cautiously approached the cowering Humbert and with one quick movement scooped up the frightened creature. Humbert would no doubt be quite happy to return to his home beneath the cellar steps where no predatory birds waited to pounce.

The knocker sounded as Julianna returned from the back of the house. She paused, took a deep breath, and went to the door, having a good idea whom her visitor would be.

"Ah, my dear stepdaughter, it has been too long." Lord Ramsden stepped inside, sweeping the tall crowned beaver from his head and handing it to her. "No servant to answer your door? A headdress fit only for the ragman in your hand? I hope this does not reflect the state of your finances?"

Julianna glanced down at the chip straw. Humbert, his courage having returned, had nibbled a large hole in the crown of his straw prison before being released. "My finances are not your concern," she replied, feeling her hackles rise as she tossed his crowned beaver and her own bonnet down on the hall table.

"But who better to be concerned than your own stepfather?" His small eyes swept over her. "You have gained weight. It is not becoming."

"Thank you," Julianna said between clenched teeth, following her stepfather as he strolled into the parlor. "I would ask you to sit down, but I know you will not be staying."

Lord Ramsden lowered his quizzing glass from an inspection of the chiming clock upon the mantelpiece.

"Anxious to be rid of me, my dear? No pretense of filial affection?" His thin lips curved into a smile. "Now, Paul was quite pleased to see me." Lord Ramsden sat down in one of the damask chairs and crossed his legs clad in elegant fawn pantaloons. "I do hope you weren't alarmed when he failed to return this morning? I was so ecstatic at finding him at last, you see, that I found I could not bear to part with him again."

"Not at any price?" Julianna asked, matching his smile with a polite one of her own.

"Ah, well, that remains to be seen, does it not?"

"And is Paul all right? He is not frightened or crying? You have some respectable person to look after him?"

Lord Ramsden twirled his quizzing glass by its satin ribbon and shrugged, looking idly about the room. "Respectability exists in the eye of the beholder," he replied. "Did not this house once belong to Carlborne?"

"You have not answered my question," Julianna persisted. "Is Paul all right?"

"At the moment. Though children do become easily upset, do they not? So it would be best for us to conclude our negotiations as quickly as possible."

"If it's money you're after, you may as well know that most of Mama's jewels have been sold and I have very little cash at hand," Julianna said quickly. "I've had an abominable run of luck."

"Luck?" Lord Ramsden raised his finely plucked eyebrows. "I've never felt that luck had any part in your play, Julianna. You are much too cool and calculating to trust to luck."

"Do you think so?"

Lord Ramsden nodded. "But let us dispense with this roundaboutation, my dear, and allow me to state my terms with the logical brevity you so adore. I have Paul. You want Paul."

"And how much will it cost to get Paul back?"

"Five thousand pounds."

Julianna gasped. "But I could never—"

"Please spare me the protestations," Lord Ramsden cut in. "I am sure you can contrive something. I need a bit of the ready, and you will supply it. If not . . . well, there is many a childless couple that would pay to acquire an heir."

"You would sell your son?"

"What good is a son when one's pockets are to let? Besides, it should be relatively easy for you to come up with the money. I have it on good authority that you count Fairmont as your friend. Persuade him to part with a bit of the yellow and Paul is yours. It is as simple as that."

Julianna turned away, the taste of blood in her mouth where she had bitten her lip. "And if I somehow raise the five thousand pounds, will you agree to leave us in peace and not bother Paul again?"

"Of course."

The reply was glibly made, but Lord Ramsden was hardly a man whose word was honor. It would not stop with five thousand pounds. The demands would go on and on; Julianna would never feel safe again. And to think she had worried about Hawkins. He was a maggot on the wall compared to Ramsden.

"When do you want the money?"

"Tonight," Lord Ramsden insisted. "I will call and collect the money tonight. I have kept the vultures at bay until now, but they are circling ever closer. It must be tonight, Julianna. And I know you will want Paul back as soon as possible in any case."

Julianna nodded, refusing to look at him, knowing how the sight of his self-satisfied smile would sicken her. "Now you will go," she said, without turning. "Leave. At once."

"But I have yet to greet my dear sister. She is somewhere about, I assume? Or have you murdered her, driven mad by her constant chatter?"

"Lady Eleanor is not at home," Julianna said, hoping the lady in question would not put in an appearance, nor the colonel arrive before she had gotten rid of Lord Ramsden.

"Ah, more's the pity. Well, you will give her my love, will you not?"

Julianna did not reply but stood, lips pressed together, eyes closed, willing him to leave.

"Tsk tsk, we are wanting in manners. Have you no loving words of farewell for your dear steppapa? However were you raised, my dear?" Lord Ramsden laughed, a high, mirthless sound to which Julianna refused to respond.

"Ah, well, I shall bid you adieu, Julianna, and suggest that you make all haste in obtaining the money. I am sure Paul would prefer his own bed tonight, and, in any case, my companion has made it quite clear she does not like to share. At least not with boys as young as Paul."

Julianna's fingernails bit into the palms of her hands as she waited, knowing that any response on her part would only encourage Lord Ramsden to linger. He enjoyed baiting her. At last she heard his departing footfalls on the carpet, the sound of the outer door closing.

Whirling quickly about, Julianna ran to the hall, slammed the chip straw upon her head, and cautiously opened the door. She had no intention of paying Lord Ramsden a single farthing. Paste jewels had served her once, they would serve her twice. But first Julianna must find out where Lord Ramsden was keeping Paul. She slipped quietly outside, her eyes on the elegant figure of her stepfather.

Chapter Fifteen

Though Lord Fairmont's imposing mansion had no human sconces lining the walk this time, Julianna had no difficulty recognizing it as she peered around a pillar of the colonnaded walkway across the street. Lord Ramsden stood on the shallow step outside the house and plied the knocker. She had followed him in the hope of finding out where he lodged and, thus, where he was keeping Paul. But what was he doing there?

The door opened, the butler greeted Lord Ramsden by name, and quickly ushered him inside while disbelief, fury, and dismay waged war within Julianna's breast. Her stepfather a welcome and obviously familiar visitor in Lord Fairmont's home?

Julianna turned around, her back against the stone column for support, one hand pressed tightly against her breast. She felt betrayed. Betrayed and bereft. Almost the way she had felt when her father died and she realized he was lost to her forever. Had she wondered who besides Hawkins could have betrayed them to Lord Ramsden? She need wonder no longer. The answer was obvious.

Fury filled the empty space that had been her heart. To think she had meant to go to Lord Fairmont for help, had meant to throw herself on his mercy. What a fool she had been! Lady Davina was right. Julianna had been taken in by a handsome face and charming manner like some chit from the schoolroom.

But no longer, Julianna promised herself, as she marched angrily across the street. No longer. She would find a way to get Paul back, and she would never trust a man again. Never!

Julianna plied the elegant brass knocker furiously, anger and fear sweeping aside timidity and caution. Paul had been gone only a few hours but it felt like an eternity. Was he frightened? Crying?

A young footman dressed in Lord Fairmont's distinctive blue livery answered the door. Julianna swept past him and stepped into an imposing hallway with marble columns.

"Inform Lord Fairmont that Julianna Seaton wishes to speak to him at once," she demanded, hands clenched at her sides, eyes dark as a storm-swept sky.

"Is there some problem?" The butler, wearing black and the somber air of authority, stepped into the hallway.

Julianna turned. "I wish to see Lord Fairmont," she reiterated. "Immediately!"

The butler took note of Julianna's bonnet with the large hole gnawed in the crown and the lack of pelisse which Julianna had not bothered to don in her haste. "I am afraid Lord Fairmont is engaged at the moment," he said, stepping behind Julianna to open the front door. "If you would care to call another time, Madam?"

"I would not," Julianna replied and walked purposefully down the hallway to a pair of carved doors which stood open on her left. "I shall wait in here. Inform Lord Fairmont that Julianna Seaton wishes, nay, demands, to see him."

Lord Ramsden, lounging in a gilt armchair near the unlit fire, raised a finely plucked eyebrow as Julianna swept into the room, but remained seated. "Well, well, what a surprise," he said, his thin lips curling in amusement. "My beloved stepdaughter has come a calling. Missing me already, my dear?"

"Don't be ridiculous," Julianna snapped. She was in no mood for her stepfather's baiting remarks. "I followed you."

"But surely that was unnecessary. You had simply to ask, and I would have informed you of my destination." Lord Ramsden gave her the innocent look of a man totally without scruples. "Though I suppose I should be gratified to see that you are following my suggestion."

Julianna frowned. "What suggestion?"

"That you apply to Fairmont for funds. He is notoriously openhanded, you know." Lord Ramsden sneered the words, as if generosity were the worst of venal sins.

"And here I thought the two of you had so much in common," Julianna replied, her own lips curling on the words. She began to pace impatiently back and forth, frowning at the walls swathed in elegant yellow stamped silk. "What are you doing here anyway?" she asked. "Come to pay your informer his reward?"

Lord Ramsden rose and walked over to a gilt and satinwood side table. "But where else should I be?" he asked, pouring himself a glass of wine from the cutglass decanter, "when Fairmont has so kindly invited me to be his guest?"

"You are staying here?" Julianna turned.

"Ah, yes," Lord Ramsden replied. "Fairmont and I are old acquaintances, you know."

"And does he—" Julianna broke off and stopped to take a deep breath. She must not lose control. Not in front of Lord Ramsden. "Does Lord Fairmont know that you have taken Paul?"

Lord Ramsden shrugged and sat down once more, sipping his wine. "Fairmont believes, quite rightly, that a boy belongs with his father."

"I see." A terrible tightness threatened to close Julianna's throat. Her eyes began to sting with tears she refused to shed. Quickly, before Lord Ramsden could see how his words had upset her, she began to pace back and forth once more, trying to requicken her anger so it might smother the aching distress that gnawed at her heart.

Why had Lord Fairmont done this terrible thing? Julianna could not understand it. Certainly he had been upset that day when she had foolishly believed Lady Davina's lies, but to conspire to hurt Paul . . . and it was not as if Lord Fairmont were some poor, penniless soul who needed the reward money. No. He had not even Hawkins's excuse of greed. Nor her stepfather's.

"Does Lord Fairmont know that you are blackmailing me?" she asked, turning suddenly on Lord Ramsden.

Lord Ramsden raised his eyebrows and finished sipping his wine before he answered. "Such an ugly word, my dear. Shall we say instead that Fairmont has no knowledge of the contribution you intend to make to my welfare? And as long as you come up with the money, he shall remain in ignorance. However, you do remember my mention of those who would pay to acquire an heir?"

Julianna frowned. "I do not see what that has to do with—"

"Fairmont is rich, childless, and fond of Paul." Lord Ramsden put down his wineglass. "Need I say more?"

"I do not believe you." Surely, even Lord Fairmont would not consider such a thing.

Lord Ramsden gave one of his elegant shrugs. "Believe what you will. But Fairmont has already discussed with me adopting the boy and mentioned a not inconsiderable amount for the privilege. Were I not so doting a father I should have agreed at once."

"But you did not."

Lord Ramsden smiled. "No. It was my dear wife's dying wish that Paul remain with you. Being a sentimental fool, I decided to give you a chance to come up with the money first."

"You are all that is kind," Julianna replied dryly. "But I have told you of my abominable run of luck. A day earlier and I would still have had Mama's sapphire necklace to give you, but it seems you might take lessons from my butler in how to extort money."

"What do you mean?" Lord Ramsden sat up, his attention caught. "What has your butler to do with this?"

"Only that Hawkins now possesses the sapphires in exchange for his silence regarding Paul's whereabouts. Ironic, is it not? Since you were already in Bath, waiting only for the opportune moment to snatch Paul."

"You gave the jewels to your butler? Have your wits gone abegging?" Lord Ramsden asked. "Those sapphires were worth a small fortune."

Julianna shrugged. "At the time I thought I had no choice. Paul is more important to me than —"

The words remained unspoken as Lord Fairmont's voice was heard in the hall. "Excellent. I am quite pleased with your work. You captured the boy's likeness with remarkable clarity."

Julianna turned towards the open door, her gloved hands clenching as she strained to hear his words.

"I must say he was not an easy subject, Lord Fairmont. The boy flits about like one of those butterflies he likes to watch and is rarely still for more than a few seconds at a time."

Julianna moved closer to get a better view. Lord Fairmont stood talking to a man who was tall and slim and . . . yes. It was the bewhiskered gentleman Julianna had seen sketching Paul in the park. The man she had seen with Eweing. Eweing . . . who had formerly been in Lord Fairmont's employ. So she had been right. Anger drained from Julianna, leaving nothing but cold despair. It did not take a mathematician's daughter to draw a logical conclusion from such obvious evidence.

With leaden steps, Julianna walked to the doorway. Lord Fairmont must have used the sketches to prove to her stepfather that Paul was in Bath. For a moment she stood in the doorway unobserved, her eyes lingering on Lord Fairmont's profile and the guinea gold of his hair, the crease in his cheek that was not quite a dimple when he smiled. Then squaring her shoulders and taking a deep, steadying breath, Julianna stepped forward.

"Lord Fairmont . . ."

"Ah, Miss Seaton. How good of you to call." Lord Fairmont smiled down at her. "May I make known to you Mr. Eweing? And, of course, you know his wife."

Julianna turned, encountering the little button eyes of her lady's maid. "His wife?"

"Whatever has happened to Madam's hat?" Eweing frowned in disapproval. "Looks like someone's been chewing on it. And Madam's hair looks as if she's been crawling through a hedge."

Julianna put up one hand to straighten her hair before recollecting herself. "None of that matters," she said in a flat voice. "Not now. How could you have done this, Eweing? You betrayed me, endangered Paul, conspired with . . . with him." Julianna gestured towards Lord Fairmont as if he were some loathsome thing she had encountered under a stone.

Instead of being affronted, Lord Fairmont's smile widened. "I shall have my man of business contact you," he informed the Eweings, dismissing them with a nod as he stepped into the small withdrawing room. Julianna was forced to step backwards or be stepped upon.

"Where is Paul?" she demanded. "I insist on seeing him. And if you have allowed my stepfather to—"

"If I have allowed Paul's father to . . . ?" Lord Fairmont asked, closing the door firmly.

"Lord Ramsden has no right—"

"What you seem to forget, Julianna," Lord Fairmont broke in once again, "is that Paul's father has every right in this matter. You are the one without rights."

"I could not have put it better myself." Lord Ramsden rose from the gilt armchair where he had been a forgotten observer. "It is a fact I have been trying to make Julianna understand for years. Unfortunately, she can be a bit thick at times, though I believe it to be stubbornness on her part rather than true stupidity such as my dear sister exhibits."

"Ramsden." Lord Fairmont nodded at the older man, his greeting curt.

"Lord Fairmont." The smile on Lord Ramsden's face was ingratiating. "Is what you have to say to my dear stepdaughter of a personal nature? Shall I remove myself?"

"If you please." Lord Fairmont held open the door to the hall.

"Of course." Lord Ramsden agreed. He walked to Julianna and took her hand in farewell. "I believe I shall see if I can interest a certain . . . Hawkins, was it? in a friendly game of whist. Meanwhile, I would remind you that it is best to keep one's own counsel in these matters." He bowed to his host and sauntered from the room.

Left alone with Lord Fairmont, Julianna put one gloved hand to her brow to ease the tension that pulled at her. She had no doubt that her stepfather would entice the butler into a card game and win the paste necklace. But any glee she might have felt over duping both Hawkins and Lord Ramsden was swallowed up in her concern for Paul and confusion over Lord Fairmont's actions. "I do not pretend to understand why you have done this," she said, all anger drained from her voice. "Do you mean to strike back at me for having refused you? For having believed Lady Davina's lies? Is not the fact that I am shunned by half of Bath society enough?"

"Julianna . . ."

"No," she interrupted. "I do not care to hear your reasons. I would only know that Paul is safe. Please." Julianna held out her hands in supplication. "You must know where he is. Any quarrel you have is with me. Surely you cannot mean to harm a small boy. Where is he? Please tell me. I will do anything. Paul will be so scared and —"

"Julianna." Lord Fairmont's voice was firm. "I do not know what you are talking about. Why do you think I would want to harm Paul?"

"Not harm him, perhaps. But you do not know how frightening it can be for a small child to be taken away from all that is familiar. I beg you. If you must hurt someone, hurt me. But not through Paul."

"Hurt you?" Lord Fairmont's words were softly spoken, but his eyes as he advanced towards her were dark with an anger that earlier had been hers. "My only thought has been to protect you. Do you not understand that if Ramsden chose to press charges against you for taking Paul, you could be transported?"

"It doesn't matter. As long as Paul is safe."

"And who would look after him while you were in some penal colony thousands of miles away? You have already said that he is frightened by that which is unfamiliar. The worse thing that could happen to Paul is to lose you. Are you so scatter-witted you cannot see that?"

Julianna pressed her lips together. "Where the people I love are concerned, I am not always logical."

"Ah, then you admit to loving me."

"What? Love . . . you?" Julianna gave a mirthless laugh. "Love a man who betrayed me to Lord Ramsden? A man who endangers Paul by his silence? Damn it, Fairmont. Tell me where Paul is!"

Lord Fairmont studied her for a moment, his eyes hard, his beautiful, chiseled countenance totally unyielding.

"Please." Julianna found herself begging.

"And if I tell you simply that Paul is safe, will you believe me? Will you trust me, Julianna?"

Julianna swallowed and looked away. He was asking for her trust. A trust she had denied him before. But how could she? With all the evidence to the contrary, how could she trust him?

Because you love him, she found herself answering. Because with love there must also be trust. And were evidence to the contrary stacked as high as the Abbey tower, it would not weigh with you. If you love him.

"If . . . if I could just see Paul?"

"I have told you. Paul is safe."

Julianna had only Lord Fairmont's word. Was that enough? Rubbing one gloved hand absently across the gilded acanthus leaves carved into the back of the settee, Julianna noted blankly that it was free of dust. A well-run household, in fact. Her eyes flicked back to Lord Fairmont's silent figure as he stood quietly awaiting her reply, his hands clenched at his sides. What had he said at that earlier meeting, that awful confrontation between them that she had been certain would be etched forever in her heart and mind? *You prate of love but know not what it is. With love there must be trust.*

"I do trust you," she said at last, and heard Lord

246

Fairmont's faint sigh. "And I believe you when you say that Paul is safe."

"He is, Julianna. You have no need to worry." Lord Fairmont smiled down at her. "Paul is in my kitchen at this very moment, no doubt charming my cook and eating enough Sally Lunns to make himself quite sick. I thought you knew he was here. Ramsden brought him earlier, I assumed with your permission."

"Paul disappeared when we were together in the Abbey," Julianna said. "I have been quite frantic not knowing where he was."

"Understandably so," Lord Fairmont agreed. "Had I known of Lord Ramsden's perfidy, I would have informed you of Paul's presence at once."

Julianna nodded.

"You do believe this?" he asked, a bit uncertainly. "And you trust me?"

"I believe you. I trust you," Julianna reiterated quietly.

"And you love me." Lord Fairmont's words were a statement of fact though his eyes still scanned her face anxiously.

Julianna's reply was a smile, a smile that lit her gray eyes to brilliant opal despite a misting of tears.

"What? Tears, Julianna? Does the thought of loving me so distress you then?"

"I do not give my trust nor my love lightly, Lord Fairmont," she warned.

"Gabriel. You must call me Gabriel," he said, his brown eyes glowing with a warmth that had Julianna breathing most unsteadily. Taking her hand, he led her around the settee where Julianna seated herself and attempted to regain her hand. But Lord Fairmont would have none of it.

"I do not take your love nor your trust lightly," he said, turning her gloved hand over and slowly unfastening the single pearl button at her wrist. "You must know that I, too, have cause to be cautious in affairs of the heart. When I thought you would not have me, I felt quite . . . lost and vowed to forget you." Lord Fairmont peeled back the glove and raised the back of her wrist to his lips. "But I found that was quite impossible."

"I . . ." Julianna swallowed and cleared her throat. "I really don't think—"

"I would merely assure myself that the cut upon your finger has quite healed," Lord Fairmont murmured, not raising his head.

She felt his teeth nibble gently on her skin.

"I should like to see Paul now." Julianna sprang to her feet.

"In a minute." Lord Fairmont pulled her back down on the settee.

"You have still not explained what my stepfather is doing here, and he spoke . . . he said something about your adopting Paul?"

"I thought to disarm the enemy by befriending him. And after all, I have hopes that he will soon be my father-in-law."

"You . . . you do?"

Lord Fairmont nodded. "And on the strength of that hope, I invited your stepfather for a visit. He arrived last night. When I mentioned that I might want to adopt Paul legally, he was quite willing but suggested that we decide the matter with a game of piquet . . . with Paul as the stakes."

"He is—my stepfather is all that is despicable. I hope you did not agree?"

"I have played against your stepfather before." Lord Fairmont shrugged. "I was sure of winning. My man of business drew up a contract in which Ramsden forfeited all paternal rights to Paul." Lord Fairmont's fingers stroked slowly up and down her throat. "And Ramsden is now badly in debt to me."

Julianna began mentally reciting logarithms to calm her galloping heart. "In that case I should warn you that he may try to pay his debt with a sapphire necklace that is not worth more than a few pounds," she murmured breathlessly.

Lord Fairmont smiled. "I thank you for the warning, but I am not so easily duped. I intend for him to pay his debt by journeying to a small estate I own in Dorset and there remaining until I give him leave. My mother shall reside there also. They will hate being immured in the country but may cheat and connive against each other for amusement. Has anyone told you what lovely skin you have, Julianna?"

"I . . . I was supposed to ask you for money," Julianna stammered. "My stepfather said unless I paid him five thousand pounds he would sell Paul to a childless couple."

"Did he?" Lord Fairmont's lips were following the path his hands had forged.

"Yes. I had already sold most of my mother's jewelry," Lord Fairmont's lips had reached her bare earlobe, ". . . which is why I am not wearing any—" She gave a soft gasp as his teeth tugged gently. "—any earrings."

Lord Fairmont did not bother to reply, having better things to do at the moment.

"Hawkins was blackmailing me as well. And—" Julianna pulled abruptly away from Lord Fairmont. "And I think you really should know that I am not a widow at all."

"Do you remember my trip to the country, Julianna?" Lord Fairmont asked, eyes half-closed as he looked down at her. "My trip concerned you. I found out exactly who you were and what you had done. I applauded your actions and would have helped you . . . had you seen fit to trust me."

Julianna had one hand braced against his shoulder. "But everything conspired to make me *not* trust you. You hired Eweing to spy on me—"

"To keep an eye on you and Paul."

"You had her husband make sketches of Paul to send to Lord Ramsden."

"Arthur Eweing is a respected miniaturist. And I had no intention of sending anything to Ramsden."

"But why—"

"Stop chattering and come here, Julianna!" Lord Fairmont commanded.

And Julianna, being a mathematician's daughter, weighed the odds and calculated that it would be foolish not to obey.

So it was that when Paul had had enough of the Sally Lunns and decided to do a bit of exploring on his own, he found Jules and Lord Fairmont in a most compromising position.

Julianna grew quite scarlet with embarrassment and would have immediately removed herself from Lord Fairmont's lap had that gentleman not firmly prevented her from doing so.

"Paul will have to get used to it," he said.

And Paul, his head tilted to one side, giggled and tugged at Julianna's skirts which were sadly disheveled.

"Me get horsie now?" he asked.

"If you promise to go back to the kitchen and behave yourself."

Paul trotted to the door. "Brownie?" he asked, a calculating look in his eyes as he turned around once more.

"If you close the door behind you, I shall ask your father to sell us Brownie," Lord Fairmont agreed.

Paul nodded and hesitated, clearly wondering if

there was anything else he should ask for while every-one was in such an agreeable mood.

"I'm afraid he has a good deal of his father in him," Julianna observed from her position nestled against Lord Fairmont's chest.

"He also has a good deal of you, Jules. May I call you that now? Or do you still prefer Mrs. Pickering?"

Julianna smiled, the cambric of his shirt soft against her cheek. "Call me what you will," she said. "But truly, we are behaving most improperly."

"Not if you agree to marry me. And you do agree, do you not, Julianna?"

Julianna nodded, though once again she felt moved to protest. "Even engaged couples do not—"

Lord Fairmont sighed and pushed her off his lap. "Very well, we shall do all that is proper. And since we have just become engaged, it is most proper for me to give you your engagement present." Rising to his feet, Lord Fairmont reached for his coat which had been carelessly abandoned on one of the armchairs. "You were curious about my dealings with Arthur Eweing, Julianna?" Lord Fairmont handed her a gold locket which he had retrieved from his coattail pocket. "If you will open it, you will see an example of his work."

It was a miniature painting of Paul. Julianna looked up at Lord Fairmont, her eyes filling with tears.

"Once I got over my anger at your refusal of my suit, I realized that what I had said was quite untrue. I had every intention of bothering you again. I never gave up hope of winning you, Julianna."

Julianna gave him a watery smile, the gold locket clasped tightly in her hands. "I am glad," she said, rising from the settee and turning her face to his so that she might more effectively demonstrate her gratitude.

"Humbert!" A small voice piped up beside them.

Lord Fairmont sighed. "Paul. If you do not leave at

once you will not get Brownie. Do you understand?"

Paul stuck out his bottom lip. "Humbert!" he demanded again. "Humbert come home?"

Julianna hastened to reassure him. "Humbert is back from visiting his family, Paul," she said, bending down to smooth a golden curl. "And says he has missed you and would like you to bring him one of those Sally Lunns you have been enjoying. Do you think you can do that?"

Paul nodded, but his small face remained puckered in a worried frown.

Lord Fairmont leaned down and scooped Paul up in his arms.

"And I promise that as soon as your Jules and I are married, we shall all go live on my country estate in Somerset — you, Humbert, and Brownie. Does that satisfy you, young man?"

A dimple appeared in Paul's cheek. "Pog like that," he said, giving Lord Fairmont a quick hug.

"Good." Lord Fairmont walked to the door with Paul. "Peters?"

"Yes, milord?" The footman appeared at once.

"Escort this young man to the kitchen and see that the cook packs some biscuits and a bit of Stilton for him to take home."

"The mouse has been found then, milord?" Peters asked. "The kitchen staff has been quite worried, wondering what to do."

"Reassure them, Peters. And tell them that I would appreciate it if Paul were kept occupied for awhile."

The footman nodded and held out his hand to Paul. "Cook's been making some of that iced gingerbread you said you liked. And there's fresh cream as well."

Paul trotted happily down the hall his hand in Peters's while Julianna and Lord Fairmont watched from the doorway.

"And now, Julianna . . . ?" Lord Fairmont asked, as he turned and walked back into the room.

"And now . . ." Julianna answered, closing the door firmly and turning the key in the lock.

He waited for her, hands on hips, cravat undone, a smile that could only be described as rakish curving his lips. "Ah, but Jules," he protested as she began to slide her arms around his neck. "This is most improper. What if someone should discover us?"

"I've calculated the odds," she whispered against his mouth. "They're infinitesimal."

"In that case," he pulled her close, "it would be a shame not to take advantage of a sure thing."

DISCOVER THE MAGIC OF REGENCY ROMANCES

ROMANTIC MASQUERADE   (3221, $3.95)
by Lois Stewart

Sabrina Latimer had come to London incognito on a fortune hunt. Disguised as a Hungarian countess, the young widow had to secure the ten thousand pounds her brother needed to pay a gambling debt. His debtor was the notorious ladies' man, Lord Jareth Tremayne. Her scheme would work if she did not fall prey to the charms of the devilish aristocrat. For Jareth was an expert at gambling and always played to win everything—and *everyone*—he could.

RETURN TO CHEYNE SPA   (3247, $2.95)
by Daisy Vivian

Very poor but ever-virtuous Elinor Hardy had to become a dealer in a London gambling house to be able to pay her rent. Her future looked dismal until Lady Augusta invited her to be her guest at the exclusive resort, Cheyne Spa. The one condition: Elinor must woo the unsuitable rogue who was in pursuit of the Duchess's pampered niece.

The unsuitable young man was enraptured with Elinor, but *she* had been struck by the devilishly handsome Tyger Dobyn. Elinor knew that Tyger was hardly the respectable, marrying kind, but unfortunately her heart did not agree!

A CRUEL DECEPTION   (3246, $3.95)
by Cathryn Huntington Chadwick

Lady Margaret Willoughby had resisted marriage for years, knowing that no man could replace her departed childhood love. But the time had come to produce an heir to the vast Willoughby holdings. First she would get her business affairs in order with the help of the new steward, the disturbingly attractive and infuriatingly capable Mr. Frank Watson; *then* she would begin the search for a man she could tolerate. If only she could find a mate with a *fraction* of the scandalously handsome Mr. Watson's appeal. . . .

Available wherever paperbacks are sold, or order direct from the Publisher. Send cover price plus 50¢ per copy for mailing and handling to Zebra Books, Dept. 3639, 475 Park Avenue South, New York, N.Y. 10016. Residents of New York and Tennessee must include sales tax. DO NOT SEND CASH. For a free Zebra/Pinnacle catalog please write to the above address.

THE ROMANCE OF LORDS AND LADIES
IN JANIS LADEN'S REGENCIES

BEWITCHING MINX (2532, $3.95)

From her first encounter with the Marquis of Penderleigh when he had mistaken her for a common trollop, Penelope had been incensed with the darkly handsome lord. Miss Penelope Larchmont was undoubtedly the most outspoken young lady Penderleigh had ever known, and the most tempting.

A NOBLE MISTRESS (2169, $3.95)

Moriah Landon had always been a singularly practical young lady. So when her father lost the family estate over a game of picquet, she paid the winner, the notorious Viscount Roane, a visit. And when he suggested the means of payment—that she become Roane's mistress—she agreed without a blink of her eyes.

SAPPHIRE TEMPTATION (3054, $3.95)

Lady Serena was commonly held to be an unusual young girl—outspoken when she should have been reticent, lively when she should have been demure. But there was one tradition she had not been allowed to break: a Wexley must marry a Gower. Richard Gower intended to teach his wife her duties—in every way.

SCOTTISH ROSE (2750, $3.95)

The Duke of Milburne returned to Milburne Hall trusting that the new governess, Miss Rose Beacham, had instilled the fear of God into his harum-scarum brood of siblings. But she romped with the children, refused to be cowed by his stern admonitions, and was so pretty that he had the devil of a time keeping his hands off her.